Praise for *Red Team E*[...]

"Another winner from an SF wizard who h[...]
self adept at blending genres for both adu[...]
—*Booklist*

"Doctorow brings a thoroughness and honesty to a subject masked by technobabble and emotional hype. . . . With unconventional gumshoe Martin at the helm, fans can expect good things from the series to come." —*Publishers Weekly*

"Outstanding. The pages seem to turn themselves."
—*The Globe and Mail*

"I can't put it down." —*The Intercept*

"Hench himself, a classic itinerant hero with a twenty-first-century skill set, [will] keep this highly readable series going."
—*Financial Times*

"I can't possibly say enough good things about Cory Doctorow's new novel. It has all the great qualities and features that one expects from a Doctorow tale, but any extra praise it accrues is due to what it does differently from past items in his canon."
—*Locus*

"Explains things to [readers] that they absolutely ought to know about—the evil crap that the complexities of the modern financial system enable." —*Crooked Timber*

"I couldn't put the book down." —Matthew Green, professor of cryptography at Johns Hopkins University

"A fascinating take on the noir detective novel."
—*Economics from the Top Down*

"A remarkably accessible examination of the inherent criminality of international finance, but in a way that radiates with a surprising sense of optimism (yes, really)." —*Boing Boing*

also by cory doctorow

novels

Down and Out
in the Magic Kingdom

Eastern Standard Tribe

Someone Comes to Town,
Someone Leaves Town

Little Brother

Makers

For the Win

Pirate Cinema

The Rapture of the Nerds
(with Charles Stross)

Homeland

Walkaway

Attack Surface

The Lost Cause

short fiction

A Place So Foreign
and Eight More

Overclocked: Stories of the
Future Present

With a Little Help

The Great Big Beautiful
Tomorrow

Radicalized

graphic novel

In Real Life (with
Jen Wang)

children's picture book

Poesy the Monster Slayer (with
Matt Rockefeller)

nonfiction

The Complete Idiot's Guide to
Publishing Science Fiction (with
Karl Schroeder)

Essential Blogging (with
Rael Dornfest, J. Scott Johnson,
Shelley Powers, Benjamin Trott,
and Mena G. Trott)

Content: Selected Essays on
Technology, Creativity, Copyright,
and the Future of the Future

Context: Further Selected Essays on
Productivity, Creativity, Parenting,
and Politics in the 21st Century

Information Doesn't Want to
Be Free: Laws for the Internet Age

How to Destroy Surveillance
Capitalism

Chokepoint Capitalism: How
Big Tech and Big Content Captured
Creative Labor Markets and
How We'll Win Them Back (with
Rebecca Giblin)

cory doctorow
red team blues

tor publishing group
new york

RED TEAM BLUES

A Tor Book
Published by Tom Doherty Associates / Tor Publishing Group
120 Broadway
New York, NY 10271

www.tor-forge.com

Tor® is a registered trademark of Macmillan Publishing Group, LLC.

The Library of Congress has cataloged the hardcover edition as follows:

Names: Doctorow, Cory, author.
Title: Red team blues / Cory Doctorow.
Description: First edition. | New York : Tor, Tor Publishing Group, 2023. |
Identifiers: LCCN 2022056780 (print) | LCCN 2022056781 (ebook) |
    ISBN 9781250865847 (hardcover) | ISBN 9781250865861 (ebook)
Subjects: LCGFT: Novels.
Classification: LCC PS3604.O27 R44 2023 (print) |
    LCC PS3604.O27 (ebook) | DDC 813/.6—dc23/eng/20221208
LC record available at https://lccn.loc.gov/2022056780
LC ebook record available at https://lccn.loc.gov/2022056781

ISBN 978-1-250-86585-4 (trade paperback)

Our books may be purchased in bulk for promotional, educational, or business use. Please contact your local bookseller or the Macmillan Corporate and Premium Sales Department at 1-800-221-7945, extension 5442, or by email at MacmillanSpecialMarkets@macmillan.com.

First Tor Paperback Edition: 2024

Printed in the United States of America

0 9 8 7 6 5 4 3 2 1

For Dan Kaminsky, 1979–2021.
Hacker, pen-tester, mensch.

Rest in peace, Dan.

red team
blues

1

One evening, I got a wild hair and drove all night from San Diego to Menlo Park. Why Menlo Park? It had both a triple-Michelin-star place and a dear old friend both within spitting distance of the Walmart parking lot, where I could park the *Unsalted Hash,* leaving me free to drink as much as I cared to and still be able to walk home and crawl into bed.

I'd done a job that turned out better than I'd expected—well enough that I was set for the year if I lived carefully. I didn't want to live carefully. The age for that was long past. I wanted to live it up. There'd be more work. I wanted to celebrate.

Truth be told, I also didn't want to contemplate the possibility that, at the age of sixty-seven, the new work might stop coming in. Silicon Valley hates old people, but that was okay, because I hated Silicon Valley. Professionally, that is.

Getting close to Bakersfield, I pulled the *Unsalted Hash* into a rest stop to stretch my legs and check my phone. After a putter around the picnic tables and vending machine, I walked the perimeter of my foolish and ungainly and luxurious tour bus, checking the tires and making sure the cargo compartments were dogged and locked. I climbed back in, checked my sludge levels and decided they were low enough that I could use my own toilet, then, finally, having forced myself to wait, sat on one of the buttery leather chairs and checked my messages.

That's how I learned that Danny Lazer was looking for me. He was working the usual channels—DMs from people who I tended to check in with when I was looking for work—and it put a shine on my evening, because sixty-seven or no, there was always work for someone with my skill set. Danny Lazer had a problem with his Trustlesscoin keys, which relied on the best protected cryptographic secrets in the world (nominally).

So I messaged him. One rest stop later, just past Gilroy, I got his reply. He was eager to see me. Would I call on him at his home in Palo Alto?

My pathetic little ego swelled up at his eagerness. I told him I had a big dinner planned the next night, but I'd see him the morning after. Truth be told, putting off a man as important as Danny Lazer, even for twenty-four hours, made me feel more important still. I could tell from his reply that the delay chafed at him. I felt petty, but not so much so that I canceled my dinner. My dear old friend was a lively sort, and it was possible we'd walk from the restaurant to her place for an hour or three before I returned to the Walmart parking lot.

Dinner didn't disappoint, and neither did the fun and games afterward. It was a very nice capstone to a very successful job, and a very good prelude to another job for one of the nicest rich men (or richest nice men) in Silicon Valley.

Danny was old Silicon Valley, a guy who started his own UUCP host so he could help distribute the alt hierarchy and once helped Tim May bring a load of unlicensed firearms across state lines from a Nevada gun show. He'd lived like a monk for decades, writing cryptographic code and fighting with the NSA over it, and had mortgaged his parents' house back east to keep himself and a couple of programmers in business in a tiny office for a decade while he and Galit lived in a thirty-foot motor home that needed engine tuning once a month just so it could trundle from one parking space to the next.

It was a bet that there would come a day when the internet's innocence would end and people would want privacy from each other and their governments, and he kept doubling down on that bet through every boom and bust, living on ramen and open cereal boxes from the used food store, refusing to part with any equity except to promising hackers who'd join him, and then the bet paid off, and he became Daniel Moses Lazar, with a 75 percent stake in Keypairs LLC, whose crypto-libraries and work-flow tools were the much-ballyhooed picks and shovels of the next internet revolution. Keypairs wasn't the first unicorn in Silicon Valley, but it was the first one that never took a dime in venture capital and whose sole angels were Danny's parents back in Jersey, to whom Danny sent at least $100 million before they made him stop, insisting that they had nothing more they wanted in this world.

Galit picked out a big place in Twin Peaks that you could see Alcatraz from on a clear day, gutted it to the foundation slab, bare studs, and ceiling joists, completely rebuilt it while being mindful of both Danny's specification for networking receptacles throughout, and Galit's encyclopedic knowledge of the Arts and Crafts Movement. One day, as she was bringing out some Mendocino grig and a cheese board for the two of them to enjoy from their half-built porch, she gasped, complained of pain in both arms, then her chest, and then she collapsed and was dead before the ambulance arrived.

It had been a good marriage: twenty-two years and no kids, because there was nowhere in their old RV to put them unless they wanted to hang them from the rafters. She'd been his rock while he'd built up Keypairs, but he'd been hers, too, rubbing her feet and helping her deal with the endless humiliations that a woman doing administrative work in Silicon Valley had to put up with. He didn't see it that way, though: after he took possession of her ashes, all he could talk about was how they'd wasted nearly a quarter of a century chasing a fortune that didn't do either of them a bit of good, and it had cost them the time they could have spent in a beach shack in the Baja while he did two hours of contract work a month to pay for machete sharpening and new hammocks once a year.

A procession of Silicon Valley's most powerful leaders and

most respected technologists filed through the Palo Alto tear-down they'd bought to perch in while the Twin Peaks project was underway. People who weren't merely wealthy but famous for their vision, their sensitivity, their insight. They argued with him about his crushing regrets and tried to tell him how much good he'd done, both for Galit and for the world, but he was un-reachable. A consensus emerged among the Friends of Danny that he was not long for this world. Not that he was going to kill himself or anything but that he would simply stop caring about living, and then nature would take its course.

They were right—given all facts in evidence, that was a fore-gone conclusion. But there was one hidden variable: Sethuramani Balakrishnan, who was twenty-five, brilliant, and had made a series of lateral moves within Keypairs: customer support, then compliance, and finally Danny's PA, a job she was vastly over-qualified for.

She helped him flip the house, then to turn Keypairs over to a management committee carefully balanced between hackers who'd been with Danny since the PDP-8 days, people with real managerial experience and proven experience growing compa-nies and running big teams. He got rid of all the shares he'd taken in over the years to sit on advisory boards and stuck everything into Vanguard index-tracker funds—the ones that *didn't* buy a lot of tech stocks.

As far as anyone could tell, Sethu didn't try to talk him out of any of this, just offered efficient, intelligent, and supremely organized help in getting Danny's life's work out of a realm in which it had to be actively managed by someone with Danny's incredible drive, insight, and technical knowledge, and into an investment vehicle managed by an overgrown spreadsheet, one that would multiply his money ahead of the CPI, year on year, until someone built a guillotine on his lawn.

What Sethu *did* talk him into was buying a condo around the corner from that Palo Alto teardown, an eight-story place, quiet, built on the grave of another Palo Alto teardown that had been snapped up by property developers in the glory days before NIMBY planning ended all high-density infill within fifty miles of Stanford.

The Camino Real had excellent security, as well as all the amenities: a pool, a gym, and a set of spring-loaded seismic dampers set deep into the bedrock that turned the whole place into a bouncy castle whenever the San Andreas Fault got a touch of indigestion.

It was steps to California Avenue and five Michelin-star restaurants—one with three stars, two with two—and it cost him eight million, plus furnishings, which Sethu oversaw, going all in on Danish woods for a midcentury modern feel that went great with the rooftop garden that came with the penthouse unit. Sethu got him interested in trying all that Michelin star food, a far cry from ramen and slightly irregular breakfast cereals, and from there, it was the chefs' tables, and then the private cooking classes, and then a major reno to the penthouse to fit it out with a kitchen that would have made Heston Blumenthal gasp and twirl.

They spent the month that the renos took in an exclusive lodge near a slightly active Costa Rican volcano, checking out the bromeliads and howler monkeys. He came back bronzed and fit from all that volcano hiking and became one of the great chefs of the new aristocracy, even pulling out the old alt.gourmand posts from the prehistory of Usenet.

I don't know when they became a couple, but I imagine it was a natural thing. Danny had a big heart, and he'd loved Galit with all of it, and with Galit gone and Danny still around, his heart wasn't going to sit idly. Sethu is beautiful and brilliant and good at what she does, and those were all the traits that attracted Danny to Galit in the first place.

The Camino Real's security gave me the twice-over and then emitted me. The elevator doors gave a sophisticated sigh and welcomed me in, and the buttonless panel lit up *PH,* and my blood pooled a little in my feet as I attained liftoff.

Danny looked at least ten years *younger* than the last time I'd seen him, craggy but handsome, and the pounds he'd put on had only filled him out so he wasn't such an ectomorphic scarecrow.

He'd definitely been hitting the kettlebells, too, and his tight Japanese tee clung just enough that I could see he'd gotten some definition in his pecs and biceps. That's hard muscle to acquire once you hit your fifties. Someone had been making Danny put in his reps.

Danny's an intense guy who believed so fiercely in the significance and beauty and urgency of cryptography that he could easily captivate a roomful of people with an impromptu lecture on the subject, and he would not relinquish that hold until they all had to leave. He wasn't a bore, but he wasn't exactly normal, and yet as far as I knew, everyone who'd ever become personally acquainted with him liked him. A lot.

"Well, you don't look like a man who got through a prix fixe at the Palmier. Even with the flights, you shouldn't be that bilious, Mart. What'd you do, stop for Oreos on the way back to your double-wide?"

I let this pour over me as he showed me into the foyer and I shucked my scuffed old loafers, the ones I saved for personal days when I didn't have to impress a client. "First of all, Lazer, the *Unsalted Hash* is a forty-foot, state-of-the-art touring bus with seven feet of internal clearance, an induction range, a deep freeze, and a sound system that can set off car alarms for a block. It is *not* a double-wide.

"Secondly, the Palmier was great, and I didn't get the prix fixe—I got a taster at the chef's table with a friend, and we stayed up later than we should have, and I *still* managed to drag myself here for a business conference at this unholy hour. I'm running on three hours' sleep and digesting a good three-thousand-calorie dinner, is all.

"Finally, I don't stop for Oreos, ever. I have a supply of 1995-vintage Hydroxes in one of the deep freezes. The original recipe contains all those great trans fats that make for excellent long-term frozen flavor and texture retention. I would offer you a package, but I won't, because they are mine, and I treasure them beyond all reason and plan to make my stash last until I can no longer consume solid food, whereupon I plan to consume the balance in smoothie form."

He took my shoes and tossed them into a closet and slammed the door, making a face, then burst out laughing and grabbed me in a bear hug that reminded me of those new biceps of his. "Man, it's good to see you, Marty. Come in, come in. We'll go out onto the roof."

I got a quick tour of a lot of teak and curves and angles, like a set dresser had been given an unlimited budget to decorate the boss's office on a midcentury period drama. Then he opened a sliding door out onto the roof-deck, which had some very nice landscaping and potted shrubs, a meandering stream patrolled by fat koi and fed by a two-foot waterfall, some comfortable-looking and elegant teak loungers, and Sethu.

She had an easel set up and was painting in oils, an impressionistic landscape of Palo Alto's nimbified one-family houses and dinky main street. It was a couple of billion dollars' worth of real estate dressed up as middle-class houses from the same midcentury dreamland as the furnishings in the living room.

She turned and saw us and narrowed her eyes, just a tiny amount, before cleaning her brushes and hanging up her smock on the easel's corner.

"Hi, hon," she said. "This must be your friend Mr. Hench."

Danny beamed at her, an expression I remembered from his most successful demos, that prideful look he got when his code performed some miracle. "Marty, I don't know if you ever met Sethu, back in the old days."

"I don't know that we were ever introduced properly," I said. She'd let me in, once or twice, when I'd come by to see if I could pull Danny out of his tailspin. But she'd been his PA then.

"Well, in that case, Sethuramani Lazer, meet Martin Hench. Marty, meet Sethu."

I'm pretty sure my facial expression didn't change when he dropped that last name on me. I'd already noticed the rock on her finger, of course—a bachelor of my age and experience takes note of these things automatically, without conscious intervention. I'm pretty sure what Danny said next was that same pride speaking, not a failure of my poker face.

"Married her last year. Or rather, she married *me,* despite being significantly out of my league."

"Lucky fella," I said. "Congrats to both of you."

He got us settled into loungers, and Sethu mentioned that she was going in for lemonade and offered us some. She brought it out in sweating tall glasses with silicone straws and then went back to her easel, far enough away that it wouldn't seem odd not to include her in our conversation.

I sipped as Danny scrolled his phone for a moment, double-checked his notes, and took Sethu in. She was beautiful, of course, but I'd known that since I'd first met her at the door of that teardown that Danny had settled into as his final resting place. Now, though, she had the kind of haircut that some very bright topiarist had charged her at least a thousand bucks for, and with it, the kind of poise I associate with very beautiful, very accomplished women who are also very, very rich. Something in the posture, a kind of deep relaxation that you rarely see. Having a very deep cash buffer can give a woman the same tranquility as any middling specimen of manhood gets for free, the liberation from casual predation that men don't even notice.

Danny put his phone down at last. "So I hear you did some work recently? Bonwick. Rearden Factoring?"

I nodded. "Yeah, Brian and I did some business, but it's not the kind of thing I can discuss. You know that. He lost something, I found it, and I made him whole."

He snorted. "Marty, you don't make people whole. Your commission still twenty-five percent?"

"It is," I said. "And I still don't charge anything to take a job, not even expenses or a retainer. I take the risk, I get the reward. That's a proposition I think you probably relate to."

"I'm familiar with the general idea." He looked around at his penthouse garden, his beautiful young wife, his view of the strivers of Palo Alto and their *Leave It to Beaver* houses, all a testament to his willingness to take all the risk and his unwillingness to share his rewards. "You ever take payment in crypto?"

"I prefer fiat"—this being the cutesy word that crypto weirdos use for real money—"I have smart accountants who keep my tax bite down to a manageable slice, and I've got no other reason to accept distributed sudoku puzzles in lieu of greenbacks."

"Very funny," he said. Cryptocurrency hustlers hate it when you point out that the whole blockchain emits billions of tons of CO_2 to help repeatedly compute pointless mathematical puzzles. "You're familiar with how crypto works, though, right?"

"Danny, I love you like a brother, but I hope I'm not about to get a sales pitch for Trustlesscoin." The only sour note in the previous night's dinner had been a couple of bros at the chef's table who spent the first hour talking about smart contracts. It was a hazard of any public space in SV, and I accepted it with good grace, but I wouldn't tolerate it in private places. Life is too short.

"No pitch, but I just want to make sure you're up to speed for what I'm going to tell you next. Forensic accounting is one thing, but when you throw in crypto, it's a whole different world."

I grunted noncommittally. Danny had been around since *crypto* meant "cryptography," and I hadn't figured him to become one of these blockchain hustlers. They're the kind of smart people who outsmart themselves, especially when it comes to shenanigans, forgetting that their public ledger is *public* and all their transactions are visible to the whole world forever. Forensic accounting never had a better friend than crypto, with its mix of public ledgers, deluded masters of the universe, and suckers pumping billions into the system. It was full employment for me and my competitors until cryptocurrency's carbon footprint rendered the earth uninhabitable.

"There are certain technical differences between Trustless and other coins. Will you allow me to explain them to you? I promise it's germane and I'm not trying to sell you anything."

"Aw, hell, Danny, you can tell me anything. I just get sick of being hustled."

"Me, too, pal. Okay, if you mentioned distributed sudoku puzzles, you know something about proof of work: the way blockchain maintains the integrity of its ledger is by having everyone in the system repeatedly do compute work that reaffirms all the entries in the ledger. So long as the value of all the assets in the ledger is less than the electricity bill for taking over the majority of the compute work, they're safe."

"That means that the more valuable all this blockchain stuff becomes, the more coal they have to burn to keep it all from being stolen," I said. It was something I'd almost said to the bros at dinner the night before, but I didn't want an argument to distract from the otherwise lovely time I'd been having with my entirely lovely companion.

"That's fair," he said. "That's what every greenie who hasn't received a couple of mil in donations from surprised cryptomillionaires will tell you. But, Marty, that's a problem with proof of work, not with distributed ledgers. If you could build a blockchain that had a negligible carbon budget, you could do a lot with it."

"Launder money. Badly."

"That," he said. "Lot of Chinese entrepreneurs and officials are anxious to beat currency controls. But it's not just money, it's anything you want to have universally available, unfalsifiable, and cryptographically secured."

"Laundered money."

He made a face. "Cynic. Not laundered money. Genocide-proof ID. Cryptographically secured, write-only manifests of a person's identifiers, including nationality, vitals, and ethnic group, but each one has its own key, held by the Blue Helmets. You get to a border and you present your biometrics, and the UN tells the border guards your nationality but not your ethnicity."

"Fanciful."

"Cynic! Yeah, fine, no one's doing it yet, but we could. All that blockchain for good shit that the hucksters talked up to make it sound like proof of work wasn't a crime against humanity. Trustlesscoin lets you do them because it doesn't need the sudoku."

I dredged up memories of half-digested podcasts I'd listened to on the road. "Is it a proof-of-stake thing?"

He snorted. "Don't try to sound smart, Marty, you'll sprain something. No, it's secure enclaves. That crypto-sub-processor in your iPhone that Apple uses to keep you from switching to another app store? It can run code. What's more, it can sign the output. So we can send you a program and check to see whether it ran as intended, because we know that the owner of a phone can't override the secure enclave. Far as Apple's concerned, iPhone owners are the enemy, and their threat model treats the device owner as an adversary—as someone who might get apps someplace that doesn't kick a fifteen to thirty percent vigorish up to Apple for every transaction, depriving its shareholders of their rake.

"Any device with a secure enclave or other trusted computing module is a device that treats its owner as the enemy. That's a device we need, because when you're in the Trustlesscoin network, that device will defend me from you, and you from me. I don't have to trust you, I just have to trust that you can't break into your own phone, which is to say that I have to trust that Apple's engineers did their job correctly, and well, you know, they've got a pretty good track record, Marty."

"Except?"

He finished his lemonade and scowled at the reusable straw. "Yeah, except. Look, Trustlesscoin is on track to become the standard public ledger for the world. I know, I know, every founder talks that 'make a dent in the universe' crap, but I mean it. You want to know how serious I am about this? I took in out-side capital."

He let me sit with that a moment. Danny Lazer, the man who ate ramen in a twenty-year-old, bent-axle RV for decades with the love of his life so he'd never have to take a nickel from any of those bloodsuckers on Sand Hill Road, and he took in out-side capital. Danny Lazer, a man who'd owned 75 percent of a unicorn, which is to say, seven-point-five-times-ten-to-the-eight U.S. American Greenback Simoleon Dollars, and he took in out-side capital.

"Why? And also, *what for*?"

He laughed. "Watching you work out a problem is like watch-ing a bulldog chew a wasp, brother. You've got a hell of a poker face, but when you start overclocking the old CPU, it just *melts*. I'll tell you why and what for.

"First of all, I wanted to create something for Sethu. She's never had the chance to live up to her potential. She's *smart*, Marty, smart like Galit was, but she's also technical, and mana-gerial, and just *born* to run things. I've never met a better candi-date for a CEO than she is. And I'm not young, you know that, and there's going to be a long time after I'm dead when she'll still be in her prime, and I wanted to make something she could grow into and grow around her.

"I'd been playing with the idea behind Trustless since the early 2000s, when Microsoft released its first Trusted Comput-ing papers, all the way back in the Palladium days! So Sethu and I hung up a whiteboard in the guest room and started spending a couple of hours a day in there. I didn't want to bring in anyone else at first, first because it seemed like a hobby and not a busi-ness, and hell, every cryptographer I know is working seventy-hour weeks as it is.

"*Then* I didn't want to bring in anyone else because I got a sense of how big this damned thing is. I mean, there's about two trillion in assets in the blockchain today, and that's with all the stupid friction of proof-of-work. When we lift the shackles off of it, *whoosh,* we're talking about a ledger that will encompass more assets than the total balance sheets of twenty or thirty of the smallest UN members . . . *combined.*

"You know me, Marty. I don't believe in much, but when I do believe in something, I'm all in. All. In. And so I brought some people in."

"What for, though? Danny, how much of your Keypairs jackpot did you manage to blow? How much money could you possibly need, and for *what*? Are you building your own chip foundry? Buying a country?"

"We actually thought of doing both of those things, you know, but decided we didn't need the headaches. The Keypairs money's only grown since I cashed out, thanks to the bull runs. I can't spend it all, won't be able to. It would sicken me to try, because I'd have to be so wasteful to even make a dent in it.

"The reason I went for outside capital wasn't money, it was connections."

I groaned. Every grifter in private equity and VC-land claimed that they had "connections" that represented value add for their portfolio companies. The social butterfly market was implausible on its face, and in practice, it was just a way of turning cocktail parties into a business expense. "Come on, Danny, you know people already."

"Not these people." And he did the thing. He looked from side to side, up and down. He turned off his phone and held his hand out for mine and carried them both to the little step next to the water feature and set them down on it so they'd be in the white-noise zone. He came back, looked around again. "I got signing keys for four of the most commonly deployed secure enclaves." He looked around *again*.

"I think I know what that means, Danny, but maybe you could spell it out? I'm just a dumb old accountant, not a cryptographic legend like yourself. And for God's sake, stop looking around. I'll let you know if I see anyone sneaking up on us."

"Sorry, sorry. Okay. The secure enclave gets a program, runs it, and signs the output. The secure enclave's little toy operating system says that it does this reliably and without exception. You see a signature on a program's output, you know the program produced it. That toy OS, it's simple. Stupid. Brutal. Does about six things, very well, and nothing else. You can't change that program. Secure enclaves are designed to be non-serviceable. Even taking them off the mainboard wrecks them. You get them into a lab and decap them and hit them with an electron-tunneling microscope, you still won't be able to recover the signing keys or force a false sig.

"But if you have the signing keys? You can just simulate a secure enclave on any computer. Then you can run any operating system you want on it, including one that will forge signatures. You do that, and you can *falsify the ledger*. You can move unlimited sums from any part of the balance sheet to your part of the balance sheet. You can jackpot the whole fucking thing."

I blew out air. "Well, that seems like a defect in the system, all right."

"It can't be helped. We call it Trustless, but there's always *some* trust in a system like this. You're not trusting the other users of the system or the company that made the software. You're trusting that a couple of leading manufacturers of cryptographic coprocessors and sub-processors, companies with decades of experience, will maintain operational security and not lose control of the keys that their entire business—and the entire business of all their customers and their customers' customers—are dependent upon. You're not trusting the other users, but you're trusting *them*."

"And yet," I said, looking over at Sethu, who was painting away and performing an excellent simulation of someone who wasn't eavesdropping, "you found someone willing to sell you some of those keys."

"Yes," he said and gave me a calm, no-bullshit, eye-to-eye stare. "I did. It's useful to have those, especially when you're first kicking a new cryptocurrency around. You make a smart contract with a bad line of code in it, you create a bug bounty with an unlimited payout. So in the early days, when you're figuring this stuff out, you do a little ledger rewriting."

"You do rewriting on a read-only ledger that no one is ever supposed to rewrite."

He rolled his eyes. "Ethereum did it early on, moved fifty mil in stolen payout from a bad smart contract out of the crook's account and back into the mark's account. No one made too much of a fuss. I mean, the immutable ledger sounds like a great idea until someone no stupider than you gets taken for fifty mil, and then rewriting the ledger is just sound fiscal policy in service to fundamental justice."

"But Ethereum told everyone they were doing it. Sounds like you did it all on the down low?"

"We were early. No one was even paying attention. All we wanted was a ledger whose early entries weren't an eternal monument to my stupid mistakes as I climbed the learning curve."

"Fine. Vain, but fine. Still, getting those keys meant a lot of power for a little reputation laundering."

He sighed and looked away. "Yeah. The thing is, I'm not the only one who makes mistakes. We are aiming for trillions secured on our chain. Trillions, Marty. Ten to the twelve. It's an unforgiving medium, and the stakes are high. The Ethereum lesson was clear: a couple of divide-by-zeros or fence post errors, a single badly typed variable or buffer overrun, and the whole thing could sink. I needed an eraser. Not on day zero but well before I attained liftoff."

"Every hacker builds in a back door, huh?"

"Don't call it that. Call it an Undo button."

"Okay, then. An Undo button in a system whose cryptography is supposed to prevent undo at all costs. But not a back door."

"You, my friend, are too smart. I miss the days when forensic accountancy and security engineering were distinct fields."

"Me, too, pal. So what happened? Your keys took a walk?"

"We built the system to be secure. You know me, I'm a paranoid old creep with a dirty mind, so everything I did, I did right.

The keys were on an air gap system. I bought that system myself off a pile of boxed HP laptops at Fry's just a couple of weeks before they closed their doors for good."

"Rest in peace."

"It was time. But back when you *could* go into Fry's, you could pick up a laptop sealed in shrink-wrap, carry it yourself to the cashier, pay cash for it, and walk out, stopping only to show your receipt to the poor door-checker. Then you could take it to the data center, badge into the clean room, lay out your workbench, unscrew that sucker, and remove every single network interface with a pair of pliers, not just snipping the traces but ripping them right off the board."

"Lucky you didn't snap the board."

He grimaced. "I did. I bought three of them so I could take a mulligan or two if I needed it. I only needed one spare, as it turned out. Then it went into a safe, a good safe, rated for three hours. There's a watchman who makes physical rounds of every safe room, every two hours. And I locked up the BIOS with a hardware token. Steal that laptop, you'd still need my token."

"And yet . . ."

"You know how they say anyone can design a security system that he himself can't figure out how to break?"

"Schneier's law."

"Schneier's law. Yeah. Someone smarter than I am figured it out."

"The watchman?"

"No, though he might have been in on it. They fired him. The safe was opened, the laptop was gone."

"And the hardware token?"

"You'll love this."

"I can't wait."

He tugged his forelock and adopted a broad Cockney accent that would have embarrassed Dick van Dyke. "Guv'nah, I was pickpocketed, so I was."

"I don't believe it. Pickpocketing is supposed to be a dead art. Who was working the scam, Apollo Robbins?"

He shrugged. "I don't reckon so. But yeah, there's plenty of Vegas acts that do pickpocketing stuff, and there's a pretty big YouTube competitive pickpocket scene with tutorials. Plus, there's the European talent, a lot of it, never really died out there. Covent Garden is like a plague reservoir for the pathogen, and you get an outbreak every year or two."

"You had the hardware token on your key ring?"

"That day, I did. I'd been in the data center. Then we went to dinner. Hydra. The prix fixe. The chef's table is nice, but the taster menu gets you the octopodi. Someone bumped me between the data center and my front door."

"Oof," I said. "Did you have to ring the downstairs neighbor's doorbell and climb out on their balcony?"

"Don't be stupid," he said. "In the first place, Sethu has her own keys. In the second place, the outside doors here are locked and armed when we're AFK."

I'd noticed the locks on the outside doors, and the break sensors, and the cameras—both the covert and overt ones. There were probably some I'd missed. I wouldn't put it past Danny to have a lidar rig in the shrubs, something to help the system distinguish between cat burglars and house cats.

"The watchman from the data center," I said. "That's your guy. Probably not the mastermind, but he'll be the key to it all."

"Looks like they socially engineered him. Matched him on Tinder, messaged him, *Oh, is that where you work? I'm just around the corner—want to meet me for a quick boba tea?*"

"Catfished. Honey trap."

He sighed. "Yeah. It was a good one."

"You reported the theft?"

"The insurance company will pay for a new laptop, which, frankly, I don't need, because I already have the spare I bought when I was going through the whole rigamarole to set up the air gap. But that's not the valuable part."

"No, it isn't. How about the keys?"

"Yeah, how about them?"

"First, have you warned your source that you lost them, so they can tell Apple and Samsung and all the other manufacturers that rely on those secure enclave chips? And second, have you warned your users that their money isn't safe?"

He looked over at Sethu, at Palo Alto, at his lemonade glass, and at the clouds in the sky. Long looks. The silence spoke volumes.

"How much money is the Trustlesscoin ledger worth, Danny?"

He looked me dead in the eye now. "About a billion."

We'd already been talking about trillions, so I shouldn't have been shocked. But tech founders are always throwing around big numbers, and I've developed the mental habit of knocking a few zeroes off any claims about "total addressable markets."

Trustlesscoin was the new crypto on the block. My unconscious estimate of its value was in the low tens of millions, which is also a big number, but not a billion.

"A billion here, a billion there—"

He cut me off. "Pretty soon, it starts to add up to real money. Yeah, I know, Marty. Don't joke, you're not good at it."

"When did you lose the keys?"

He checked his watch—a mechanical one, not ostentatious, an old wartime Rolex, from when men's Oysters were the size of a nickel, not these giant tourbillon monstrosities that cost a million bucks and looked like a poor man's idea of a rich man's watch. "Seventy-four hours and thirty minutes ago."

"Give or take."

"You're not good at comedy, Marty. We've established that."

"What fallout has there been?"

"Not much," he said. "In fact, maybe none. We have a pretty good statistical picture of what normal Trustless transaction activity looks like, and nothing has rung the alarm bells yet."

"Yet. But maybe not ever. Maybe they can't figure out how to exploit what they got."

"Or maybe they're biding their time. Or running an old-school salami-slice grift, shaving a lot of pennies, getting ready to cash out."

"Can you block that? They have to convert Trustlesscoins into fiat to get away with it, right?"

"They do, but we can't stop them. We're on every major exchange, not just to other tokens but also a bunch of different kinds of fiat and stablecoins. How do you think we got to a billion dollars so quickly? Trustless is both highly liquid and highly efficient. That's why it's the future of finance."

"And money laundering."

For a second, I thought he was going to throw his lemonade glass, dash it to the cool flagstones of his roof garden. He took a deep breath and then another and then set the glass down. "And money laundering. Marty, stop fucking with me. I am keenly aware that there are money launderers using my service. That has been apparent since the start. Some of these money launderers are very far away and would struggle to reach me if my technology did something to upset them. Some of them are closer."

He shook his head violently. "Marty, I am shitting bricks here. There's another shoe getting ready to drop, and when it does, I'm going to go down with it. Hard. I'm not just talking about losing my reputation and my fortune, I'm not just talking about ruining the life of that woman over there who dragged me back from the brink. I'm talking about being targeted for physical violence by unreasonable, sadistic, powerful criminal men who amassed their fortunes by spilling an ocean of blood and who cannot be placated. Nor can they be fended off, not unless I want to live my life inside a bunker.

"I don't know who stole those keys, Marty. I shouldn't have had them in the first place. I am now in a position where everything I hold dear is on the line, and so I called you. You and I go way back, you're my friend and I trust you, but I didn't call you because I wanted to cry on your shoulder."

"You called me because you think I can get the keys back."

"Bullshit. I called you because I'm desperate. I don't think anyone can get those keys back. I think that inside of a month, everything I care about will be in ruins. Major technology platforms that depend on secure enclaves for things way beyond Trustlesscoin will be exposed because of my recklessness, and they will be fucked. Secure enclaves are designed to be tamper-proof. You try to take one off a board the way I did with those air gap laptops' network interfaces and you render them permanently inoperable. They can't be field updated. They have no flashable BIOS. A vulnerability in a secure enclave is permanent.

"But the trillions of dollars in damage that I will do to the largest tech companies in the world will not worry me, because I will either be on the run or dead. Not a good death, either, Marty.

"So I called you because before that happens, I plan on exhausting every avenue of mitigation available to me."

"If I recover them?"

He snorted. "You do that, you might save my life and rescue a third of the top performers on the S&P 500 from their worst earnings call since the Great Financial Crisis."

"I mean, what do I get?"

The transformation was incredible. One minute, he'd been a scared old man, desperate, literally pleading for his life. In a flash, he was calm, back in the realm of numbers, and I was making a deal with a guy who'd eaten ramen for twenty-two years rather than surrender any more of his future fortune than was absolutely necessary.

"Well, a twenty-five percent commission is obviously out of the question. We're talking about a billion dollars here."

"That's if I recover the keys before they exfiltrate any of that money. My commission is based on value at recovery, not initial value. So if any of this goes public and the value of a Trustlesscoin falls to zero, then I get twenty-five percent of nothing."

He looked sour. "If that happens, you won't have anywhere to send your invoice for your twenty-five percent, either. But,

Marty, you can't seriously expect a two-hundred-and-fifty-mil upside here."

"Daniel Moses Lazer, you just got through lecturing me on the trillions in *downside* if those keys aren't recovered. Note that I did not say that I expected any share of the positive externalities a successful recovery would generate. Just the direct benefit to my client." I nodded at him.

"But a quarter of a billion dollars—"

"Or maybe it's nothing. Or maybe I'll find myself face-to-face with these killers you say you'd have to cower in a bunker over until the end of your natural life. Danny, I'm surprised at you. You know who I am. You know what I charge. You know I don't haggle."

He smiled, and I saw a little of the happy, well-fed, successful second act that he'd projected when he answered his door. "Yeah, I know. But I had to try. Two hundred and fifty mil is two hundred and fifty mil."

"A quarter of a billion dollars here, a quarter of a billion there—"

"Yeah, yeah. Pretty soon, we're talking real money. You think you can do it?"

I shrugged. "Can't say. I have some ideas about how to start, covering the bases, being my normal, meticulous self. You'd be surprised how often that works. If there's a fast resolution to this scam, it'll be because the people on the other side of it forgot to dot an i or cross a t. They have to make zero mistakes; I just have to find one error. They have to be perfect; I just have to be systematic. It's why I play the red team. Advantage to the attacker, as always."

"As always." He checked his watch. "Shit, I got to get my phone for a second here. Can you give me a minute?"

"Sure," I said as he grabbed his phone and mine, giving me mine back absently as he powered his up and logged in to it even as he slid through his sliding doors and into that picture-perfect living room.

I didn't power up my phone right away. First, because it was a game I played with myself: How long could I go without ramming its phosphors into my eyeballs? Second, because I wanted to mull over this job. And third, because I had a sense from Sethu's body language that she wanted to have a word with me.

She stepped away from the painting. She really was very good. Whatever she'd done to it while Danny and I had been talking had brought it to life in a way I couldn't exactly articulate, making it seem *energetic,* hinting at all the feverish activity in the home offices and garages and cars in that impressionistic landscape. She gave it *hustle.*

"Danny tells me you've done this work before," she said, hanging her smock on the easel and wiping her hands with an oily rag.

"Since the earliest days," I said. "Most accountants saw the spreadsheet as a tool for making their lives easier. A smaller group realized its potential for covering up financial crimes. I think I was the only member of that second group that wanted to prevent the crimes, rather than creating them."

"So there were three groups," she said.

"I guess so," I said. "The bean counters, the crooks, and me. Pretty sure we used to all hang out in the same Usenet support group for advanced Lotus 1–2–3 users."

"You've solved a lot of cases?"

"You make me sound like a detective. Yeah, I've made some of my clients pretty happy."

"Danny said you just had a big victory?"

"Rearden Factoring. They're financial engineers, leveraging supply-chain desperation. If you're a big blue chip, you tell your suppliers that you're paying them on one hundred and eighty days net unless they sign up with Rearden, which will process their invoices in thirty days in exchange for a two percent commission. Rearden doesn't charge the buyers anything for this; it just leverages up that free cash flow, turning it into capital for big bets in the capital markets, rotating its positions with every billing cycle. It's a lucrative business."

"It sounds like a dirty business," she said.

"No dirtier than any monopoly scam. The bigger the bigs get, the better the terms they can extract from their supply chain. It's the golden rule: they have the gold, they make the rules."

"And you helped them?"

"I did. Insider job, but he made a mistake. I caught it."

"That is a lucky break. Why would someone so competent in one domain be so foolish in another?"

"That is a mystery that I have pondered since I first figured out my old man was a brilliant mechanical engineer and a dribbling idiot when it came to politics, Sethu. If I ever figure out the answer to that question, I'll be sure to let you know."

She and I exchanged a look that meant something, though I couldn't have said what. If Sethu was a gold digger who'd tricked Danny into having something to live for, I wasn't going to fault her for it or begrudge her any of Danny's holdings, assuming he had any holdings in a week or two. Teaming up with a young, beautiful, devastatingly intelligent woman wasn't a lapse in Danny's brilliance as far as I was concerned—it was his smarts carrying over from one domain into the next.

"Thanks for the history lesson," she said. "Always fascinating to hear these tales from the electronic frontier."

"Anytime," I said as she picked up the easel and went back indoors, passing Danny in the doorway as he came out to me.

"Did she grill you?" he asked.

"Just a friendly chat," I said.

"Well, then, you got lucky. She's my equal partner in Trustless, and she's also the beneficiary of my estate. She has as much at stake as I do here. Even before this incident, she told me I was too trusting. *Me!* If she's willing to trust you, you should take it as a standing ovation in your little one-man show, *Martin Hench: Stand-Up Guy.*"

"It's a performance that's wowed 'em for a generation," I said.

"Well, maybe this will be your grand finale. An old player who happens on a quarter billion dollars doesn't need to perform for his grubstake anymore."

"But you didn't quit when you had the chance," I said, before realizing with a wince that he *had* quit, quit everything and made ready to quit life itself.

He saw the wince, and his eyes and voice softened. "I nearly did. Maybe I should have."

2

The next morning, I visited the data center. It was inland, past Stockton, in a small town that was growing so fast that almost every storefront on its two-block main street was under renovation. To judge by the Airbnb listings, every house for miles was a "rustic cabin" with "scenic vistas." But on the outskirts, where the big, refrigerated freight warehouses nestled alongside the rail sidings, the vistas weren't so much scenic as empty—nothingness stretching to nowhere, forever.

The warehouses had been converted to data centers, not Amazon distribution centers, because this close to the Bay Area, the economics penciled out that way.

These data centers catered to a specialty trade: people whose applications didn't fit into one of the big clouds because of some weird technical characteristic or because of some weird threat model (I guess Trustless had both). The high-security refit was good enough that I stopped trying to find the holes in the system within the first ten minutes; every bright idea I had for a vulnerability—a way to tailgate on a pass, an unsecured roof approach—was visibly and obviously countered, and that meant there was a whole universe of stuff I *wasn't* seeing that would be even securer.

I'd have come straight from Danny's place if I could have, but you don't get to just walk into a place like that. I had a friend who had just taken the CSO job at a fintech start-up with stupid Saudi money (the Saudis purely love money laundering) reach out to them, intimating that they were worried about a breach at their current bespoke data center and asking if their security consultant could come out and tour their facilities.

I was warned to bring a REAL ID–compliant driver's license or my passport, and they did the biometric matching carefully at the front desk before escorting me to a room of lockboxes, where I was politely but firmly instructed to stash all my electronics.

"How do your customers perform diagnostics and trouble-shoot with outside experts if you don't let them bring in phones and laptops?" I asked.

"The rules are different for customers," the short, no-nonsense Latinx security guard told me. She moved well, like someone who knew down-and-dirty fighting, and she had a Taser on her hip. After I emptied my pockets, I went through a millimeter-wave scanner and a magnetometer.

On the sanitary side of the checkpoint, I was met by the facilities manager, Vikram Zain, an ex-marine who'd grown out his high-and-tight but still had some visible ink on his forearm, peeking out from his polo shirt. He had three devices slung from his belt—black rectangles that could have been tablets or Tasers—and a smile that he could turn on and off like a light switch.

"Mr. Hench," he said.

"Mr. Zain. Thanks for taking the time."

"My pleasure," he said with uncaring insincerity. "I hope Es-katerina made it clear that the tour's going to be pretty limited. The way we do business here means that you can't enter any of our tenants' spaces."

"I should hope not," I said mildly.

"Good. Well, so long as we're both on the same page on that, I can show you the generation facilities, the main punch down for our fiber, the mini-kitchen. Unless you want to see the dump-ster?"

I sighed. "Look, Vikram, I'm just doing a favor for a friend who's in a tight spot. Masala's got to move to a new data center fast, and they don't want to move again anytime soon. They need a space they can grow into and stick with. Normally, that's a slow and measured process, but this time around, they've got to do it fast. That's a rotten way to do security, and Zeldo knows it, so he's asking me to do whatever I can to help him not screw it up. I understand that you can't show me much here—hell, it's a mark in your favor. But I'll see whatever I can see, I'll ask some questions, and I'll report back as honestly as I can."

He shook his head, then smiled, on-off. "No one ever does security right in advance. It's always a reactive posture. Everyone wants to play on the red team."

"Even you?"

He smiled even bigger and left the smile on his face this time. "Not me, bro. Blue team all the way."

"Sounds like you were born for this job."

As it happens, I hate playing blue team, even though I spend a lot of time thinking about it, even playing it in war games. Defenders have the disadvantage. My day job has always been on the red team, and blue teaming in the exercises makes me a better adversary, gives me a sense of how real-world defenses fail.

After that, Vikram and I set up an easy rapport. The facility was impressive, especially considering how quickly it had been converted from a cold-chain meat-and-produce warehouse to a secure data facility. I asked him about the patch process for his sensors, and he and I spent a lovely half hour walking through the unique ops challenges in an environment that had a high likelihood of supply-chain attacks.

He showed me the mini-kitchen and nodded approvingly when I turned down a pod coffee, then took me to his office where he made me an AeroPress using an electric kettle and a little corner sink.

"Okay," I said. "I guess that about covers it. Wish I could have seen inside a cage, but I get it."

He shook his head. "Hell with it. We're just provisioning a new private facility for a tenant that's upgrading. None of their servers are there, but I can get you into the room, show you how it works. They're a high-sensitivity customer—got their own air gap and safe room." I knew the customer was Trustless. They'd demanded—and received—an upgrade and a year's free rent after the break-in. I also knew that it was right next door to their existing space, to make the move easier and minimize downtime.

"Vikram, I don't want to be any trouble."

"It's no trouble," he said. "It's on the way back out anyway. Come on, there's not much to see, but since you've come all this way . . ."

There wasn't much to see. There was the empty cage with its racks and power supplies, RJ45 plugs, cable troughs, worktables. The doorway was steel-framed, and when I thumped my knuckles along the drywall, they made a solid noise as the Sheetrock contacted the tempered steel grid beneath it.

I checked out the punch downs and brackets for CCTVs and motion sensors, the dry extinguisher, the primary and backup chiller vents, the thermostat and backup thermostat. The cages were bolted deep into the structural members, as was the air gap room's walls and doorway. The locks were excellent, warded and properly installed.

Vikram trailed me by a respectful distance as I examined each feature, loaning me a penlight at one point.

"This is really good," I pronounced, handing him back the light. "How the hell did someone rob it?"

His smile blipped out of existence. He didn't rise to the bait, though.

"Come on, Vik. It's not exactly common knowledge, but Danny Lazer's a plugged-in guy. When he gets taken, word gets around. What I hear, he had a setup a lot like this one."

"Mr. Hench," Vikram began.

"'*Mr. Hench*' now? What happened to 'Marty'?"

"Mr. Hench, we don't discuss our clients' business with anyone. Your client will be glad to hear that, I'm sure."

"I'm sure he will. But he's also not going to move his operation into this facility if there's a big old unpatched vuln that was just exploited."

Vikram's jarhead stone-face act got even stonier. Mount Rushmore by way of the subcontinent. I decided I never wanted to play poker against Vikram Zain.

"Look, Vikram, let's be serious. I got hired for this gig because I'm good at my job. Part of being good at my job is finding out things like this. And part of being good at it is getting to the bottom of it. You are good at your job. What would you do if you had my job? Would you shrug and say, 'I'm sure it's all fine now, Zeldo, you go ahead and move all of Masala's servers here, and don't you fret at all about that physical security issue'?"

"I would not," he said.

"Yeah, that's what I figured. Everything I've seen suggests that you folks are careful and professional, imaginative and thoughtful. This is a *good* setup. But when you're on the blue team, you've got to be perfect, and the red team—"

"—merely has to find a single mistake." He relaxed one iota, then another.

"Let's go back to my office," he said.

3

Ales Kocourek was at SF State and Jia Hak was at Stanford when they met. No one would have pegged them for romance. She was a grind, in that Korean American success story way, while he was second-generation Czech and more interested in e-sports than comp sci.

But they shared a passion for digital laptop reggae, and she loved his hardware, the weird synths powered by SID chips harvested from actual Commodore 64s and 128s, even reject pulls that he called the "serendipities" for the weird tones these defective chips would insert into the mix.

Meanwhile, he loved the music she made with them, her hair flying around her head as her fingers flew over the knobs and faders while she mixed in real time.

She tutored him in comp sci, and he got pretty good at physical security, with a gift for building easily maintained and reliable networks of heterogeneous sensors and actuators, sometimes writing his own compatibility layers to merge the data from a heat sensor, a motion sensor, and a camera into an anomaly-reporting system.

Vikram hired Ales in his sophomore year based on a personal recommendation from an old retired friend who taught the program part-time just to keep busy. Vik also tried to hire Jia, but she wasn't interested—Stanford undergrads didn't need to haul ass all the way past Stockton to get a side hustle. But she'd come by to get Ales, Ubering out while grinding on her assignments on a laptop, using mobile data the whole way, then driving him back in his car when he'd put in too many hours to drive safely.

Vikram had suspected they were gobbling Provigil and/or Adderall and partying all night, but that was their business.

After Trustless's cage got ripped off and the poor watchman had been investigated, disgraced, fired, and sent a stern letter reminding him of the bowel-loosening consequences of violating his NDA, Vikram had gone looking for the actual insider threat. The watchman wasn't a dummy, but he also wasn't into the kind of locksport and digital shenanigans that would have let him pull off the Trustless air gap stunt.

Drawing Vikram out wasn't easy, but once I made it subtly clear that I wasn't trying to bust his balls, only trying to find a way to reassure my "client," he opened up some.

The list of possible suspects just wasn't that long. Thing was, Ales had written so much custom code for the sensor grid that a supply chain threat was just about unimaginable. Even if someone at the company that made the camera or the motion detector installed a web shell and tried to penetrate the network that way, Ales's abstraction layers meant it wouldn't be able to exfiltrate a single bit.

So if Ales's code meant that no one on the outside could have disabled the security systems while the break-in took place, it meant that someone on the inside must have.

"He hasn't answered his phone or email since the day of the break-in," Vikram finished. "No social check-ins for him or the girl. No one's tagged either of them on any public posts since, and the open-source intelligence people haven't recorded any pings. They've dropped off the map."

"Well," I said, "that feels significant."

He made a face. "Don't be funny. He can't stay underground forever. There's too much open-source intel, too many off-the-books facial recognition social-monitoring services. He'll surface, and then things will happen."

"I have no doubt."

4

Sit in the same Walmart parking lot long enough and eventually every RV bum you've ever known will show up. The *Sectoral Balance,* Raza's tour bus, was one spot away from the *Unsalted Hash,* freshly detailed and proudly emblazoned with its name and a stylized Kasey the Kangaroo logo.

Raza had cranked out her pop-outs and unfolded her back deck, thus neatly skirting Walmart's prohibition on setting up lounge furniture and a grill. She was slow-cooking something meaty and fragrant, augmented by applewood chips that were puffing away like a roomful of teenage vapers.

I parked my Leaf and plugged it into the charger, then walked back to the RV parking. She saw me coming and poured me a bourbon. She liked the artificial stuff, which was all right by me. The number of organic chemists that were replicating wood extracts and blending them with pure grain alcohol had shot up over the past couple of years, and competition was fierce to produce the most surprising and smooth varietals.

"Look who it is," I said. "Thought you were still in the Midwest."

"I was, I'm not. Come on up and I'll tell you about it."

She did something to her grill and then unlocked the RV doors. I climbed up the stairs and threaded my way through her living room and back onto her deck.

I'd known Wilma Razafimandimby for thirty years. She'd been the sole voice of sanity at the first conference on virtual currencies ("e-gold," God help us all) and forensic accounting, speaking in her soft Malagasy accent with infinite patience and even more firmness, telling the audience of goldbug cranks that money came from taxes, not gold.

"Gentlemen," she'd told her nearly all-male audience at the closing panel on the first day, "if the government taxes your money first and spends it second, where does your money *come from*?"

The derision was palpable and also pretty close to openly racist (is it really a dog whistle if a human can hear it?), and her co-panelists had refused to engage with her. If it weren't for the angry dudes in the audience who'd called her out during the Q and A, she wouldn't have had the chance to say another word. As it was, she'd dominated the last thirty minutes of the panel and stepped off the stage with her head held high.

She got her own miniature table and four people's worth of hors d'oeuvres to herself. I went to the hotel bar—eschewing the crowded open bar in the back of the conference room—and got two glasses of passable French Burgundy and brought them to her little Coventry. I handed her one and told her how much I'd appreciated her interventions, making it as clear as I knew how that I wasn't trying to get her up to my room. A beautiful friendship was born.

"They say Missouri is part of the South," she said as she set out a dish of pistachios and a saucer for the shells. "But that's only from May to September. The rest of the year, it is definitely part of the Midwest. I told my UMKC colleagues that all my future residencies would have to be timed with the Southern months. I'm an old lady now, and it gets into my bones."

If you got up early enough and the weather was nice, you could see Raza doing yoga out on her deck. I'd seen her do things to her body that I was pretty sure I'd never been supple or strong enough to match. But if she wanted to chalk the end of her patience with midwestern winters up to senescence, I wouldn't argue with her.

"I was heading to San Diego, but I thought I'd look up some old friends in the Bay Area. When I saw the *Hash* here, I knew it had to be serendipity. You socializing or working?"

"That," I said, "is a long story."

"I brought Kansas City ribs and rub," she said. "They've been slow-cooking for, oh, ten hours now. Why don't you and I discuss it over dinner?"

She set the tone for the evening with a huge tub of wet wipes, followed swiftly by platters of meat that literally fell off the bone on the way to my mouth, staining the jeans and holey dot-com T-shirt I'd changed into in anticipation of such an event. Soon, we were in the midst of a glorious murder scene, our hands and wrists and mouths smeared with red, drifts of tomato-stained wipes on the pop-out deck, and everywhere bones, bones, bones.

"I think you'll find him," Raza said.

"Well, I'm glad one of us thinks so," I said. "I've missed your optimism."

"Oh," she said, tipping two more fingers of bourbon in a glass, "I'm not optimistic. Your boy won't have the keys."

"All right, Watson, explain."

"Watson?" She sipped her bourbon and gave me a cool look. The sun was down, and the Walmart parking lot lamps made everything look like a bleached-out Polaroid. It turned her greenish and me mustard-colored.

"Okay, Sherlock, if you must. I never claimed to be smart, just diligent."

"And that, ladies and gentlemen, is how an accountant brags." She poured me more bourbon. "Follow me here. Your boy, Alex?"

"Ales," I said. "It's Czech."

"Ales. He's a kid. That's the most important clue of all. He's not a criminal mastermind. He's a kid who likes making goofy synthesizers and who got a high-security job because everyone who's actually qualified to do those jobs already has a job. Someone offered him money to get those keys, enough that a life underground for him and his girl sounded like a fair trade. Now these two are Silicon Valley techies, so they don't impress easily. I'm guessing it's in the tens of millions, at least."

"I got that far, too."

"Right, so your Ales, he cooks up a plan to get away clean. I'm sure he's erased all his old social media posts by now."

"Yup."

"Of course he has. But what he can't do is erase all his *friends'* social media posts. What you want to do is find those friends and comb back through them for any kind of remote place where he might go to ground for a while, while things cool off. There's no way his clients made payment in full, not yet. They're going to want to validate the keys, then make sure that they can get away with whatever they were planning."

"Why wouldn't he wait somewhere far from U.S. law enforcement? Venezuela? Cuba? Hell, Tonga?"

She smiled. "Because he doesn't know anything or anyone in those places. The kinds of people who contracted with him for this gig, they're powerful and ruthless. If things go wrong, he's going to want to be close enough to whatever kind of power bloc he can summon: college friends whose parents are lawyers. His girl's at Stanford, right? That puts her three handshakes from a congressional majority and two from the senator whip, tops."

"Okay, so he's close by. Call it somewhere on the continental U.S."

"California," she said. "The farther he drives, the more of a trail he leaves. The boy is good at information security. So he's close by."

"Where?"

"That's where social media comes in. College kids go places. Beach houses. Lake houses. Campsites. Deserts. Burning Man. He's been to some places with a big group of friends for epic weekends, and he saw how empty and isolated they are when the kids go home. Of course they're isolated; no one wants to be next door to a party lake-house full of synthesizer hackers partying for four straight days.

"If I were you, I'd get into that boy's friends' social media archives and look for places where they tagged him in during long weekends. Those parameters should make it quick: tagged photos from long weekends with two or more of his friends present. Piff, paff, pouf."

I thought about it. "You are a very smart person," I said. "I don't know that I could have come up with that on my own. Maybe I'm getting too old for this job."

She waved her hand at me. "Foolishness. Keeping up with children is easy. You just need to guest-teach some undergrads for a semester every year. You've never bothered because children don't usually steal enough to make it worth your while."

"*Now* you're in my territory. Raza, young people in their twenties steal like crazy. They know the deck is stacked against them, and they're bright, and they have no executive function. Cryptocurrency lights up those tender pleasure centers like cocaine."

"All right, Marty, I concede the point. Can we say that children don't steal enough *and get away with it* to be worth your while?"

"That's an excellent friendly amendment." I scooped up my drift of red wipes and stuffed them into the trash bag she'd tied to the porch railing. "I guess I've got some social media scraping to do."

Of course, *I* don't scrape social media. I've got subcontractors for that, in several time zones. I got some bright folks in Amsterdam on the line and gave them Raza's parameters, telling them to build a social graph for Ales by pulling the intersection of digital laptop reggae, synthesizer manufacturing, SFU, and Jia's computer science class at Stanford. The Dutch kids spoke better English than I do, and they grasped the project's scope quickly. I could hear keys clattering before I hung up.

Then it was just me, washing up in the *Unsalted Hash*'s little bathroom, checking the tanks and noting that I'd need to sludge it soon. I brushed my teeth and turned back the sheets and did all the usual things before you go to bed, and then I just . . . lay there.

Sleep used to come easily. In the heady early days, when there was always a good reason to work a seventy-hour week, sleep was something you filled the corners with—rolling up a jacket as a pillow and commandeering an empty office at a client site, reclining the passenger seat in your car and parking in a dark corner of the lot, checking into an airport hotel for two hours' rest before catching a flight.

Now, sleep eludes me. It's not just the 2:00 a.m. piss-call (or the 3:00 a.m. one, or the 4:00 a.m. curtain call). It's not just the rib I got busted for me once when I happened upon a client's CFO in a supposedly empty office, taking a high-speed drill to a stack of hard drives. I was lucky: I kicked the drill cord out of the wall before he saw me and then kicked the drill out of his hands when he whirled around.

Sleep eludes me because I am *fraught*. The compartments I once housed my work in while I slumbered have long rotted away. Everything mixes now, a greatest-hits reel of my worries, my fears, my regrets. Those most of all.

I practice good sleep hygiene and set the do-not-disturbs on all my devices when I turn in, but you don't need an audible alert when you get up from bed and check your device every twenty minutes.

The Dutch kids took two hours to build up a dossier of eight places where Ales had gone to weekend-long parties since his junior year in high school. As soon as I caught sight of the list, my brain entered a recursive problem-solving mode, trying to find an optimal traveling-salesman route between all eight spots. Then I got to the seventh spot and realized I didn't need the route plan. There was only one place I was likely to find him.

After that, I slept just fine.

Jordan's Mill was not the most famous victim of last year's Mendocino fires. The little town didn't have any picturesque wineries or a nice old gold-rush-themed Main Street. What it had were some retirement places, a diner, a gas station, and a few lake houses.

One of those lake houses had been an especial favorite with Ales and Jia's friends, a place that had been lavishly photo-documented as a site of foolin' around, dancin', cuddlin', and even some swimmin'.

Those pictures seemed haunted now, considering the eighteen people who'd died when the wildfire blew through town, taking every tree and cabin and the gas station and all those cozy little retirement places that boomers had despaired of flipping after their parents finally died. Lucky them: the insurance payouts were far more than the market value of Ma and Pa's homestead.

I came to the burned-over lands thirty minutes before I got to Jordan's Mill: a flat landscape of concrete foundation slabs and charred tree stumps and automobiles. There were green shoots there, thriving in the moisture from the fall's freak atmospheric river and the nutrient-rich ash of all those incinerated lives.

The road out to the party house had decayed quickly in the year since the fire, with major potholes and cracks, further complicated by the melted, rusting remains of so many cars. The *Hash* has got the kind of miracle suspension you'd expect from an $800,000 touring bus, but I decided I'd park and lock it and unhook the Leaf from the bumper hitch. The little electric car was a lot more maneuverable than my forty-foot traveling home.

It wasn't easy finding the lake house. Google Maps had erased the roads that once led to it, on the sensible grounds that they weren't roads anymore. By combining satellite photos and paper maps I'd downloaded from the California Geological Survey, I was able to steer through the ashes and stumps and foundations until I found the right place.

There wasn't much left of the house; it had been built on a slope heading down to the lake dock, with wraparound decks resting on wooden pilings. All that wood was gone, and the cinder blocks of the bottom half of the place had tumbled in on each other and been partially buried when the hill caved in on it—probably during the atmospheric river floods.

But there was the lake, receding in drought, leaving behind vast, geologic-scale bathtub rings as it dried up. And between the lake and the cabin's wreckage, hidden from all land approaches, was a dirty white Kia Niro with a roof rack that supported a grid of solar panels. All four of its tires were flat, and its rims had sunk into the ash and mud of the blackened beach.

Not far away was the shelter, a futuristic-looking silver foil thing with quilted walls and circular zip-out portholes, as well as a fabric vestibule. It was a Shiftpod, a legendarily easy-to-assemble shelter I associated with Burning Man types I'd run into at campgrounds. It listed slightly, a couple of its ropes dangling loose, the stake loops resting on the ground.

The flats and the tilted shelter gave a strong impression of being abandoned, but what really did it was the cooler that had been tipped over beside the Shiftpod, its contents scattered and left to go moldy. I picked my way through the sweaty cheese and disintegrating sliced loaf of brown bread, holding the Leaf's crowbar in one hand. As I got closer to the entrance, the smell hit me, and I doubled back to the car and retrieved the gaiter I kept in the glove compartment, then lined it with two thicknesses of eucalyptus-scented disinfectant wipes, so I was breathing through the cotton and the wipes.

Standing at the Shiftpod's vestibule entrance, I peered into the darkness, then got out a little Maglite and shone it inside. The beam sliced through the dim interior, illuminating a bare leg. A man's leg. The toes were so dark with pooled blood, they were almost black. I played the light over the rest of the space, following the leg up to a bare man's ass, crusted with dried blood and dirt. He was on his stomach, his face turned toward me. The dead only bear a cursory resemblance to the living, but it was Ales Kocourek.

Ales was lying in the wreckage of his go bag, all his survival gear and rations spread around him on the Shiftpod floor. Someone had unzipped part of the floor and pulled it away from the wall and had probed the dirt they'd uncovered with a shovel. The shovel was right there. It was probably what had caved in poor Ales's head.

Amid the wreckage was the remains of an HP laptop. Smashing a laptop—really taking it to pieces, snapping the internal boards and components into pieces small enough to use as a weapon—wasn't easy. They'd only partially managed the trick, but that was enough. They'd produced a long, tapered sliver of circuit board, and they'd impaled Ales on it, shoving it quite some ways up his rectum. I could only imagine they did it before they beat his brains out.

I found Jia on the other side of the caved-in lake house, next to what I guessed was the cement pad for a boathouse. She answered the riddle of what had happened to the stakes from the Shiftpod's support ropes: one through each wrist and another through her heart. Her face was livid with bruises.

I almost missed the third kid, because he was actually mixed in with the cabin's rubble, and enough dirt had sifted over him that he was well camouflaged. He might have been handsome once—certainly, he was in excellent shape, like a gymnast or a rock climber, and his long hair probably flattered him. His hands were tied behind him with wire, and his pants were around his ankles. They'd mutilated him and then left him to bleed out. There are big arteries in that region, so maybe it was quick.

I'd left my phone behind in the *Hash,* not wanting to leave any kind of record of where I'd gone or how long I'd spent there. It wouldn't have done me any good from inside its Faraday pouch anyway—I'd buttoned it up five miles before the Jordan's Mill off-ramp. But I had a little point-and-shoot in my pocket, and I dithered over whether to use it. The images had already gone into long-term mental storage, the vault that I got an involuntary tour of between 2:00 and 4:00 a.m. most nights. Digital pictures were just evidence—the basis for a future obstruction of justice indictment.

I hefted the point-and-shoot, looked through the viewfinder. Looking at the dead in the little scratched screen didn't make it any easier to contemplate them.

I'd taken a lot of pictures of terrible things with that point-and-shoot. Its memory card had a lot of ghosts trapped inside of it, file fragments, partially overwritten scenes of terror and sorrow. It was a cursed object.

I decided I didn't need any more photos. Then, just as I was reaching the Leaf, I jogged back and took some pictures of the smashed shell of the laptop, its shattered drive. Danny would want to see it.

6

I used the Wi-Fi at a truck stop Starbucks outside of Ukiah to get onto the Tor network, then used that to contact WeTip. The crime reporting form was easy, and the system promised to instantaneously route my description of the crime scene to the Mendocino sheriff's office.

When I unbuttoned my phone, I found a message from Raza inviting me to a berth she'd established on Muir Beach, in a field behind a friend's house. The friend had a septic system we could sludge into and had offered the use of his garden hose hookup and a two-hundred-foot extension cord plugged into a twenty-amp receptacle in his garage, where he kept a little hobby wood-and-machine shop. He had been something, once: a computer pioneer of some kind or another, his achievements forgotten but his fuck-you money growing year after year thanks to the miracle of over-the-counter financial products. Raza had known him since they were both larvae, and he was happy to let her park the *Sectoral Balance* in his back forty.

She and our host were out for dinner somewhere when I arrived, so I parked and unhitched the Leaf and plugged in, pumped out, and filled up all the *Hash*'s compartments, tanks, and batteries, and then I showered off the stink of the burned-over place and bagged the clothes I'd worn that day, storing them in a compartment under the bus. I warmed up some chili I'd stocked up on and frozen in individual portions during a swing through New Mexico.

Once I'd eaten, drunk, evacuated, and managed all my logistics, it was time to stick the point-and-shoot's memory card in a reader I plugged into my laptop and download the photos to a plausible deniability partition on my laptop, one I could securely erase with a few clicks, leaving no record of its existence.

I looked at the photos of the smashed laptop and tried to think only about the laptop and not about the people who'd been around when it had been reduced to flinders. I'd found most of the back panel intact and had gotten a couple of good photos of the serial and model number stickers and their bar codes. I cropped those and got a good shot of the remains of its hard drive, collaged them all into a single image, and sent it off to Danny.

That was that. If they'd gotten the keys off the laptop, then either Ales and Jia and their friend would be alive and much, much richer; or they'd have a bullet hole in their foreheads and they'd been in a shallow grave somewhere. The scene at Jordan's Mill was the result of the keys *not* working. Someone wanted information out of these kids, and they didn't or wouldn't hand it over.

Either way, it was done.

> Wrong laptop.

Two words from Danny, waiting on my phone when I unwisely flipped it over and checked the notifications on my way to the toilet at 2:00 a.m.

I stared at the dark for a long time after that. I must have fallen asleep eventually.

7

Danny answered the door in jeans and a Stanford sweatshirt, barefoot with long toes whose knuckles were dotted with tufts of gray hair.

"Sethu's out running errands," he said. He picked up a vacuum flask of coffee and handed me a couple of mugs. "I take it black, but let me know if you want me to bring out milk or sugar?"

"Black's fine," I said and followed him out onto the roof-deck.

Sethu's easel was still there, a fresh canvas on it, an abstract form of slashed colors taking shape on it. It was midmorning, the city streets largely empty beneath us, all activity squirreled away in those unassuming little buildings.

"How sure are you?" I asked after he'd poured us both coffee in thick-sided diner mugs.

"About the laptop? One hundred percent. Wrong serial number. Wrong model number. Remember, I bought three of those and only used two. I double-checked the final spare, just to be sure."

"What if you accidentally grabbed two very similar models?"

He shook his head. "First of all, these two models aren't very similar. They both have twelve-inch screens, they're both from HP, but that's where the similarity ends. Second of all, the serial numbers don't match. I scanned the receipt and expensed the machines to Trustless, and I went into our financials to double-check."

"Okay, but—"

"Shut up and let me get to third of all, okay? Third of all, that's a computer that came out this year. I set up my system, the missing system, *last year*. That computer was manufactured *after* I put the missing laptop in the safe in the air gap room."

"Wrong laptop," I said.

"Wrong laptop."

After the third cup of coffee, he convinced me that he wanted to know what I'd found. I'd been pretty clear with him that he could live out the rest of his days without those details and he'd die a happier man for it, but he said he needed to know.

So I told him.

No matter how many times you describe a thing like that, it doesn't get easier. Or at least, it never got easier for me. If anything, it's gotten harder, poisoned by the looming possibility that whatever I said would be echoing in my ears in some 3:00 a.m. piss call, echoing long after I got between the sheets.

Danny turned gray as I told the tale, then went a little green. His hand shook as he poured the last of his coffee into his cup.

"What a thing," he said.

They were hollow words. I didn't have any better ones. I kept my mouth shut.

"What do you think happened?"

I wanted to be done. I wanted to get in the *Hash* and drive down to the Baja and find a beach where I could park, set up my hammock, do some snorkeling and fishing, and not think about the three kids. Not think about the blood on Ales Kocourek's hindquarters or the shovel-shaped dent in the back of his head.

But I owed Danny something. I'd taken the job. I'd thought about the deaths and tried to figure out what could have led to them.

"Danny, I think Ales and Jia got cute. I think they figured out what they'd stolen and how much it could be worth, and they knew that they had to have the hardware token that you got relieved of to cash out. So they bought a second laptop and configured it so it would pass a cursory inspection. Maybe they rigged it to clone your hardware token, or maybe they had a plan to switch the tokens during the handover.

"They met their connection and staged a canned demo for him, or them. They gimmicked the new laptop to demand a hardware token to boot. Doesn't matter which token, of course. It's not like the connections would bring a second one along so they could do a double-blind randomized trial. The laptop had a random key on it, just some long random number they generated. They were betting that would be the convincer and that the connections would pay them off, then they could recover the real laptop, unlock it with the token, and disappear. Disappearing is hard, but a billion dollars pays for a lot of help."

"But it didn't work."

"Evidently not. The connections were the suspicious sort, the type of people who didn't just want to recover the key and move on—they actually had the hardware and expertise on hand to determine if the key was any good." I imagined how Ales and Jia and their friend must have sweated it out as their connection's techie ran the checks on the laptop and the keys, knowing they were going to be caught, knowing there'd be hard consequences. They were only kids. He liked building stupid synthesizers. She liked thrashing her hair around while she played them, wearing headphones the size of cartoon earmuffs. The other boy was pretty, like a dancer. Maybe he was their boyfriend.

"And then the 'connections' realized it didn't work and decided they'd been crossed," Danny said, nodding. "But why didn't the kids give up the location of the real keys? Why let themselves be tortured to death? A billion dollars doesn't help you once you're dead."

I shrugged. "Maybe they understood that they'd be dead no matter what. Or maybe they gave up the information and got killed anyway. Maybe that's why they were killed in three different locations. First, the bad guys did Ales in the tent, then sent someone off to check the location he'd given up. Get the laptop back and kill Jia, just to show the pretty boy they meant business. Then they confirm they have the right computer this time and get rid of the last kid rather than leaving him around to identify them.

"Or maybe not. Maybe the bad guys have no executive function to speak of and that's why they're in their line of work. They clock the double cross, see red, and take it out on these three idiot kids. If I ever meet these characters, I'll ask them about it."

"Do you think the laptop is out there?"

"It's a computer, Danny. It's going to be out there for a hundred thousand years before it biodegrades."

"Don't be an asshole, Marty. I know you've had a shitty couple of days, but I have to be pragmatic here. There's a lot riding on those keys. Not just Trustless's future. Lots of bystanders who depend on the integrity of secure enclaves."

"You could warn them."

He stood up and stalked away from me, his hands balled into fists, stared at Palo Alto for a while, then came back. "I never should have bought those keys. I thought I was doing the right thing."

"You talked yourself into thinking you were doing the right thing."

"Fine, yes, that's what happened. But it's *happened.* Now I need to know, do I go public about this? It would probably mean financial ruin for me, maybe prison. Sethu would be ruined, too, and she's got a lot longer for that to sting than I do.

"I'll do it if I have to. If it comes down to ruining my life and Sethu's life, or risking the safety and integrity of millions of people, I will take the hit. But can't you see, Marty, *I want to be sure.*"

Everybody liked Danny. He was the kind of guy you wanted to do right by. He had integrity. He'd made a stupid mistake and he would pay for it, but he wanted to be sure.

"What would 'being sure' look like?"

"I'm assuming that the adversaries have the token but not the laptop. I want to recover or destroy that laptop before they gain access to it. And if they have the laptop, I want to know it."

"You'll know if they have the laptop," I said. "The missing billion dollars will be pretty obvious."

8

The kids' Kia was probably in a Mendocino impound lot or forensics lab. It might have a record of its final journey in its onboard systems, but I was guessing not. Ales was reckless and greedy, but he understood embedded systems. Same goes for their phones—it was possible that they'd forgotten to turn them off and bag them when they were on their way to stash the laptop, but I didn't think they had. Jia got into Stanford. Ales had spent a year in the paranoid company of Vikram Zain, threat-modeling physical, digital, and hybrid attacks on the data center.

And if he didn't think about mobile information leakage, their friend probably had. The Mendocino sheriff and the FBI press release identified the third boy as Sergey Preobrazhensky, a Stanford grad student working on a double master's degree: an MBA and a master's in cybersecurity. Smart kid. Maybe the kind of kid who'd get ideas about the usefulness of a billion dollars in exfiltrated crypto-assets. He had family who could certainly help; his father was one of the most powerful bankers in Azerbaijan.

What had they done with it? They'd only need it momentarily, long enough to extract the keys from it, and then they could stick it in a giant shredder or a brick of thermite. Wherever they planned to go, they didn't need to lug around 2.3 pounds of electronics just to house a few kilobits of randomly generated keys. Still, they couldn't risk damaging it while they were waiting to get the token from their clients. That probably ruled out FedExing it to Baku or wherever; the number of short-fingered customs agents and butterfingered parcel sorters and light-fingered carriers between here and there exceeded prudence.

They'd taken it somewhere that it wouldn't be disturbed. Somewhere dry and safe. Somewhere they could get to without taking too much of a detour between San Francisco and Jordan's Mill.

Maybe they'd stopped into a Comfort Inn, unscrewed a ventilator grating, and pushed the laptop as far down the ductwork as it would go?

When Laura Poitras needed to give Snowden a mailing address for him to send that hard drive to, she'd gotten a friend of a friend's place in Brooklyn, and it had sat on the doorstep for a day before it had gotten taken inside. If a porch pirate had gotten to it first . . .

Thirty years ago, this job involved a lot of legwork: flying around the country to doorstop people with a microcassette recorder and a fifteen-pound "portable" computer. Today, I can call up some Dutch kids and email them a photo and get a full dossier within hours.

Every time I set out to do some old-fashioned shoe-leather work, I have to remind myself of all the labor-saving tools I enjoy, all the hours they save. Time I can spend doing productive work, or just catching up on my sleep after a night haunted by three kids in a burned-over place, staked out, mutilated, tortured, head bashed in.

I did the legwork. There aren't too many ways to get from San Francisco to Jordan's Mill, and I worked backward from the burned-over lands toward the city. I reasoned that they'd want to have the laptop close by so they could retrieve it after they got paid and then get lost with it, maybe head to Vegas or Seattle, someplace where you could rendezvous with a private jet.

I stopped into every diner, every grocery store, every gas station, every motel, every roadside produce stand. I boomered it up, dad jeans and a blazer over a polo shirt, polarizing clip-on shades over a pair of glasses with obvious bifocal zones (I left my everyday glasses with their progressive lenses in the glove box of the *Hash*). I topped it off with a pair of readers in the breast pocket.

I'd have preferred to ask about Jia. People like to help a dad whose daughter has gone missing. But I wasn't going to pass for Korean, and Jia didn't look like she had a white dad. So I had to be Ales's dad, and I worked up a good patter about him and his friends and the camping trip that had gone wrong. I found that I could even cry some. Then, to my alarm, I found that it was hard to stop crying.

I struck out all the first day, working my way from the burned-over lands back to SFO. The Leaf's battery was bottoming out, so I parked at a charger in the Terminal 2 short-term lot and went and looked at the exhibits in the little museum, savoring them in ways that almost no one would. I like airport museums: so much love poured into those display cases, only to be rushed past in a stressed-out whirlwind or to be stared blankly at during a long layover.

After half an hour, I headed back out to the garage, got in the car, and drove back to Raza's friend's spread, where I could charge overnight.

Raza had done laundry and was stringing it up on a line she'd strung between the *Hash* and the *Sectoral Balance*. That reminded me that I should find a wash-and-fold the next day, and I threw my laundry bag into the trunk of the Leaf.

"You look miserable," she said.

"That's not surprising," I said.

She made a face. "You need to chat, just knock. If not, I understand. Either way, the sunset is in twenty minutes, and I'm low on bourbon."

"I'm well supplied," I said. "Meet you in fifteen."

A friend you don't have to talk to is a gift. The sunset was spectacular. I chewed an indica gummy and lay down in bed. I had more shoe leather to lay the next day.

9

The cannabis gave me a hangover that no coffee would dispel, but once I got off the highway and rolled down the Leaf's windows, the fresh air did wonders. I got out the printed maps I'd been working from and looked over the day's itinerary. I'd followed 101 yesterday. Today, I'd work 128.

A lot of wineries. Would they have stopped at one? Jia and Ales were too young to buy wine. Maybe Sergey had gone in for them. I hadn't seen any wine bottles at their campsite. I decided I'd stop in at a couple of the wineries anyway, find a couple of decent bottles: one for Raza and one for our gracious host.

Graciela's was a little Mexican restaurant just over the Mendocino county line, where 128 and 101 merge again, a good location. Laura, the young woman who served me, turned out to be Graciela's daughter-in-law, and Tomas, the cook, was her husband.

"Graciela only works the busy shifts now," Laura said. At 2:00 p.m., the place was empty except for me, and Laura was warmly impersonal in that way of great restaurant servers. "She earned it, twenty years in this place."

"Nice to see it in the hands of a new generation. This is really excellent food." It really was. I'd skipped over the main part of the menu and gone straight to the "Specialties of Jalisco" and opted for a bowl of tripe soup and a *lonche* sandwich.

She thanked me and promised to tell Tomas. I found that mentioning a new generation had made me mist over, which would have been great acting if it had been acting. She made a concerned frown and asked if I needed anything.

"Sorry," I said, patting my face with my napkin, swiping at my eyes (I'd taken off the bifocals so the tripe wouldn't steam them up). "It's just—" I got out the photos of Ales and his friends that I'd printed on the inkjet in the *Hash*.

Before I could tell her the tale, though, she gasped and stepped back with a loud "*Oh!*"

"Laura?" I said, but she had recovered herself and was stepping back from the table, reaching for her waitress pad like she'd suddenly remembered some restaurant-type errands that meant she'd have to leave her customer to his thoughts for now.

I made a split-second decision as to how I'd play it. I got up out of my chair and stepped to her, keeping my voice low but intense. "Laura, if you know something about my son—"

She shook her head. "No, I just—I saw them on the news. I saw they'd been—"

Tears in both our eyes now. "Laura, please. A father wants to know. I've been driving up and down these roads, trying to find out a little more about his last days. Please, Laura, a father wants to know."

She got a look so tender I felt ashamed. Then she looked at Tomas in the kitchen, who was looking at us, holding a big metal spatula that quivered slightly from his tight grip. She made a sign that it was all right and the spatula stopped shaking and Tomas went back to his grill, but not without looking at us for another long moment.

"They were in here," she said, sitting down opposite me at my little two-top. "Nice kids. They seemed happy. So excited, even. They kept laughing, and they ordered a whole second dinner to go that they said they'd eat in their motel that night. They tipped well, too, not like some college kids."

"But you didn't tell the police," I said. It was a hunch. I didn't know anyone at the Mendocino sheriff's office, and my contacts hadn't come up with a connection yet, though they were looking.

She was silent. I had another hunch. "Laura, I don't care if you're documented or undocumented. Honestly, I don't. And I understand if you didn't want to talk to the police."

She smiled, though fat, silent tears were rolling down her cheeks. "It's been eating me up. I knew those poor kids had parents and that my information could mean something. But I couldn't risk it. I never talk to cops. *We* never talk to cops."

I touched her wrist gently. "It's okay," I said. "I'm grateful to you. Thank you."

"Wait here," she said. She went into the kitchen, and she and Tomas had an intense, hushed conversation, too quiet for me to make out even if I could have followed the Spanish. Then he nodded in understanding and gave her a short, hard hug.

She left the kitchen and went into what I took to be a storeroom, then came back carrying a laptop bag, black nylon, cheap, new looking.

"They left this behind," she said. "Hung it on one of their chairbacks. I found it before they'd left the parking lot and ran out to get them, but they didn't see me. I knew they'd be back for it, so I just held on to it."

I had a wild surmise. Ales and Jia and Sergey had seen this good woman and her good husband and had decided they were the kind of people who'd put a forgotten laptop away for safe-keeping until its owner called for it. It was the kind of plan you might make on the spur of the moment when the nice waitress brought you a free *jericalla* for dessert just because you looked like you could use fattening up. It was the kind of lateral move that would be hard for an adversary to outguess.

And maybe it was why they hadn't told their clients where the laptop could be found.

10

I sent a pic of the bar code to Danny by Signal, setting the message to delete itself after one day. Then I deleted it from my phone and drove back to the *Hash* for a very large bourbon and two of those gummies. Danny called before I dropped off, and I bumped him to voice mail with a text message:

> > Taking the rest of the day off.

There was a long pause, then he replied:

> > You've earned it. Talk tomorrow.

Another pause.

> > Is it secure?

The gummies were starting to kick in, making me feel gloriously stupid and discorporeal. All I wanted to do was sleep, but obviously, he deserved an answer.

> > I'll sleep with it under my pillow.

I set my phone to Do Not Disturb and slid the laptop under my pillow.

———

This time, Danny opened his door in a pair of genuinely fantastic pajamas: regimental stripe, heavy cotton, cut to flatter an older body by hanging, rather than clinging, monogrammed *DML* over the right breast pocket. I'd seen a set like that in the men's section at Fortnum & Mason near Piccadilly Circus once. They'd been £350, and I couldn't justify spending that kind of money, not even for genuinely fantastic pajamas.

Maybe I'd charter a jet to London and buy a pair.

He shook my hand solemnly as I came through the door, then accepted the bag from me. I'd stuffed the laptop bag into a gym bag and padded it with a couple of my clean hand towels from the neatly tied parcel I'd picked up at the wash-and-fold in Muir Beach. I didn't want to walk into the Camino Real apartments carrying a laptop bag last seen in the possession of Ales Kocourek, Jia Hak, and Sergey Preobrazhensky.

He hefted the bag. "I need a few minutes. Would you mind showing yourself onto the roof? You know the way, right? Help yourself to anything you need from the kitchen. Sethu is out."

No pretense that she was running any errands. She'd been sent away. This was a meeting between Danny Lazer and me. For a very brief moment, I wondered if he'd try to kill me. It was only a fleeting thought, because Danny Lazer wouldn't lift a finger to me—or anyone else, for that matter. He was passionate and brilliant, but gentle. Nevertheless, I had the thought, considered the thought, and then dispelled it, because having that kind of thought is my job, which is why I was ready to retire.

I found a pitcher of fresh-squeezed blood-orange juice next to a hand juicer and a bowl of juiced-out orange rinds. I poured myself a glass and went out onto the roof-deck to admire Sethu's canvas.

It was still an abstract. She'd scraped away a lot of the bright colors I'd seen the last time, replacing them with moody grays. It was all jangles and angles. I didn't think I liked it.

He joined me after about half an hour, carrying the laptop. He opened its lid and showed me the holes he'd drilled through the keyboard, popping off the key caps from the Shift to the V, the Caps Lock to the G. They were through-and-through holes, right through the hard drive beneath them.

"Never saw the use for a Caps Lock key," I said.

He gave me the ghost of a smile. "This is just a temporary measure, best I could manage with my little hand drill. I have a secure disposal company coming by in an hour. They bring a truck right up to the entrance, then take the machine and drop it in this grinder, like a paper shredder that can handle a whole laptop, reduce it to fragments no bigger than a fingernail clipping in under a minute."

"So you're out of the keys business."

"I am," he said. "I never should have been in that business. It was stupid. Vanity. Not wanting to have my mistakes on display forever. Jesus, what an idiotic thing to worry about."

I shrugged. "Mistakes happen," I said.

He grimaced. "Those kids certainly learned that."

I nodded. They had. They'd paid a price for their mistake. Danny was going to pay, too, but he'd get to walk away from his mistakes, alive, regretful, and 25 percent poorer.

"I'm certain that the people who stole your authentication token never touched this computer. That means that the keys were never accessed and the Trustlesscoin system is completely intact."

He stared at Palo Alto, at the staid boxes, full of frenzy. "I concur with your assessment."

"Danny, can I ask, what is the value of the assets in the Trustlesscoin ledger?" I'd looked it up that morning, but I wanted to hear from him.

"I make it one point two billion."

That was a little higher than the analyst's report that I'd read had put it, but then, Danny had better information about the status of the Trustless ledger.

"Well, I guess that's a little too much for a cash transaction," I said. Twenty-five percent of $1.2 billion was $300 million. That was the kind of number I'd kept out of my mind as much as possible over the preceding week and especially over the past twenty-four hours. I didn't want my thoughts about that payday mingled with mental images of those three kids.

He looked at me for a very long, very considering moment. He tried to close the laptop's lid, but more of the key caps had popped off, and so he had to settle for mostly closing it and setting it down awkwardly on the roof-deck. It was weird to see him handle it so daintily, as if he hadn't just drilled it to pieces. As if he wasn't about to drop it in an industrial shredder.

"Marty, do you really think you should get three hundred million dollars for a week's work?"

"You know the joke about the photocopier repairman, Danny?"

"The one that goes, 'No, I kicked the machine for free, the seventy-five bucks was for knowing *where* to kick it'? Yeah, I know that joke."

"Yesterday at this time, you were facing the near-certain prospect of losing everything. Your honor, your reputation, your fortune. Ruination for you and your young wife, the years you've got left together and the years she's got left after you pass away.

"Today, you're back to building Trustlesscoin. As I recall, you believe that you can put trillions of dollars into that blockchain in pretty short order. Ten to the twelfth power dollars, as you put it. The reason for that sudden change of fortune is that I knew where to kick."

He grimaced. "When you put it that way—"

"Danny, you and I never signed a contract. We've been friends a long time, and you knew what my deal was. So I trusted you. Remember how you told me your coins weren't really trustless, that they just moved trust away from people like Danny Lazer in favor of the security engineers at a couple of chip foundries?"

He nodded warily.

"I don't trust those engineers. As I think we can both agree, they can be suborned. If I ever put any money into Trustlesscoin, it won't be because of my faith in those engineers. It'll be because of my trust in Danny Lazer."

He opened his mouth, shut it again.

I stood up and walked to the railing to look out at Palo Alto for a while. Danny joined me a few minutes later. "Danny," I said, still looking at the city, "if you can't afford my bill, you just say so. We've been friends a long time."

He snorted. "Martin 'the Mensch' Hench strikes again. You'll get every penny. You earned every penny."

But you can't just hand over $300 mil.

For one thing, Danny didn't have $300 mil in cash. His money was in units of real estate investment trusts owned by Estonian companies that were owned by Scottish companies. It was in SPACs based in Cyprus whose directors were numbered Nevada companies. It was in LLCs that owned luxury flats in impossibly tall, thin spires in New York and London. It was in shares of art stashed in climate-controlled containers in the free port of Geneva.

Transferring those assets was both simple and complex. Recording changes of shares in Bermuda and Edinburgh and Nicosia was a fiddly business, but there were lawyers who specialized in it.

One of them was right there in Palo Alto. Ira Hermann: a genial fellow in a loose-fitting, camel-colored cardigan who had his own notary stamp and a smart-looking woman whom he was training up who served as a witness on the signature blanks. I had to drop into his office four times that week, producing "wet signatures" on documents that were stamped, witnessed, and FedExed to distant corners of the world. He kept records on a laptop that was disconnected from the internet, making printouts on a big, humming laser printer and clipping them neatly and putting them in folders.

All those folders went into a fireproof lockbox, along with a USB stick containing digital versions. Ira handed me two of these and advised me to put one in a safe-deposit box and give the other one to my lawyer.

I asked him if *he'd* be my lawyer. I liked the way he operated, even if the majority of his work was in service to helping crooks of one kind or another hide their assets from the law and the government.

He took off his readers and folded them and tucked them into the cardigan's breast pocket and gave me a brief smile. "Mr. Hench, all appearances notwithstanding, I am no longer practicing. This kind of work is something I do for a few, valued old clients who predate my retirement, like Danny Lazer. I've worked some very long hours under a lot of pressure, down through the years, and I'm taking the time I've got left to do some good work in this world."

"Well, that seems laudable. I might be in the market for doing some good with my time. Do you mind if I ask what you've found to do?"

"I raise money for climate charities," Hermann said. "Direct aid for solarizing and weatherizing housing in the ten percent poorest U.S. zip codes. There's a group of us who raise the funds, but they're locally administered by community groups that are right there on the ground."

"That sounds like good work, all right." I swallowed my next words.

"You look like you've got something more to say," he said.

"Not really," I said.

A tight-lipped smile. "Mr. Hench, I know what you did for a living. You could say that we're both veterans of a long guerrilla war between people who want to hide money and people who want to find it. I'm guessing that you're thinking about how much money those local communities might have if the landlords and business owners and other beneficiaries of the wealth created there hadn't been able to make their winnings disappear."

I smiled. "Something like that."

He shrugged. "You'll get no argument from me here. It's what I'm good at, and I did it, and it paid well. One day, I realized that I had enough hidden away, myself, that I didn't have to do it anymore. And I decided that would be it for me. But because I'm an honorable man—for certain values of 'honorable'—I couldn't just walk away from it all. I had to wind up loose ends for the people I'd served."

"I guess if Danny Lazer were my client, I'd want to do right by him, too."

"Danny is good people, but not all my clients are. A lot of them are monsters. Real monsters. The great monsters of history, of our era. But I have my honor."

"Which is why you didn't just hand your hard drives over to the IRS and start a new life under a false identity in remotest Mali," I said.

"The thought never crossed my mind," he said mildly. "I don't pretend that these men—and a few women—that I served are better at allocating that capital than a democratic government might be, assuming such a thing can be found. Like I said, many of them are perfectly monstrous. But despite that, I am in no hurry to tell the authorities where those assets are stashed."

"If you did, you'd have to tell them where *your* assets are, too, I suppose."

He smiled again, lips even tighter. "You say things that other people mostly just think, Mr. Hench."

"You did ask, Mr. Hermann."

"Yes, I suppose I did. Let me ask you something: Now that you have all this money, what do you plan to do with it? Are you going to declare it as income, pay tax on it? If you do, you will still have something like two hundred million to your name."

"That's a fascinating question," I said. "It's certainly one I'll be giving some thought to."

"I'd be interested in knowing what your answer is."

"I'll let you know. In the meantime, I still need legal representation, if only to have someone to hand this strongbox over to. Is your assistant in the market for new clients?"

He chuckled, apologized. "Zoe's practice is going to be a lot more . . . *active* than you're likely to need. She's got ambition.

"Mr. Hench, with a fortune of under half a billion, you don't really need the services of someone like Zoe or even me. Any of the Big Four consultancies will be glad to put your affairs in order. They'll do a perfectly respectable job and charge reasonable rates, provided you check the invoices over closely at least once a year to make sure no one is padding his billings at bonus time. You have a very large fortune, Mr. Hench, but it's an *off-the-shelf* sort of fortune, the kind of thing that fits very neatly into a standardized template. The kinds of bespoke services offices like this provide are for people in pursuit of global domination, of a dent in the universe, of a dynasty, of their own libertarian island nation, or just their own senator. I get the strong impression that your pursuing days are over."

"That's true," I said. "Like you, I find myself with enough to tide me over and no desire to do more of the kind of work that produced it."

"Wise choice," he said. "Let me know if you'd like to make a donation to my fund."

"Put me down for a million."

He didn't bat an eye. "Easily done. I'll have the paperwork in a moment."

I almost jumped in to say I'd been kidding. I had been, sort of. But not quite. And why not? I literally wouldn't miss a million bucks at this point. I couldn't do it every day—a million here, a million there, pretty soon, etc., etc.—but I had the feeling that any charity Ira Hermann ran would be an effective one.

I waited patiently while he did the donation paperwork. He'd transferred title to a piece of undeveloped land on the Big Island to a numbered company. Zoe came in and witnessed the paperwork and gave me a smile that made me feel a little good about myself.

They both stood there while I gathered up my document safe and put on my jacket and my uncle's old air force mechanic's hat, frayed and soft as felt.

"It was a sincere pleasure to meet you, Mr. Hench."

"Make it Marty," I said.

"It's Ira, then," he said and shook my hand.

"Zoe," I said and shook her hand.

Just before he left, Zoe put her hand on my elbow. "Marty, before you go, can I ask you something?"

"Anything," I said. I didn't care. She was smart and lovely and thought I was a good guy. She had pledged her life to helping the monsters of history hide their money, but so what? If no one did her job, I wouldn't have been able to do mine. I think maybe I was finally getting the giddiness of all that money. Ten to the eight dollars isn't ten to the twelve dollars, but it's still a heady, heady sum.

"Ira told me what you did for a living. I understand you were very good at it."

"I suppose I was." Talking about it in the past tense gave me a little thrill. The money and all it meant were growing realer by the second.

"Well, you've seen how we operate. What I want to know is, if you were up against us, could you beat us?" She held my gaze coolly, like she wasn't asking my help to commit unsolvable crimes.

"Funny you should ask. I've had a fair bit of time to sit around here and think about just those questions, waiting for this or that to happen, a document to print or for a revision to be made."

"Yes?"

"Yes."

She cocked her head. "Yes, what?"

"Yes, I could unravel it. Not all of it, but most of it. Enough to get your clients into a position where they might tell the rest to negotiate a settlement."

"I see," she said. "Would you be willing to share any of these methodological weaknesses? I'm always interested in understanding how the audit process works."

I thought about it. "You know, I don't think I want to do that. The IRS isn't going to be able to do what I do. For one thing, they have to tell you when they're coming after you, and then you can pay a very good firm of lawyers to slow them down. I get to work in sneaky ways that aren't available to the taxman. And given how starved the high-net-worth audit initiative is, your clients are more likely to be struck by a meteor than a tax penalty. But if someone *really* wants to track down the money you've hidden, I like the idea that they'll be able to recover some of it. Call it professional honor." I winked at Ira showily, and Zoe rolled her eyes.

"Fair enough," she said. "I guess my self-improvement project will be an individual affair."

11

Three hundred million dollars changes everything, and then again, it changes nothing at all.

The *Hash* had started out as a very slightly used $800,000 tour bus, taken in lieu of payment from a grateful retired Top 40 front man whose manager had disappeared with $2 million worth of his money. He was happy to round up the payment, based on generous depreciation and the fact that he would not have to go out on tour ever again thanks to the money I'd recovered for him.

Over the years, I'd upgraded her in this way and that, but I hadn't had to do much. My rock star had mercifully subdued taste (by rock star standards, at least), and had specced out an interior that felt more like a houseboat than a camper. Between the mortgage-free lifestyle and the bus's excellent engineering and minimal maintenance budget, my major expenses were food, good whiskey, and gasoline.

I looked at the possibilities for an electric bus and decided the ranges were still too short, especially if I was going to keep on towing an EV for more maneuverable trips. I looked into houses but couldn't decide where I'd want to live. I looked at vacations but couldn't decide where I'd go.

Raza had agreed to write a paper with a colleague at UCSB and had driven down the coast to meet with her. I'd gotten to know our host a little at Raza's farewell dinner and had hung around on his back forty for a few days afterward while I looked over cars and houses and buses and vacation destinations.

But he was Raza's friend, not mine. I called the travel concierge that came with my new "relationship manager" at KPMG and asked him to find me a quiet and beautiful place to park the *Hash* for a week while I stared at the waves and counted the seagulls. He came back an hour later with a private hookup near San Luis Obispo. It had its own natural hot spring. That sold me. I gassed up the *Hash* and hit the road and settled in to figure out what I wanted to do when I grew up.

Two weeks stretched to four. First, because SLO is a nice town to hang out in, and second, because a section of the Pacific Coast Highway crumbled into the sea the day after I arrived, leaving me with no easy path southward. I didn't want to go back north, at least no farther than a day trip to Hearst Castle.

I got to know the town, its greasy spoons, its one good restaurant—where the university president could take visiting parents who were good donor prospects—and of course the Madonna Inn, where I had the obligatory pie and milkshake and then went and hiked it off in the state park.

I also found a jeweler, supernaturally good at what she did, far too good for a college town, making very small, very understated pieces that were easy to overlook, but which balanced metals and design and stones in ways that were fierce and lively. Her work should have been in Fortnum & Mason, one floor down from the £350 pajamas, or a few streets away off Savile Row, by the Vivienne Westwood boutique. As it was, she was easily the most upscale seller of any merchandise in all of SLO, and she was horribly underpriced at that.

I went in one day on a whim and then couldn't get those pieces out of my mind. When you live in a tour bus, you don't tend to accumulate a lot of worldly goods, but I had half a mind to buy ten or twenty of her pieces, just to have on hand as gifts should I ever find a woman I wanted to make very, very happy.

And then the next morning, I realized that I *did* have a woman

I wanted to make happy, my old chum Raza, not far up the road in Santa Cruz. There are academic economists who make a killing on their private contracts, but Raza didn't do that kind of economics. If you were looking to pay an academic who'd swear blind that your company's planned merger wouldn't create anti-competitive concerns, she would not be your go-to.

Still, she was an economist, good with money, tenured and then pensioned, and could live well, if carefully, until she was done. That wasn't such a bad deal. Plenty of people had worse ones.

But I'd known Raza a long time. I'd met her while she and I were in town for some conference or another, seen how she dressed up for the rubber-chicken banquets. I knew what kind of stuff she liked to wear when she was dressing up. I knew she'd go crazy for this jewelry. In fact, it was so perfect for her that picking out just one piece presented a serious and protracted dilemma.

At last, I had the item: a brooch the size of a silver-dollar pancake, with a twined platinum-and-gold form that looked at first like an abstract but that was, on closer inspection, the sea at sunset, and set in it, sapphires and emeralds, sparkling like seafoam. It was a piece that looked wonderful at first glance, then, with enough study, became *profound*. She was going to love it.

I took it to a pack-and-ship near the Cal Poly campus and parked around back in an EV charge bay and swiped my card. I figured I'd ship the gift, find a coffee shop, and get a 50 percent charge in twenty minutes from the supercharger. The Leaf's charge port had developed idiosyncrasies lately, and I'd been meaning to take it to a dealer for service, but in the meantime, I'd managed to not quite plug it in the night before, and the battery was running low.

A nice college kid in the ship-and-pack did a good job with the jewelry box, and I double-checked the c/o address of Raza's colleague on campus before he shipped it. I found a coffee shop and read a campus newspaper for a quarter hour and got back to the Leaf to discover that the battery was still nearly dead. I guessed the idiosyncrasies in the charge port had reached the point of no return. I looked up Nissan dealerships and found one close by and headed out for it.

I was in the middle of the left turn onto the PCH when the Leaf's dashboard lit up, every warning light going at once. I smelled a burning plastic smell, and I yanked the wheel to the right, mounting the curb and putting it in park as I leaped out of the door, seconds before the entire undercarriage of the car burst into flames with an electrical *crackle*. An instant later, the entire car was engulfed.

As I watched it be consumed by the flames, I smugly congratulated myself on my excellent reflexes and mentally cataloged the things I'd lose with the car while I dialed 911. There was a sack of laundry on the back seat; I'd stripped the bed linens that morning. There was the normal detritus of a driver—parking passes, change for meters, a pocketknife, and a nail clipper. Some wipes. Not much, considering that I'd owned the Leaf for seven years.

The fire department used chem extinguishers on it, then called me a tow. The guys were properly impressed with the Leaf's act of self-immolation, and one fellow made a point of telling me that he'd never trusted EVs.

We ended up at the same dealership I'd been headed to at first. The manager on duty turned gray as we rolled into the parking lot and whistled up a group of mechanics to get the wreck out of sight of the paying customers and into a distant service bay.

I was given a cup of pod coffee and a seat in the manager's office while he and a senior mechanic listened to my description of the symptoms. They fixated on the problems I'd had with the charge port and the low battery, and I gathered that the bad charge had probably saved my life. A fully charged Leaf battery would have done more than burst into flame—it would have blown, with a ten- to twenty-yard blast radius. *That's* why the manager had turned gray when we rolled up: he was imagining that he was looking at a bomb that had just blown a serious crater in some quiet SLO street.

The car was a write-off, of course. I'd called my insurance company while the firefighters were working the car over, and they'd called the dealership. It was pro forma: I'd be getting the Leaf's Blue Book value, less my deductible.

Eventually, we ran out of exclamations about how terrible it all was, and how lucky I was, and how *great* the Leaf had been . . . until it exploded, and how the manager could set me up with a nice replacement, though I could forget about a trade-in, har har har. They said they'd call me an Uber, and I asked if they could get me a real taxi instead, so they looked up a number and did so. They were eager to please, so I asked if I could go and retrieve the plates off the wreck: I'd once scrapped a car only to get a fistful of tickets a month later, the bounty of some entrepreneur who'd pulled all the plates in the scrapyard and rotated them around on his badly parked cars.

The mechanics had it up on a lift and were going over the charred remains. I saw right away that I wouldn't be getting the license plates off the Leaf; they were warped beyond all recognition. As I turned to go, the chief mechanic tapped my shoulder, led me under the lift.

He spoke in Spanish to one of his mechanics, a young guy with a lazy smile and very sharp eyes, *"Show the man."*

The kid pulled a flashlight out of his breast pocket and shone it toward the front of the car. They'd already chipped out most of the battery, so I was looking up at the charge port and a little box full of charred electronics. The kid narrowed his beam.

"See?"

"Not exactly." My Spanish wasn't great, but I could get by.

"There. In the front. The marks."

I squinted. I couldn't see it. The chief mechanic took out his phone and scrolled it for a while, then showed me a picture of what that assembly was supposed to look like. The fire had done a number on it, but there was also something else—a black box in my car, one that wasn't in the assembly in the picture.

"Did you do any aftermarket modification of this car, sir?"

"Well, I put in an air freshener once, but I decided I didn't like the smell."

He made the smallest smile of all. "Javier thinks someone tampered with your car and that led to the fire. That box there, it looks like it bypassed the safety interlocks on the battery. If someone did that, and then messed with the battery . . ."

"Whoosh," I said. "Well, I can say with some certainty that I never installed any aftermarket modifications in this car. It's possible that was there when I bought it. I'm the second owner. That seems a lot more likely than someone trying to blow up my car."

He looked skeptical.

"This is America. When a person wants to kill another person, he generally buys a gun and keeps it simple. Even in California, this is still a common practice."

That got a slightly bigger smile. "I'm sure you're right," he said. He squinted out of the maintenance bay. "Your cab is here."

"Thank you," I said. "*Gracias,* Javier."

"*De nada.*"

12

When you suddenly find yourself $300 million richer, it probably helps to be unselfconscious. Back at the *Hash* that night, I paid for a year's subscription to *Consumer Reports*, springing for the full package after a moment's hover over the "Digital Monthly" option. I directed the print edition to an old college friend who was serving ten years at Folsom, and ticked off the auto-renew box.

From there, I maneuvered to this year's car listings, checking the box for all-electric and unchecking the box for Teslas. I just don't like the man. I've spent enough years around enough bull-shitters that I can spot them a mile away. In his case, I could spot him from orbit, using one of his overpromised, underdelivered satellites.

It was a good year for EVs, with all-electric models from the Germans, the Japanese, the Swedes, and the British. Some of them were awfully pretty, too. I got the sense that the designers were finally waking up to the liberatory potential of all-electrics, the form-factor freedom that you couldn't match in a vehicle powered by exploding microscopic dinosaurs.

But here's where the self-consciousness comes in. All my professional life, I'd strived for forgettability on the job, anonymous cars and anonymous clothes, dad jeans and bifocals. I'd cultivated the art of boring bartenders to tears so that they'd quickly forget about me once I'd finished asking nosy questions. It's not who I was, really. I liked well-made clothes and well-made cars, top-rail booze and really good coffee. But more than I liked those things, I liked being good at being invisible. In my business, the flashy guys were the prey, and predators like me were so matte that we absorbed all visible light.

You can buy a car on the internet these days. The dealers list their inventory and prices, including delivery. If I laid down the Amex Black card that my KPMG fixer had messengered to me the day after I signed up, there would be a sub-twenty-four-hour interval, and then a white-glove delivery crew would be at my doorstep with a new car, hand-rubbed and fully loaded. A custom paint job would add a mere two days to the process. In seventy-two hours, I could have a bright orange, all-electric Porsche or Audi or even a Lambo in hand, with acid-green trim and custom plates. Such a car would be a flashing status symbol, and the status it would convey is: "Here is a pathetic specimen of middle-aged manhood, with more money than brains." Never mind the fact that it would be a delight to drive and fun to look at. The self-conscious mind cares not for such frivolous considerations.

In the end, self-consciousness won. I closed my laptop and called the dealership that had taken custodianship of the Leaf's ashes and asked them if they had anything used on the lot that was roughly comparable. They had one in "champagne," a color I'm not very fond of, but I bought it anyway, along with a manufacturer's warranty, and they even promised same-day delivery. The Black card absorbed the charge without blinking.

The new car rolled up just as the sun was setting, along with a follow car that the delivery woman would ride back in. She apologized for being a little late, explaining that they'd had to wait until someone could mount the trailer hitch. I told her it was no problem, looked at my champagne-colored Leaf and the folder of paperwork it had come with, signed some paperwork, and waved the delivery team goodbye as they disappeared into another perfect, bloody-orange California sunset.

I like eating dinner alone, especially on an evening like that. I'd moved a porterhouse from the freezer to the fridge the night before, and I'd set it on the counter after I ordered the car to let it come up to room temp. I used the induction top to get a thick-bottom pan *very* hot, added oil, rubbed salt and pepper into the steak, and seared it for two and a half minutes in the oil. Then I transferred it to a cutting board, turned it over, and cut it into half-inch strips, still in place around the bone. I added a couple of big pats of unsalted butter, some sprigs of rosemary, and three or four garlic cloves, then stuck it under the broiler for three more minutes. It came out tender, pink in the middle, herbed, and so tender it cut with a fork.

I ate it on a little folding table in the last rays of the sunset, then put the trash away and stripped down and brought a glass of bourbon up to the hot spring. It was hot enough that I had to ease my way into it, and it smelled not unpleasantly of the earth, the sulfur notes joined by less offensive smells. I lowered myself into it by inches until I was in up to my neck and then sipped my bourbon and listened to the nighttime sounds of the wilderness: night calls of birds, the rustlings of nocturnal rodents and their predators. Eventually, I felt as tenderized as that steak, like my meat might slide off my bones, and I eased myself back out into the sea-cooled night air that made all my skin pucker at once. I sucked in a breath that tasted of salt and whiskey and braised tallow and garlic and made myself pad in slow and measured pace, past my brand-new car, and back to the *Hash* for a shower.

It was only after all of that that I saw my phone was blinking on the kitchen table next to the unwashed skillet on its trivet. I unlocked the screen and read the notification. It was a text from an unknown number.

> Marty, I have bad news. My husband died today. It was very sudden, and he didn't suffer. He wasn't observant, but he always told me that he valued the Jewish custom of fast burial. We will bury him tomorrow afternoon in Colma. I am sorry to have to pass on such sad tidings. Danny thought the world of you, and the work you did for him was very important to him. Please let me know if you can come. If not, we will have a memorial in a

month's time, on April 12th, which would have been his 75th
birthday. (this is Sethuramani Balakrishnan)

I stared at my phone for a very long time. I'd brushed my
teeth, but I'd missed a shred of steak. I found an interdental
brush and worked it out and spat it in the sink, then threw away
the brush. Then I picked up my phone and read the message.
Then I read it again.

> I'll be there.

What do you say?

> I'll be there. I'm so sorry.

I've written messages like this, and that's not how they go.
What do you say?

> That's terrible, Sethu. I'm so sorry. Of course I'll be there.
Thank you for writing.

I almost hit Send. Then.

> You can call me anytime if you need to talk or if I can help in
any way.

13

Seventy-five-year-old men die all the time, even very rich ones. You can improve your odds by getting a personal trainer and a chef and a younger wife who loves you and wants you to live as long as possible and so makes sure you avail yourself of the services of both. You can buy very good medical care and very good screening. But sometimes, you can get a little bulge in a blood vessel in your brain, like a ripe red berry, and if you're lucky, it causes headaches, makes one pupil smaller than the other, all the telltale signs that something is impeding blood flow, the signs that might get you into an MRI and then, *very* quickly, an operating table. You get a big, fat bill, an interesting scar, a fun story, and a chance to see what shape your head has always been under all that hair.

If you're unlucky, the little berry forms in an innocuous place, and it sits there in quiet peace and contemplation, until, one day, a thin spot forms in its curved wall, and that weak tissue strains and strains, and then it rips a little, and then a lot.

If you're unlucky, you go to bed beside your smart, beautiful, loving young wife and never wake up. When they autopsy you, they find the spot where the berry burst. They can't miss it. They just look for the place where the blood flooded out, damaging your brain until your autonomic nervous system tapped out, and your heart and lungs fluttered a little and were stilled.

The funeral home laid Danny out in a winding sheet and a plain pine box. The service was secular, given by one of the curators at the Computer History Museum, who had known Danny since they were both fresh kids and had spent a month with him for an oral history of the cypherpunk movement. There were lots of cypherpunks in attendance, old and hippie-looking, and there were cryptocurrency kids, too young and hungry.

After the main eulogy, Sethu spoke movingly about their love and gave Galit her dues, describing Danny as a gift that one woman gave to another, a man made gentle and good by a good woman, Sethu treating his care and maintenance as a sacred debt to the woman who'd been Danny's first soulmate.

Then one of Danny's business partners from Trustless spoke, ex-Intel, a chip guy who'd cashed out and started a successful fund, then an unsuccessful one, then a successful one. I wondered if he was the one who talked Danny into buying those secure enclave keys. I wondered it so hard that I missed everything he said, and then it was time to hoist poor Danny's body up into the hearse. I was a pallbearer and I sort of knew two of the other guys, and we nodded awkwardly while the funeral director told us where to hold and how and then gave us a one-two-three--up signal. Carrying that box out to the hearse used up the attention that I might otherwise have devoted to thinking about what was inside the box, and I was grateful for the distraction.

I'd come to the service in the Leaf, leaving the *Hash* in a Walmart parking lot in San Bruno. On the way out to the car, I spotted Ira and Zoe standing by the entrance, poking at their phones in the telltale manner of someone trying to page a rideshare service. I hailed them.

"You two need a ride?"

They smiled, and Zoe said, "Yes, please. We split a Lyft here because we thought we might go out for drinks with some of Danny's friends afterward, but there are no cars available now."

"Hop in," I said and unlocked the doors with my fob.

Ira took the passenger seat, and Zoe rode in back. He was in a black suit, nicely cut, a white shirt, open collar button, no tie. She wore a black skirt, white blouse, black blazer. I had steamed my funeral suit in the RV's shower that morning, and I'd put on my black tie because I thought pallbearers ought to wear one. As it turns out, none of the other bearers agreed.

We made noises about it being a nice service and a terrible shock and a great mercy that he'd gone so suddenly. We talked about what a picture of bravery and resolve Sethu was and how our hearts went out to her.

We ran out of things to talk about somewhere in the Outer Sunset, and it felt wrong to turn on the radio. After a moment's silence, inching through traffic, Zoe said, "Can I ask you a question, a personal one?"

"Of course," I said. "Is my answer privileged?"

I was being flip, but she took it seriously because she was a good lawyer. "It can be. Ira's your lawyer, I'm his partner, so it's all in the firm. But I don't think you'll need it for this."

"Shoot."

"I just wondered what you were doing with your money."

"You know, that is a very interesting question. I haven't talked to anyone about it, not apart from you and Danny. It feels strange talking about that much money. Like it's a dirty secret."

I saw her smile in the rearview. "That's pretty typical. I spend a fair bit of my time coaching my clients on how to talk about large sums of money with their families: parents, spouses, kids, no-good cousins with crackpot schemes. It's hard for them to talk about money with their families, but they're plenty relieved to talk about it with *me*. Just to have someone they can talk about it with."

"Well, I'll tell you the truth: I haven't done *anything* with it."

She was a good lawyer, but would make a lousy poker player. A fleeting glimpse in the rearview revealed that she thought I was lying.

"Seriously," I said.

"Nothing?" she said. "You got a three-hundred-million-dollar windfall and you haven't bought *anything* with it?"

"When you put it that way, okay, I've spent a little. I bought a small piece of jewelry for an old friend, kind of a woman who wouldn't treat herself and deserves a little something." Raza had sent me a picture of herself wearing the brooch at a beachside place in Santa Cruz, smiling and toasting me with a large glass of white wine. It looked great on her, and she'd asked for the artist's name so she could buy a few more pieces.

"And that's it? A small piece of jewelry?"

"Well, that, and a car."

Ira had been silent through this, but he let out a grunt of satisfaction at that news. Maybe he was proud of his protégée for getting to the truth, or maybe he was just vicariously pleased for me for treating myself a little.

Zoe, meanwhile, was beaming. "I see. What sort? How much? You can tell me; it's all privileged."

"You're sitting in it."

I savored the silence that followed.

"You bought a Nissan Leaf to celebrate earning three hundred million dollars?" Zoe's millennial incredulity made me feel absurdly, indecently pleased with myself.

"No," I said. "I bought it because my old Nissan Leaf spontaneously combusted and the dealer felt bad for me and offered me a deal on a used replacement."

They both seemed even more uncomfortable.

"Don't worry," I said. "It was a freak thing. Unheard of. I'm sure this one won't blow up or anything."

By then, we were in Colma. I got us parked at the cemetery and shook both their hands and let them thank me for the ride before hustling away. I had a feeling they'd be getting a Lyft back, even if it meant a long wait.

The other pallbearers and I met up and moved the box to the place it needed to go, atop the straps and the winch over the grave. It was a good, bright day, and all the shiny black shoes contrasted nicely with the green grass.

The graveside service was mercifully short. The Computer History Museum fellow said some brief words and the winch unrolled and then we all took turns with the shovels. I waited until all the family members and business partners had thrown in their shovelful, then I took a turn.

There was a line to hug Sethu and offer condolences. Rather than join it, I moved a few yards off to Galit's headstone, in the adjacent plot. They'd bought together at some point, and Danny either hadn't wanted to change those arrangements or hadn't thought to. I wondered if Sethu would be able to buy a plot on Danny's other side and whether she'd have another husband by then who'd need his own plot beside hers.

I looked at Galit's headstone, read the epitaph—I AM. I AM. I AM.—heard the heartbeat in the Plath quote, the brave drumbeat of our lives, echoed in my own ears, as always when I contemplated those words. Someone slipped an arm through mine.

I turned to see who it was. It took me a moment to recognize her because it had been some years.

"Ruth?"

"Hi, Marty."

Ruth Schwartzburg had been the first office manager at Keypairs, back in the days when they were still called *secretaries*. Ruth didn't let anyone call her that, though. As the company grew and more customers came on board, everyone technical was too busy writing code and patching bugs to address customer support, so she became the "customer support manager," too, and then, because she was good at her job, she decided that Keypairs needed real documentation, not just the man pages you could read off the command line after you installed it.

So she became the company's first tech writer, then its first documentation specialist, then, as her docs and organization of support requests produced solid sales leads and high customer satisfaction, she got a team. She hired people like her: ambitious, young, not especially technical. People from working-class backgrounds, like hers, who understood the value of hard work and could empathize with befuddled users of Keypairs' products.

Danny Lazer was a likable guy because he was the sort of person who could recognize talent like Ruth's, give her the resources and respect she deserved, recognize her accomplishments, and pay her accordingly, including stock grants.

Even before Galit had died, she was a paper millionaire, VP of customer experience. After Danny sold the company to Oracle, she became a cash millionaire. That made it easy for her to quit ten minutes into her first meeting with Larry Ellison, handing him her employee badge, getting up from the table, and walking out of the boardroom. She didn't tell anyone about it, but word got around anyway, and she was a Silicon Valley queen for life on account of it.

"You look good," she said.

"You, too," I said.

We hugged.

"You actually look like shit," she said.

"Thank you for your honesty."

We both laughed. It was our turn to go and drop a shovelful of dirt on Danny, so we did that together, and walked back to the cars together.

"I hear people are getting together for drinks after this," she said.

"I heard that, too, but I don't think I'm up for it."

She snorted. "I was thinking the same thing. Not in the mood for a big group, especially if those blockchain creeps are going to be there."

"Yeah, that's about where I netted out. I remember when *crypto* meant 'cryptography.'"

"I remember when you had to either be a techie or a money freak. Seeing the two merged into one identity is uncanny, like something out of the *Monster Manual*."

She was driving an old Prius C with a paint-scrape all down the driver's side. As she unlocked it, she looked me straight in the eyes. "Actually, I would like to talk and have a drink. Just not in a big group. Maybe with a good old friend."

"I'd like that," I said. "I'm staying in San Bruno."

"Really? Airport hotel?"

"Walmart parking lot," I said.

She cocked her head, then snorted. "You're not still living on that bus?"

"If it works, why mess with it?"

"Well, I'm in San Mateo, and I know a good place. I'll text you the address."

It was the kind of place that they drummed out of San Francisco a long time before: dark wood, red leather, lots of booths, waiters in black suits. If a place like this still exists in the city, it's an ironic revival. This was the original. Their steaks weren't as good as mine, but the creamed spinach was incredible, and the bar's top shelf had two excellent bourbons: a Willett Pot and a Cabernet-finished Jefferson's.

We made small talk while we ate, and I didn't let her split the check.

"I'm pretty flush," I said, silencing her weak objections. "You can get the next one."

She tried to make light of it, but I could tell she was relieved. I could also tell she'd been sitting on something she wanted to tell me and hadn't found the nerve yet. Once the server picked up the signed bill—and smiled at the 30 percent tip—there was an awkward pause as she chewed her lip.

"Ruth, if there's something you wanted to talk to me about, I'm here. If you want to think about it awhile, you can always call."

"No," she said, and I saw there were tears standing out in her eyes, glittering in the candlelight. "Don't go just yet. Thanks for the push, Marty. There *is* something." She patted her eyes with a clean corner of her napkin, opened her mouth to speak, then closed it again and wiped her eyes harder. She took some composing breaths, and I concentrated on projecting calm and readiness.

"It's about Lorrie," she said.

Oh. I hadn't said anything about the pale stripe around her ring finger, but I'd wondered.

"You know, you weren't the only one who had a private talk with me about him." I remembered it well: I'd caught up with her at a Keypairs Christmas party at a swish restaurant at a hobby farm where all the food was literally farm-to-table, served by farmhands who could tell the tale of every morsel. It was charming enough, but I had come stag and been seated next to a junior coder who was unhealthily interested in all that backstory and it got to be a bit much, so I excused myself to go see the night sky—it was a clear, moonless night, and we were an hour from the city lights, and a couple of the Keypairs people had brought out their telescopes and were giving tours of Saturn's rings and Jupiter's moons.

I found her out there, leaning against a tree with her arms folded over her chest, making an anxious silhouette. She'd confessed that she was having second thoughts about her engagement to Lawrence Lin, and asked for my honest opinion.

"Ruth, if you're asking that, I think you know the answer."

She choked up but managed to get out, "I think I do, but I want to hear it anyway."

"All right, then. I'll give it to you as straight as I can make it, without any emotion. I have known Lorrie since his first job, over at Apple, back in the 68K days. He made a good first impression, and Jobs took him with the NeXT. But it was all surface. He was sloppy. Made stupid mistakes and wouldn't admit it. Didn't like getting chewed out by Steve in front of the whole team. When he got fired, he sued. That's where I came in, asked to check on his history.

"He was a cheater, Ruth. Cheated his way through Caltech, squeaked out with a degree because they knew he'd make a stink if they pushed it. He'd taken credit for other people's work at Apple. The whisper network knew it, but it never got up to management. I told the NeXT CFO that any settlement they paid Lawrence Lin to go away peacefully would be cheaper than the fight he'd put up and the stink he'd make.

"All of that is just background. Here's the worst part: he never accepted any responsibility for any of it. It was all other people's fault. He was being singled out. He was being targeted. He was being persecuted.

"I've known a lot of hustlers, aggro types who cut corners and bull their way through the consequences. It's a type, out here. Move fast and break things. Don't ask permission; beg forgiveness. But most of those people, they know they're doing it. You can manage them, tack around them, factor them into your plans.

"The ones who get high on their own supply, though? There's no factoring them in. Far as they're concerned, they're the only player characters in the game and everyone else is an NPC, a literal nobody.

"Lawrence Lin is the second type, Ruth."

She married him anyway. I sent them a nice German blender.

She sighed and reached over the booth back for a napkin from the empty table behind her. "At least five people told me that there was something off about Lorrie, but none of them had his number the way you did. For them, it was just a feeling. You diagnosed the pathology, and you did it perfectly."

"I spend more time cleaning up after grifters than your median friend, Ruth. It gives me an outlook."

"Fair enough. I wish I'd listened to you."

"But you left him," I said, tapping her bare finger with my own fingertip.

"Too late," she said. "By the time I realized it wasn't ever going to get better, it was just going to keep getting worse, every account was empty, even the ones that were supposed to be locked up until I turned sixty-five."

"Ouch," I said. "What did he take you for?"

"Eight million," she said. "But here's the worst part: he claims *I* pissed it all away. I have a little condo down here, a one-bedroom place worth a hundred and fifty k, and he's suing for half of that. And he wants half of my pension, once that kicks in. Oracle assumed Keypairs' pension liabilities, and they start paying out in two years."

"Community property state," I said.

"Good old California," she said. "The Golden State. Look, I heard you were retired, but I wondered if you might have some tips . . . Just something I can try to find out where he's hid it all. Or maybe a name, a protégé or a competitor? I have a line of credit on the condo; I can use that for a retainer."

I realized I could just call up Ira or Zoe and meet them at their office tomorrow with Ruth and sign over beneficial ownership to an LLC on a distant treasure island and make her whole, and I'd never even feel the loss. She didn't know that, and I wondered how she'd take it if I offered.

"As a matter of fact, I *am* retired, but I find myself with nothing much to do to fill my days. I haven't found any hobbies I'd consider taking up, and I was going a bit stir-crazy in the old mobile home. How about if I have a quick poke around, see what I can find?"

She started to cry in earnest then, and I poached two more napkins off the booth behind me before our server noticed what was going on and quick-walked to the check-in stand to poach a box of tissues, which she discreetly dropped off on our table with a small nod of sympathy.

I got Ruth into an Uber and slow-drove the Leaf back to the *Hash*. As I reached the Walmart parking lot, I realized I was humming. Three hundred million dollars was an abstract problem, amorphous as all offshore funds. Outwitting Lorrie Lin was a crisply defined problem, as engaging and irresistible as a cross-word puzzle.

Three days later, I met Ruth in the lobby of the SFO Aloft Hotel. I'd moved in after the first day, when I realized that I was wasting valuable Lorrie Lin time driving the bus around looking for a place to dump my sludge and refill my water tanks. I Pricelined all the hotels within twenty miles, and the Aloft came in cheapest for five nights in a room with two doubles, which the clerk kindly swapped for a king at check-in.

"Here you go," I said, handing her a manila envelope as she hung her light jacket over the back of the low lounge chair. She was wearing a sleeveless black shirt under it, showing off her good arms. I had her figured for sixty, but she wore it well, with silver hair in a neat bob and soft eyes that missed nothing but forgave much. She deserved better than Lorrie Lin.

She got a guarded expression as she opened the envelope and looked at the sheets of paper I'd printed in the hotel business center. They'd charged me enough for the printouts that it might have been cheaper to order an ink-jet from Amazon for same-day delivery. I put it on the Black card and silenced the whispering frugal imp nagging me from my right shoulder.

She skimmed the first page, then got to the bottom of the sheet and gasped when she saw the number there. It was a hair over $9 million. Lorrie had taken stock options to sign onto three start-ups and had kept them when he was asked to leave. One of them had paid off well.

She shuffled the pages, looking at my supporting documentation: account numbers, true beneficial owners, the Delaware LLCs, the insurance policies, the brokerage accounts.

"Marty—"

"Lorrie Lin is a very bad crook," I said. "His problem is that he thinks he's smarter than everyone else. Anyone can design a con that he himself can't think of a way to beat. That doesn't mean he's built a system that works. It just means he's built a system that works on people stupider than he is."

She laughed, a clear, ringing, relieved, wild sound that drew stares from around the lobby. "Spoken like a lifelong red teamer," she said. Then she shook her head, put the papers down very carefully, rose from her chair, and motioned for me to do the same, and she stood up on tiptoe to get her arms around my neck and practically chinned herself on me to pull me into a bear hug that made my old, injured rib creak. I didn't mind.

She was a good hugger, and she followed it up with a kiss on each cheek, then a soft one right on my lips, and I remembered how beautiful she was. Not just handsome nor merely well preserved. A knockout.

I hugged her back, then set her down and took note of the audience we'd drawn. I didn't care. I could afford to make a scene, and the occasion warranted it.

She sat down with tears streaming down her face and riffled through her smart little black purse for a tissue, did the necessary, then returned the papers to the envelope, folded it in half, and stuck it in the purse with the dirty Kleenex.

"Where do you want the money sent?" she asked. "Do you have an LLC or somewhere I can transfer it to? It's going to take some time for my lawyer to get ahold of all of this, but once he does—"

"Ruth, I'm retired. This one was a favor for an old friend. Besides, with community property, you still might have to sign half of this away to Lorrie Lin, even with all the evidence of shenanigans you're going to put in front of the judge."

"Don't be absurd. You're a professional, you did your job, you deserve to be compensated. If I give half to Lorrie and split the remainder with you, I'm still a millionaire with an unmortgaged home and a pension due in a few years. Who needs more than that?"

"I don't," I said. "The month before Danny died, I did a job for him. A big one. And that one wasn't a favor. I'm okay, Ruth. All set." I almost named the figure, but I did not. My extended network of OG Silicon Valley types included paupers and billionaires, and long ago, we all figured out that the best way to stay on friendly terms was to keep the figures out of it.

"So here we are, a couple of one percenters at an Aloft Hotel by SFO, with something to celebrate," she said. "You'd think we could come up with something fancier than this."

So I finally did it. I finally spent the money the way they all seem to think you should, when it arrives. My man at KPMG got us a limo, a table at the French Laundry, a suite at the Nikko with its own *onsen* for afterward, with a bottle of Pappy Van Winkle next to an eyedropper and a little frosted blue-glass flask of mountain spring water.

Ruth and I ended up in the *onsen*'s deep, scalding tub with glasses each containing $500 worth of bourbon. We had laughed a lot that night, and the move from the restaurant to the hotel to the tub had been as natural as an old married couple, or two prepubescent cousins taking a bath together during a sleepover.

It was only once our meat had tenderized and our faces had reddened from the heat that I seemed to sober up all at once and realize that in the space of a few days, I'd gone from doing this on my own in a hot spring down in San Luis Obispo to doing it here, high atop the Nikko, all of San Francisco laid out in the picture window, and, close enough to touch my dear, old, gorgeous friend Ruth Schwartzburg, gloriously naked, lit golden and gray by those city lights, her eyes smoky and brown and large and smart and forgiving, like you could fall into them.

"Come here," she said and patted the bench beside her.

I did, and she slid her arm around my shoulder, worked her way onto my lap, so she was in a mermaid's carry. She tilted her face up to mine and looked at me with those big, brown eyes.

I don't often have mornings after. Notwithstanding the stories about rock stars, there aren't many women who want to spend the night in a luxury tour bus. And I'm the kind of old-fashioned gent who doesn't want to hang around like a bad smell after the deed is done, making toilet noises and raiding the fridge the next morning. There've been a few years where there was a woman in my life, or I was a man in hers, and that could be nice, but on the whole, I'm a person who tends to wake on my own.

It's a tribute to how good a friend Ruth was to me that there was no awkwardness the next morning. Even her snores were cute, and when she felt me stirring, she rolled to face me, flung an arm over me, and pulled me spoon-wise to her, kissing the back of my neck with sleepy softness.

We took it easy that morning, got room service Japanese breakfast delivered with smooth, cheerful efficiency by the club-floor staff, who set up the low table and laid the many dishes on it with perfect, squared precision.

We sat on the floor for a while, legs under the table, making delighted and surprised noises as we tried different foods, sometimes offering each other a choice morsel on our chopsticks. We showered separately, and those catfooted concierge staffers stole in and cleared it all away while we were out of the suite's dining room.

"Well," she said, wrapping a towel around her hair and retying the striped linen robe.

"Well," I replied from my perch on the sofa. They'd brought in a facsimile edition of the day's edition of the *Asahi Shimbun*, printed on heavy tabloid printer paper and bound with silk ribbon, and I'd been reading the day's news in Tokyo while she did bathroom things.

She sat down next to me and cuddled up a little. "That was a perfectly wonderful way to wrap up a perfectly terrible nightmare. I can't believe I flushed away ten years of my life. And there's still some very unpleasant stuff ahead of me."

"You can pay to make most of that go away. Get an attack lawyer who'll make Lorrie's life a living hell. It will cost far less than you were planning to give me, and if you choose wisely, you'll get someone who'll terrorize him into settling. Especially if they can convey to him that every day he delays the inevitable means deducting thousands of dollars from your joint assets to pay the legal bills."

"You're right," she said. "That's exactly how I should play it. Oh, God, I needed this good break. Needed it so much." She took the newspaper out of my hands and set it beside her, then gave me a long, hard smooch right on the lips. It had the air of the period at the end of the sentence.

"All part of the service, ma'am," I said, then looked into those deep, shrewd eyes. "Listen, Ruth, just so you know, I don't expect you to make this a regular thing. We both had something to celebrate, and we were both lucky to have someone to celebrate it with. At this point in my life, that's all I'm after."

Those eyes softened even more. How could one person look so loving and smart at the same time? Oh, Lorrie, you have no idea what you threw away, you dumb fuck. "Thank you, Marty. I was trying to find a way to say that myself. How the hell are you still single?"

"Well, for one thing, no woman wants to marry a man who lives out of his car," I said.

She snorted.

We strolled out to Union Square, holding hands like kids. On impulse, we bought tickets for the cable car and rode the running board all the way to Fisherman's Wharf and got lobster rolls and tossed fries at the seagulls. Finally, we found a bench with a view of the bay and watched the people, the gulls, the beggars and the grifters, and the sad and broken people. We got aggressively panhandled, and I was about to tell the kid—skinny, sad, strung out, a little girl no older than eighteen—to buzz off, when I remembered that I was worth $300 million, and I gave her five twenties. She smiled in a guarded way and scurried off.

"That was nice," Ruth said.

"It won't make a difference in the long run," I said.

"But it will in the short run. That's dinner and a room."

"And a fix," I said.

"If I lived like that, I'd need something to take the edge off, too." That was Ruth all over, smart and kind.

An interval occurred. She snorted.

"Something funny?"

She pointed out at the sea. "Us sitting here, staring there. All it needs is Otis Redding whistling 'Dock of the Bay.'"

"That was Danny Lazer's theme song," I said. "He used to drive me crazy, humming it."

"You think I don't know that? Believe me, buster, he drove his coworkers a lot crazier than his pals. That's why I thought of it. Poor Danny."

"Poor Danny," I agreed. "But all things being equal, not so bad. Seventy-five, healthy until he wasn't, then it was quick, died rich, in love with a beautiful and capable woman who was good for him."

"You approve of Sethu, then?"

"You don't?" I asked.

"Oh, I approve. But I know you, Martin Hench. You're on the red team. You're always looking for weaknesses in others' defenses. Danny had plenty of those. When Sethu first came to Keypairs, she was an oddball, so smart about finance, but she was in my department, doing customer support. She could have been running the department's books instead. Hell, anytime I couldn't figure out our budget, I roped her into it.

"And then, after Galit went and she took over Danny's life, a lot of us got worried. We loved Danny, even if he did sell the company out from under us. Galit was his life. He was just waiting to die. Between Sethu's business smarts and Danny's vulnerability, and the age difference—"

"I had the same thought," I confessed. "But it wasn't my business. And besides, before long, it became clear that if she was going to inherit whatever Danny was going to leave behind, she'd earned it. Without her . . ."

"Yeah," Ruth said. "Yeah. I know he was an old friend of yours, and I didn't know him as long as you did, but, Marty, I think I knew him better. I saw him five days a week, *at least*. Lots of weekends, too, especially in the early years. It was scary to see him decline after Galit died. Like someone had pulled out his plug and he was deflating. He aged so fast, and he just wasn't . . . *there* when I visited. So I agree with you: whatever Sethu's getting now, she deserves."

That night, back on the *Hash* in the parking lot of the Aloft, I turned those words over and over in my mind. Finally, I sent Sethu a text.

> Sorry I didn't tag along after the funeral. Too many people. But I'd love a chance to pay my condolences properly, whenever you're ready. Say the word and I'll swing by.

The reply took less than a minute.

> Tomorrow at lunch? Noon?

14

This time, it was Sethu who greeted me at the door, giving me a stiff hug instead of Danny's customary ribbing. She wore loose men's pajamas with a monogram and a regimental stripe. Danny's. Her hair wasn't brushed, and she still had yesterday's makeup around her eyes.

The photo-ready midcentury living room was notably disarrayed, with visible dust, cushions on the floor, and a blanket balled up at the foot of the sofa, which had suspicious indentations in it. If I woke up next to my dead spouse, I wouldn't want to sleep in my bed again, either.

Passing through the kitchen on the way to the roof-deck, I saw empty wine bottles ranked on the counter, the sink full of long-stemmed wineglasses clinking in cold, soapy water.

She'd done work on her last canvas, removing the few bits of color she'd left behind, replacing them with slashes of black and charcoal. She'd left her palette on the ground beside the easel with brushes stuck in dried blobs of paint.

I sat down in my usual chair. It was a nice day, and there was a nice view. The noontime city was uncharacteristically busy as the busy people burst out of their workhouses and scurried to find lunch, then scurried back again, faces glued to phones.

Sethu sat next to me. She smelled unwashed. Something flashed on her wrist. The little wartime Rolex Oyster that Danny had worn, back when they made them the size of a lady's watch. It suited her. I noticed it wasn't running.

"Sethu," I said, "I'm so sorry about Danny. I can see it's hurting you. Someone once told me that asking how to help a grieving person was no good, because it puts the obligation on them to think of something, so how about this: I'll clean up your kitchen and tidy the living room while you get ready to go to lunch?"

That earned me a sad and grateful look. "Thank you, Marty. I'd like that. I'm not quite up for going out to lunch just yet. I'm still gathering myself, a bit."

"Take as long as you'd like, Sethu. I've got all the time in the world."

So we sat there, watching the lunchtime rush under the noon sun. I thought about Danny and his withdrawal after he was widowed. I wondered if Sethu needed someone to do for her what she had done for him. I hoped she found someone and that he didn't turn out to be another Lorrie Lin.

Finally, she stood and touched her hair and made a wry expression. "Okay," she said, "time to gird my loins. You don't have to clean my house, Marty. Honestly."

"I know I don't," I said, "but I will."

As the saying goes, she cleaned up real good. She emerged from her bedroom with her hair under a tan kerchief, wearing wide-legged black slacks and a stiff white cotton shirt tailored narrow and high at the waist, exposing a millimeter of torso. She stepped into a pair of leather sandals and lifted each foot like a yogi to buckle the straps.

She thanked me for the tidiness of the living room and kitchen and took the bag of wine bottles from me and dropped them down a chute on the way to the elevator. We heard them shatter and tinkle from afar.

"Where to?" I asked when we reached the sidewalk. She didn't answer. She was busy scanning the road, squinting at the parked cars from behind her sunglasses, her whole affect tense and fearful. Then she took my arm and set off down the street at a fast clip.

"Everything okay?" I asked as we hustled along the sidewalk.

"Fine," she said, practically dragging me into a sandwich place with plastic tables and a menu over the counter. She slid into a table toward the back, out of sight of the window, and gave me her order, toasted egg salad with tomatoes and cress. I lined up and ordered for both of us.

Seated across from her, back to the window, I caught some of her nervousness. "Look, Sethu, I can tell this is hard on you. If you're worried that someone's going to see us together and think you're romancing some stranger days after your husband died—"

She made a startled sound that quickly turned into a laugh. The laugh went on, getting more and more cracked, until she forcibly choked it down. "That's not something I'd ever worry about. First, because it's none of anyone else's fucking business who I'm fucking; and second, because Danny and I were poly and out. He took his girlfriends out around here all the time. I did the same with my boyfriends."

She took her shades off and gave me a frank, defiant look. "You didn't know?"

"Nope. Don't care, either. Like you said, none of my business."

The sandwiches came. They were better than I'd expected, tall and wrapped in butcher's paper, skewered on toothpicks, then sliced through. Mine was tongue on rye with swiss, the order scrawled in grease pencil on the paper wrapper.

"Ew," she said.

"To each their own," I said and waggled my eyebrows. It cheered her a little, which cheered me, a little.

"Sorry to be such a head case," she said, lifting off the top slice of her sandwich and taking a dainty, open-faced bite of the remainder. "It's been a week."

"You have every right to be shook up," I said. My sandwich was piled so high that I gave up on trying to get a bite out of it and opened it and forked up a couple of mouthfuls of meat and cheese, planning to eat it down to manageable girth. "But, Sethu, you seem like you're not just grieving. Forgive me, but you seem like you're scared."

Her lips tightened. "That's true." She nibbled her sandwich, gathering her thoughts. "That's why I wanted to see you. To warn you."

"Warn me," I said.

She set down the sandwich. "Maybe it's nothing. But I thought you should know. Danny would have told you. He was going to."

I pushed aside my lunch. Suddenly, I wasn't very hungry. I had a premonition, a flash. Those three kids. The goofy expression on Ales's swollen, staved-in face, like a cartoon character who's had his head run over. People lost their lives over the cryptographic keys I'd recovered. I'd assumed that whatever mechanism led to them knowing of the keys' existence in the first place would have let them know that those keys were now gone and totally unrecoverable. But maybe not. Maybe they were willing to keep killing to get them.

"What is it, Sethu?"

She pondered her open-faced sandwich, then seemed to lose her appetite and set it down.

"Three young men paid us a visit last week, the day before Danny died. Their English was excellent and almost entirely unaccented, but there was just a *little* Russian in there."

"Did they want the keys?"

She cocked her head like I'd surprised her. Then she realized which keys I meant and closed her eyes, like she was looking inside for the right words. When she opened them again, she said, "No, Marty, they want *you*."

Only a couple of Danny's business partners knew that he had the keys to begin with. He didn't tell any of them that the keys had been compromised until I'd returned the laptop to him and he'd destroyed it. He had been thinking on the same lines as I had—there was a leak somewhere in his org, and that leak had led to the theft. If he wanted to get the word out that there was nothing to steal, he had to tell the same people who knew about the keys that he'd shredded the laptop; otherwise, things would get even hotter.

When three young men presented themselves at the Camino Real's security desk, he'd scoped them out through the lobby camera and was about to send them away when one of them said something to the security guard, who said that they were here to discuss real estate at Jordan's Mill.

He didn't want them in his home, so he'd gone down to meet with them, and they'd talked in one of the conversation clusters in the lobby, three low armchairs and a table with a live orchid. One of the guys had stood. The building's security staff didn't need to be told that Danny would like them to keep their distance, but watch out anyway.

"When he came back up, he was shaking," Sethu said. "He'd recorded the conversation on his phone, and he played it back for me. They were polite, well-spoken, sounded like they'd been in the U.S. for some time, maybe since college. Guys in their late twenties. The conversation was all ellipses, talking around the issue. *Such a tragedy, those three poor children.*

"That's when they mentioned you. They said they'd heard you were the last known person to see the kids alive and they wanted to ask a question. One of them claimed to be there on behalf of the Russian kid, Sergey—"

"He's Azerbaijani. Probably ethnically Russian, though, with a name like Preobrazhensky."

She shrugged. "They pumped Danny for information about you. They weren't subtle. They said that a father wants to know about his son's last moments. They said that they understood that maybe you felt you were compromised, involved somehow in whatever had gone wrong, and they weren't looking to get you into any trouble. They said—"

But I'd tuned out because of the rising buzzing in my ears and the plummeting feeling in my stomach. They were paraphrasing my conversation with Laura, at Graciela's. I wasn't the only one willing to do some shoe-leather searching for the place that those kids might have stashed their laptop on the way to Jordan's Mill.

"Do you have the recording?" I said. "From Danny's phone?"

She shook her head. "I didn't have a login for any of his devices. He left instructions with his will for unlocking his business files, but not his personal ones. Danny was a cryptographer, Marty. He knew that if he died without revealing his keys, no one would ever be able to access his papers." Tears streaked her face. "I knew about it, but I didn't realize he'd put all our photos in his personal partition. Gone forever. That asshole."

I forced myself to be present, though all I could think of was Laura and her husband, Tomas.

"I'm sorry, Sethu. I'm sure he didn't mean for it to happen. He must have just had one drive for 'personal' and the other for 'business,' and your photos weren't 'business.'"

She blew her nose on a napkin. "I know, I'm not an idiot. But Jesus, it's all gone. He didn't use social media. I have a few photos he sent to me over the years, and the ones I took, but there's so much of my life that I thought I'd be able to see, and I'll never see it again." She cried for a while more. "I'd give anything to see those photos."

"They asked for me," I said. It wasn't a question, but she nodded.

"Danny was so worked up about it. I didn't have to ask why. The way those kids were killed, and if these three were connected somehow—" She pushed the rest of her sandwich away. I realized I didn't want any more of mine, either. "He didn't tell them anything that wasn't public information. The way they talked, those ellipses, they made sure they knew about the keys, and there was the implied threat that they'd let other people know if Danny didn't help them find you. So he told them things, but nothing"—she fished for the word—"sensitive."

She bit her lip. More tears welled in her eyes, and she blotted them. Feeling a sense of déjà vu, I nabbed some napkins

off the next table and handed them to her. "I can't help but—"
She couldn't get the words out. She breathed in and out, mastered herself. "I can't help but think that the worry about what
would happen next is what—" More blotting, breathing. "Maybe
it killed Danny."

This was my cue to say that I was sure it wasn't, but I wasn't
so sure.

15

I'd parked the Leaf a couple of blocks away. I was dying to get back to it and see if there was any bad news about a little out-of-the-way restaurant named Graciela's, set close to where 101 and 128 merged. But I needed to get Sethu home, and she had every reason to want an escort to get there. I'm an old guy and I've lost half a step, but I've emerged from more bouts standing than on my back. Of course, I'm not bulletproof.

The walk to the Camino Real was uneventful, though some paranoid pattern-matching part of my mind kept overfitting the surroundings and finding things to be alarmed about in them: Had that Tesla been parked there before? Wasn't that the same tech bro with a man-bun we passed earlier? (There are a lot of Teslas in Palo Alto. Ditto man-buns.)

I got her to the elevator. We'd hardly said a word on the way back, but once we got into the Camino Real's lobby, she grabbed my arm and murmured, "Come upstairs. Please."

I had another wild surmise, something about widows and polyamory and the way some people distract themselves when life gets too real. I didn't want that. Not because Sethu wasn't desirable and not because she was "Danny's girl." Even before I heard of ethical nonmonogamy, I had been painfully disabused of the idea that an adult woman was any man's "girl." I had some patient women to thank for that lesson and a few impatient ones who'd made sure it stuck.

Once we were in her home, she became visibly anxious. Re-tidying the living room that I'd tidied before we'd gone out: minute adjustments to the cushions and meaningless perturbations of the houseplants' leaves. I sat upright in a streamlined teak armchair that was designed for reclining, watching her without staring, letting her gather her thoughts or her courage or both.

"Marty," she said at last, while putting on a performance of concern for a potted palm, her back to me.

"Yes?"

"I've never been entirely comfortable around you, and I'm sorry about that. Danny really cared about you, and I know you two went way back. I wish I'd tagged along when you two got together. He always asked and I always turned him down, and I could tell that disappointed him."

"It's okay," I said. "Everyone doesn't have to be everyone else's best friend. For the record, I confess I was a little skeptical when you and Danny went from PA and boss to, uh—"

"Boyfriend and girlfriend?" She stopped fussing with the plant and turned to face me with a sad smile. "I felt that. You and all of Danny's oldest friends, really, and of course I knew why. Young woman, rich older widower. It's not exactly subtle. And I confess that I *was* seeking security as much as love, but, Marty, I did love Danny. I loved him so much it ached." Tears again, and she had tissue boxes on hand, and I studied the view out the picture window while she took care of herself.

"But that's not why I wasn't comfortable around you. I could get over that. The real reason—" She stopped. "I'm going to get a cup of tea. Would you like something?"

"No, no, I'm fine. Thank you."

"I'll be back in a minute."

The view was very nice. Palo Alto had emptied again, all the activity retreating indoors. It looked like a soundstage, ready for the crew to move in and set up the shot. That reminded me of some friends I had in Burbank, right next to the Warner lot, and how we'd made a tentative date to hike out in Angeles Forest and finish it with dinner at the Smoke House the next time I came to town.

She came out with an earthenware mug and fussed with a

coaster, settling herself on an angular sofa. "You're a pioneer, Marty Hench."

"Came over in a covered wagon," I agreed.

"I mean, in digital forensic accounting. The way Danny told it, you were born at the same moment that the first computerized finance crimes were being committed."

"Something like that."

"Something like that. So you'll know all the legends, all the watershed moments."

"Most of them," I said.

"So you'll know the name Jim Hannah."

I held myself very still. "I know the name," I said. "I never met him."

She looked me in the eyes. Hers were welling over again, but her voice was steady. "I knew him. I lived with him for five years."

Hannah had been a finance guy, but not the regular kind. In a region where they were happy to launder Saudi money and Russian money and Chinese money, Hannah took the money no one else would take. He called himself a "portfolio manager," but he never said whose portfolios he was managing. He often came in on deals where there was a prestige partner who wanted to put up a little money for a lot of equity, leaving the founders scrounging for more money to bulk up the round without giving up too much equity. Hannah was that guy. He'd buy in big, expect little in return, and that got him in on a *lot* of early deals. Tiny amounts of equity early turned into lots of money later at the exit, and Hannah's brag sheet made him out to be the shrewdest investor in the Valley, early on RISC, SGI, Pixar, Netscape, Yahoo!, LinkedIn. Lots of smaller companies, too, little start-ups that weren't ever supposed to be standalone businesses, just targets for acquisition by one of the bigs.

When he died, word got around that he was an investor in *twenty-seven* of Apple's acquisitions. That sounds more impressive than it really is; Apple buys companies more often than I buy groceries.

He died showy. He'd bought a performance car, a stupid car, a "supercar" from Bugatti, and he liked to bomb up and down El Camino Real and 101 on it, racking up traffic tickets and citations that he fought in court like a demon. Larry Ellison liked to buzz the Valley in his surplus fighter jet; Jim Hannah liked to tear up the roads in his Bugatti. Neither of them truly believes that other people are really *real,* not the way they are, and thus the danger and misery they inflict on the rest of us isn't worth a damn.

The Bugatti flipped on the San Mateo bridge, right over the guardrail and into the bay. They say he hit his head hard on the wheel at some point because there wasn't much left of his face when they fished him out of the water.

"I met Jim when I was twenty. My life had been pretty chaotic up until that point. I always knew that I was smart, but I choked up every time I sat down to take a test. I got a string of report cards with straight Ds and comments from my teachers saying that I was very bright but needed to apply myself.

"For my parents, that was just proof that I had grown up to be a lazy, stupid American girl. There was talk of shipping me back to Kolkata, maybe for university or maybe to just get some proper discipline. I dodged that, but the situation at home only got worse after I graduated high school. Not even the junior colleges wanted me. The only educational institutions that welcomed me made Trump University look like Yale. My parents wouldn't accept that, though, and gave me an ultimatum: if I wanted to go on living under their roof, I had to enroll in a degree program.

"So I left. I know that eighteen-year-olds have moved out on their own for centuries, but I was not a mature eighteen-year-old. I bounced from group house to group house, renting the worst room, working four gig economy jobs at a time to make rent and still coming up short. Eventually, I'd get so far in arrears that my roommates would invite me to live somewhere else. A lot of the time, that somewhere else was my car, which got broken into twice. My clothes were stolen, my laptop, my phone. I'd scrounge money for more, thrifted and used, and sign up for more gig work. I had to quit driving Uber because my car was no longer up to their standards, so then it was just delivering takeout and doing home-cleaning shifts.

"That's how I met Jim. And yes, it was every bit as creepy as it sounds: a fifty-year-old guy with a lot of money sends out for a broke young girl to clean his house and then puts the moves on her. But it wasn't purely a quid pro quo. The situation I was in back then, I wasn't just broke and desperate: I was *lonely*. Most days, the only conversation I'd get was with the people at the restaurants who handed me bags of takeout to deliver to people who barely grunted thanks when I dropped them off.

"Jim's interest was obviously carnal, but not *exclusively* carnal. He was funny, smart, and knew a lot about a lot of things. I've always been a dilettante, ten miles wide and one inch deep, and talking to Jim was complete catnip for me, leaping from subject to subject, making connections I wouldn't have seen coming but couldn't unsee in retrospect.

"I didn't get any cleaning done that day, but Jim didn't mind. He booked me the next day, and the next, and the next. It was so flattering that this powerful, intelligent man wanted to just sit and talk with me, that by the time he made his move, I was half in love with him.

"It wasn't entirely transactional. Jim set me up in his place, gave me spending money, took me to parties and meetings, introduced me to his friends. I had my own room, but most nights, I ended up in his room. I didn't mind. I liked it. I had other boyfriends, and he had other girlfriends, and that was fine, too.

"Best of all, I learned from him. A lot of business went through his little one-man shop, and he was very careful about what he put in writing, which made it all more complicated. Little by little, he enlisted me to be his second-in-command, teaching me how the forms and procedures worked, teaching me how to do international company formation and do untraceable transfers in and out of them.

"The first time he heard about Bitcoin—at a little dinner party with just two other couples—it was like he'd been electrocuted. He was *vibrating* through the rest of the meal, champing to leave and go home and get on top of it. He even built a little mining rig, adding a sixty-amp circuit to power the AC in his TV room, which was taken over by caseless PCs with bare video cards that he blasted with the biggest fans he could find.

"But what really interested him was off-ramps and on-ramps: ways to convert fiat money to Bitcoin, and Bitcoin back to fiat money. He had such deep expertise in moving money around without the blockchain, and it gave him a huge advantage. He knew how to detour around real-world bottlenecks with cryptocurrency and how to beat cryptocurrency controls with old-school financial secrecy techniques. He called himself a centaur: a human being assisted by a machine, more powerful than either could be on its own."

She stopped and sipped her tea. It must have been cold by then, but she clearly needed a moment to regroup.

"I heard that about Jim," I said. "He had quite a reputation."

"Yes," she said with a sad smile. "That was his weakness: he loved for people to know how clever he was. He said it brought in business, but it was all about his ego. His own childhood wasn't much better than my own, and we bonded over our mutual need to prove we were better than anyone else." She took some more tea, and now her hand shook when she set down the mug, making it rattle on the coaster.

"Bragging like he did, that was what brought in the Azeris. Officials, top of the treasury, and they had a *lot* of money to move. More than he was comfortable with, which is saying something, because Jim loved big deals, the bigger the better. But the sums involved . . . Even Jim balked at them. But the Azeris were . . .

forceful. Jim dealt with a lot of tough guys, but the Azeris gave him the fear. He worked very long hours on their project, unable to sleep, getting up at 2:00 a.m. to pace or drive around.

"Finally, he said he had it cracked. He wouldn't tell me anything about it, insisted on handling it himself. He sent me away to Palm Springs for a week while he closed the deal. Three days later, he was dead."

"Forgive me, Sethu, but he wasn't exactly a careful driver."

That actually got a laugh out of her, but it came out as more of a bark. "He wasn't, no, especially not in that Bugatti. But after the funeral, a couple of guys I had never met asked me very nicely if they could have all of Jim's computers and phones and any passwords I had lying around. They said they wanted to be sure that none of that information fell into the wrong hands and that they'd be happy to compensate me well if I could manage that for them.

"And I did it, because I needed the money, sure—I wasn't in for anything from Jim's will, and he had a brother who made it clear he wanted me to vacate the premises as soon as was humanly possible—but also because they strongly implied that the alternative was that they'd come and take Jim's devices and that they'd remember that I was the person who got between them and what they wanted. I'd met some tough guys while I worked with Jim, but these guys were, I don't know, next level."

She shrugged. "I mean, why not? Jim was dead. His clients were scumbags. And I knew for a fact that he kept almost no records and flushed any files as soon as they weren't needed anymore." Shrugged again. "I did it."

"Sounds like you made the right call," I said. "It wasn't your job to keep Jim's old clients' secrets, and getting roughed up and then kicked out penniless wouldn't help them anyway."

She sighed and drank tea. "That's what I tell myself. Jim's brother was furious when none of the computers or files were in the house, threatened to sue me or call the police. I laughed at him. I was young and heartbroken and frightened of the men who'd surely killed Jim. I wasn't going to be afraid of that piece of shit. He owned a photocopy store in an Ohio college town. Hadn't spoken to Jim in twenty years. Had a wife and family waiting for him back home. Even if he'd had Jim's records, he'd have had no idea what to do with them."

"Do you think he found Jim's money?"

That got a better laugh out of her. "Fuck no. No way. *You* could have found it, I bet. I knew where a lot of it was, but I wasn't going to touch it. It wasn't mine, and those gentlemen with Jim's devices might decide to retrieve it, in which case, I didn't want them to discover that I'd gotten there first. If there's one thing I learned from Jim, it was that there was always more money out there."

"So what did you do?"

She cocked her head like she didn't understand the question, then said, "Oh! I got a job. At Keypairs. First in customer support, then in the finance compliance department, and then as Danny's PA."

My turn to laugh. "That makes sense," I said. "You knew the tricks, so you knew what to look for."

"I did. Danny ran Keypairs clean. He knew that cryptography could be used by people who had legit reasons to hide things from the government—Iranian dissidents, say—but he didn't want the company to become a haven for crooks. Not just because of his morals but because of the company's reputation. He'd built that company up with Galit; it was as much hers as it was his, and she didn't like any funny stuff, so he made sure there was as little funny stuff as possible."

"Danny was always a pretty straight arrow," I said.

"Yeah," she said. "But it was different with Trustlesscoin. I helped design the trip wires, you know? Danny didn't want any obvious criminality in his system. He knew that the best he could do was to keep all the stupid criminals out, but that was okay with him. Deep down, he knew that without money laundering and criminal payments, there just wouldn't be the liquidity Trustlesscoins needed to be a real currency. So I worked with the engineering team to create business rules that would catch all but the smartest crooks, without presenting too many hurdles to the legit speculators. They don't want to have to call an 800 number every time they try to move assets in or out of Trustless because the algorithm had flagged them.

"I was good at it. I *am* good at it. I'm technically on a grief leave, but the board has let me know that they expect to name me as interim CEO whenever I'm ready to come back, and then to make it permanent at the next quarterly meeting. I mean, of course they will; by then, Danny's estate will have been probated, and I'll hold his shares and mine. Any board member who doesn't want me as CEO can hit the bricks."

"Do you want to be CEO of Trustless?"

She set her cup down with a click and stared at me for a long time. She had always been a beautiful woman, but grief had matured her, made her look *formidable* as well as beautiful. She hadn't been a kid for a long time, but now she was well and truly an adult.

A single tear slipped down her cheek. "I owe it to Danny," she said. "He built Trustless for me. He knew I'd outlive him, wanted me to have a legacy from him, an empire I could build that would be mine and his together. That's why he wanted those secure enclave keys, you know—not because he was worried that he'd make a mistake but because he was worried *I* would. That my compliance code would let someone like Jim into the system, someone who'd make Trustless synonymous with finance crime. He wanted an insurance policy, a way to reverse those transactions if he ever caught them. He wanted to keep Trustless safe for me." The tears were coursing down her cheeks, but she kept her face still. Now it twisted into naked anguish. "For *me*. Oh, Danny," she gasped.

I crossed the room and stood beside her, my hand gently on hers. She grabbed it and pulled me to her and hugged me in a death grip that made my rib hurt, but I didn't let it get in the way. My shoulder grew damp with her tears. I held her and rocked her while she cried, letting her get it out for as long as she needed to. Eventually, the tears slowed, and she sat up. The slanted afternoon light that fell on her face made a tragedy mask of it and gave me an unexpected pang. I had lost so many of the people that mattered to me over the years, and the tempo was only accelerating and would only accelerate from here on in, as everyone got older, and it would only stop when I did.

When had I stopped crying like that for my dead? Why hadn't I cried like that for Danny? I would have, once. Now, my grieving was a numb thing in a distant place, honored only through empty solemnity, raising a solitary glass to him and trying to actually think about him, rather than thinking about how I was thinking about him.

She wiped her eyes, then wiped her hands on the sofa's upholstery. "Thank you for that," she said. "Really. Thank you. It's hard to know how to help someone who's feeling upset, but you did just perfect."

That wasn't something I'd have ever thought to say to someone, but I discovered that I felt good about someone saying it to me. I guess that's what they call *emotional intelligence*. Maybe I should spend my remaining years cultivating it.

She stood up and smoothed her hands on her thighs. "I think I need a nap. This day has been . . . a lot."

"I can only imagine. Thank you, Sethu. Anytime you need anything—"

"There is something," she said softly, but looked right into my eyes.

"Anything."

"Will you . . . lie down with me? Just to be there? Since Danny went, there's been this empty, sad place next to me, and it takes forever for me to drop off. It's like there's something missing, nagging my subconscious, and it can't let go. Just stay there until I drop off."

This is a perfectly terrible idea. "Of course," I said.

Funny thing. I fell asleep, too, fully clothed, still in my socks, on top of the covers, in that dim room with half a sandwich in my belly and a million things I should have been doing, some of which might have meant the difference between life and death.

Maybe it was the night I'd spent with Ruth. Sleepovers weren't my thing. Truth be told, it wasn't just that no one wanted to overnight in my white elephant rock star tour bus. It was me. I wasn't an overnight kind of guy.

But maybe I was becoming one. The sleeping hours next to Sethu were some of the most profoundly restful of my life. I woke to find Sethu snugged up behind me, knees tucked behind mine, arm across my chest, face in the nape of my neck, where her breath tickled.

I lay awake for a long, slow, warm, syrupy moment, eyes closed, taking stock of the unprecedented circumstances and distantly understanding that this was all unwise, and reveling in it. Sethu smelled good. It was the fresh-baked version of the sour smell I'd gotten a noseful of that morning when I'd first seen her: a warm smell with floral notes, and beneath it, a very human smell indeed.

She was awake, too. Her hand began to stroke my chest in small, gentle circles, and her breath got hotter on my neck. Then her lips brushed the skin and kissed me. Softly, then firmly. Then a little nip of her square little teeth.

I caught her hand in mine. It was hot and small, and it squeezed me back hard.

"Sethu—" I started.

"I know," she said. "I know. But let's. Let's anyway. It won't hurt anyone, and it's something I need." She kissed the back of my neck. "Danny would have been fine with this when he was alive. He certainly won't care now."

We were in his bed. She was his wife. Ethical nonmonogamy

was a fine-sounding concept, but I'd always preferred the grand American tradition of serial nonmonogamy. It was safer. You didn't have to talk about your feelings quite so much.

She kissed the back of my neck again, and her hand escaped mine and began to trail over my chest and stomach. Someone moaned. It was me. I turned around and found her lips.

16

"I'm not one of those guys who falls asleep right afterward," I said, by way of apology as I got up, having calculated that I had waited a decent interval. It's a calculation I'm eminently familiar with.

She sat up, unselfconsciously nude. That tragedy mask I'd been so skewered by earlier was still there, but overlaid with a kind of lazy satisfaction. Any worry I'd had that she was a fragile thing, unsure of her own mind, vanished. She was the picture of vivid self-knowledge.

"I wish I could paint you," I said. "Honestly."

She smiled. "I've done some self-portraits. Never wanted to hang them; it always seemed so self-indulgent. Maybe you can take one."

There was nowhere for me to hang art in the *Unsalted Hash*. It didn't matter. I'd take one. I had a storage locker inland, and I was overdue for a visit to it. "I'd love that."

She took me to a studio where the canvases were stacked deep against the walls. She flipped through several before pulling one out. It showed her head-and-shoulders, three-quarter profile, and there was something in the expression on her face, a kind of hardness that was frankly ugly. The real Sethu had a little of that hardness, but nothing like the way she saw herself. I wondered if the real reason she didn't hang her self-portraits was because of what they revealed about how she saw herself. Looking at that painting felt more intimate than anything we'd done in the bed Danny had died in.

I took it and let her show me to her door. She grabbed me for another rib-aching hug and pulled my face down to hers for a soft kiss on the lips. Then she whispered in my ear, "Jim had a friend, Sebo Szarka. He's the one who brought the Azeris to Jim. No one from the region moves a ruble in or out of the global finance system without his knowing about it. He might know about the men who were asking about you, if you want to know."

I turned the name Sebo Szarka over on the drive back to the *Unsalted Hash*, and then again as I took the *Hash* out to get sludged and to refill its water tanks.

This was getting stupid. I was worth hundreds of millions of dollars and I didn't have a permanent water hookup for my luxury bus. I called the KPMG concierge and told him to find me a campground in central San Francisco. Five minutes later, I had a berth at the Chabot Campground, across the bay in Oakland. It had all the amenities, plus a lake and forest. The greenery in San Luis Obispo had made an impression on me, reminded me that I'd been missing all that in a string of lazy berths at Walmart parking lots.

I hooked up the Leaf to the *Hash*'s tow hitch and climbed back inside and punched up the route, but the traffic on the Bay Bridge was deep red and entirely immobile. Instead of setting off, I started plugging *Seb Szarka* into search engines.

There was a reason I'd never heard of Mr. Szarka: he was clean. Partner at a boutique firm that specialized in tech finance, a significant donor to the Computer History Museum but also SFMOMA. He was the kind of old-school tech lawyer who didn't need a LinkedIn profile and was also the kind of clean operator who you couldn't find on a police blotter or a mug shot site. There were thousands of these guys operating in the Bay Area, mere millionaires who facilitated agreements between the representatives of billionaires and techies who dreamed of becoming billionaires themselves.

If Sethu was right and Szarka was the go-to guy for former-

Soviet money deals, then he was good at his job, because not a hint of that stuff came through in his digital footprint.

I decided to pay him a visit. After all, I had a lot of money and I might decide to invest it in a tech company. I had my concierge at KPMG get in touch with him to set up a meeting, then checked the Bay Bridge traffic. It had gone from red to orange, so I fired up a playlist of Preservation Hall Jazz Band's live shows, put the *Hash* in gear, and pulled out of the Walmart parking lot.

The KPMG kid had picked a winner. My berth had a view of the lake and a nice Black family next door in an RV with a pup tent, who came by to tell me to let them know if their kids got too rambunctious. The kids were cute in the way that other people's kids can be, grinning and messy and clearly having the time of their lives. I found some It's-It bars in my freezer and passed them around and assured Mom and Dad that I was a major fan of the sounds of merriment.

KPMG had also gotten hold of Mr. Szarka and set up a meeting for the next morning. As I'd expected, inquiries from the high-net-worth office of a Big Four accounting firm with a global reputation for financial engineering carried a lot of weight with that kind of lawyer.

I unhooked the Leaf and dropped a load of laundry at a wash-and-fold, picked up a sack of groceries, and stopped at a fancy liquor store for a new bottle. I picked out a bottle of Widow Jane bourbon and then spotted a $2,000 bottle of twenty-two-year-old Willett behind the counter behind locked plexiglass. It reminded me that I was incredibly, stupidly rich and that I was going to play on that idiotic wealth to get away with asking snoopy questions of an important stranger the next day.

"I'll have the Willett," I told the clerk, handing her my Black card. She was a middle-aged, bored Korean woman who'd nodded politely to me when I came in and smiled briefly when I brought up my purchase. Now, she actually looked at me, measuring me.

"The one up there," I said. "The two-thousand-dollar one." In case there was any doubt.

She took the Black card from me, then keyed the purchase into her till and ran it on the chip-and-pin machine, comparing the signature. She hovered over the register for a moment after the transaction cleared, as if waiting for the phone to ring with a call from Amex's fraud-prevention team. Then she locked the till, pocketed the key ring, and unfolded a step stool, which she used to fetch the bottle down, locking the case before descending. She got a cloth bag with the name of the liquor store on it from behind the counter, put the Willett in a paper bag and then in the cloth bag, added my Widow Jane, and carefully passed them to me.

"Free bag for purchases over one hundred dollars," she said.

"Thank you," I said. I didn't really need a tote bag.

"Are you a big fan of this bourbon?" she said, pointing at the bag.

"No," I said. "I've never tried it. But I figured a two-thousand-dollar bottle must be good, and I'm celebrating."

"Well, congratulations," she said, and I drove back to the campground.

The campsite came with a little grill. I fired up a chimney of hardwood charcoal and added some cherrywood chips, then I pounded some chicken breasts flat with the bottom of a heavy skillet, marinated them in red wine vinegar, olive oil, garlic, and dill, and charred them quickly over the hot coals. I steamed some asparagus while they cooked, drizzled chili oil and sprinkled salt over the spears, and made myself a plate. The picnic table that came with the site was in bad need of a power wash, so I set up my little folding table and camp chair and ate slowly.

The kids from next door showed up as I was getting seconds, carrying a bowl of strawberries and cream from their mother, and I thanked them courteously and asked them to pass it on to

Mom, along with an invitation to come have some chicken, as I'd made far too much.

Dad came by a few minutes later and explained they had plenty of dinner themselves, but thanked me for my generosity. I mentioned that I'd been planning on having a drink with the sunset and did they want to join me and he said that sounded very neighborly and introduced himself as Vernon and his wife as Khloe and affirmed that both of them enjoyed bourbon, though Khloe liked hers with Diet Coke and would bring her own mixer.

And so we consumed about $500 worth of bourbon, much of it mixed with Diet Coke, as we watched a perfectly lovely sunset and the two boys chased each other and I learned about Vernon's work as a graphic designer and the sound engineering degree Khloe was nearly finished with.

The bourbon was . . . fine. The $80 bottle of Widow Jane was every bit as good, to be honest, as was Raza's synthetic stuff, which went for $25 a bottle and was cheaper in quantity—no one would even sell you a sixty-ounce mini-keg of Willett or Widow Jane.

Much better than the bourbon was being around two perfectly normal adults with their perfectly normal kids, sharing their vacation in the East Bay with a friendly stranger. I wondered if this kind of thing ever happened to people who had hundreds of millions of dollars. I imagined how the mood would turn irretrievably awkward if I told them how much the whiskey I was pouring into Khloe's glass of Diet Coke was worth. Well, not what it was worth—what I *paid* for it.

"All this talking," Vernon said, "and we haven't asked you what you're up to. Taking a little vacation?" He had this big, wide-open face, framed by a bushy beard, and artists' fingers, clever and restless.

"Oh," I said, "I'm recently retired. Trying to figure out what I'm going to do when I grow up."

"That's a fun way to put it," Khloe said. She had short hair and round cheeks, an easy smile that lit up whenever she saw her boys. They bombed up to us then, clutching scribble drawings they'd done with Sharpie on scrap paper and shoving them at their dad. Vernon took the Sharpie and quickly filled in the scribbles with deft, sure strokes, turning them into improbable fantasy creatures—a lopsided dragon blowing bubbles and a farting unicorn with epic stink lines. The boys howled with laughter and bounded off.

Khloe's radiant smile followed them into the night. "Do you think *not* growing up is an option?"

"I may find out," I said. The bourbon was getting low. Two thousand dollars, gone in an instant and never missed.

"What did you retire from, Marty?" Vernon asked.

"Accounting," I said. When I wanted to talk about the job, I answered that question with *forensic* accounting. When I didn't, I just said *accounting.* No one wanted to talk about accounting.

Vernon nodded. "Well, that's a job that's hard to leave. Every CPA I know, retired or not, ends up taking contract work filling in at tax season."

Not that kind of accounting. "I think I'll be able to stay away," I said. "I've had enough of that business for one life."

Sebo Szarka had an office in the Financial District, near the Transamerica Pyramid, in the 555 Montgomery building, several floors down from the Morrison Foerster complex, a homier kind of floor where a lot of small practitioners doing law and finance had their offices.

His secretary, an efficient young man with Cossack cheekbones and a friendly manner, came down to the lobby to get me and made courteous chitchat about the rain and the traffic as we shot up in the elevator. He opened the biometric door lock with his face and then showed me in, offering me coffee, tea, or Hungarian apricot juice. I got the juice, which came in a heavy crystal lowball glass with two rounded-off ice cubes, along with a small plate with a slice of a layered walnut-apricot cake iced with chocolate that he told me was a "Zserbó." It was sweeter than I liked, but I still took a second bite.

Sebo came out of his office presently and shook my hand and told me how glad he was to meet me and did I need some apricot juice or a piece of Zserbó, and I assured him I'd had my fill and followed him into his inner office.

He was a jowly, fit sort of person in his late sixties, a little old-fashioned looking with an out-of-date but bespoke suit that revealed starched cuffs and heavy silver or platinum links, a thick wedding band, and some kind of signet ring like you'd get with your engineering degree. He exuded that elusive "old-world charm" and seemed supremely calm as we seated ourselves on a pair of conversation chairs, mine with a view of the picture window and the San Francisco fog.

"Tell me, Mr. Hench, how I can help you today."

I had come in prepared for this to go either way, to play it like I had money that needed moving around and see what he could do for me, or to just play it straight. His confidence and calm made me decide to play it straight.

"Mr. Szarka—"

"Sebo, please."

"Sebo. I got your name from Sethu Lazer, who used to be Sethu Balakrishnan. She knew you through Jim Hannah."

His facial expression did not change at all, a neat trick. He thought a moment, then nodded very slightly. "It was so sad, what happened to Jim," he said.

"It was," I said. "I didn't know the man personally, but it certainly presented a tragedy from Sethu at a critical juncture in her life. Nevertheless, she landed well, because she's a competent and resilient person, and despite some recent tragedy in her life, she is thriving."

"I'm very glad to hear that." He had the smallest bit of deliberate boredom showing through, a busy man with important things to do.

"Sebo, I don't want to waste your time. I came here because

three kids got murdered in Jordan's Mill, over an idiotic mix-up that may or may not have something to do with some Azerbaijani families. A boy from a prominent banking family was among the dead, name of Preobrazhensky."

Again, his expression did not shift, but he made another minute nod.

"Sethu told me that you might know the family."

"As it happens, I do." He gave a minute headshake. "What an ugly thing."

"Sethu told me you are the person to speak to if I had questions about the way the . . . community . . . is dealing with the tragedy."

Finally, he allowed himself to look a little frustrated. "Sethu has a very active imagination, I'm afraid. I came here in '56, after the tanks came to Budapest, and helped a few others who left my country and the region, doing what I could here and there. From that, some impressionable people have gotten the impression that I am some sort of *mafiyeh* banker or oligarch fixer. The reality is far less exciting. I'm just a lawyer with a small practice, I'm afraid."

I allowed myself to look a little frustrated, too. "Yeah, but that's not what Sethu thinks—"

He cut me off, raising his voice. "Sethu—"

And I raised *my* voice. "*Sethu says* you set up the deal that got Jim Hannah killed. A deal to use cryptocurrency to move half the GNP of Azerbaijan." He tried to interrupt, and I stopped him. "And now there's a dead Azeri oligarch's kid, and someone's been asking Sethu about me, and also, someone tried to kill me. So please, Sebo, can you and I have a frank and open discussion?"

He stood up and walked to the window, contemplating the white fog, the shrouded nearby buildings barely visible through it. "Mr. Hench, I'm afraid I can't help you."

"I think you can, Mr. Szarka. And just to be clear, I'm not looking for a freebie. That killing? It involved something that had been stolen from Danny Lazer. Something very valuable. Something that shouldn't have even existed in the first place. I helped

Danny recover and destroy that thing, and in so doing, I discovered the bodies. Danny paid me well for my work, and I'm about ready to retire. And I need a money manager and attorney who can handle my finances for me. I hear good things about you."

He turned and glared at me. "Mr. Hench, I don't know how much you understand about this situation—"

"Very little," I said.

"—but you seem to have gotten yourself into something very ugly indeed. Something dangerous. The family is very upset. They are motivated and have a lot of resources to bring to bear addressing what was done to that poor boy. I'm sorry to be the bearer of bad news, but no matter how much money Danny Lazer paid you, I have a feeling you're not going to get much of a retirement out of it."

"But I didn't have anything to do with it," I said. "I'm just the guy who found the mess first."

"That's not how they see it," he said. He went and sat behind his desk, settling into an ergonomic chair and trying to look like the upstanding citizen he played for the public. "Mr. Hench, here's the only piece of good news I can offer you: your name isn't out there. Yet. If it were, I would never have met you. But every friend of the Preobrazhenskys knows that there's a man out there that they're coming for, a man who they hold responsible for Sergey's death. That man is you, it seems, and you seem like a nice guy, but I'm afraid that there's nothing I—or anyone else— can do to help you.

"I'm telling you this because I feel bad for what happened to Jim. Yes, I introduced him to one of my clients, and yes, it did not go well for him.

"Sethu has romantic ideas about me, but she's not altogether off base. There were a lot of people who wanted out of the USSR, and I helped them, here and there. And then after the Wall came down, there were people who helped rebuild their countries, and I helped *them*. I like to do good works, Mr. Hench, to help people. That's all. Believe me when I say if I could help you, I would."

"I believe it, Mr. Szarka." Ice had stolen over my guts as he spoke.

"I'm sorry I couldn't be of further assistance," he said and began to get up again, to see me to the door. I stopped him.

"Mr. Szarka, can I ask you a small favor?"

"Of course, Mr. Hench. If I can help, I will be glad to."

"If you find yourself talking to any of the Preobrazhensky family's friends, could you tell them something?"

He made a moue of distaste. "I am unlikely to have that opportunity, Mr. Hench."

"Nevertheless. If the opportunity arises, please tell them that Sergey and his friends stole something for someone and then tried to keep it for themselves. The children's switch was discovered, and their client grew upset with them. I was not the client. I was working for the man whose goods were stolen. I have no part in the family's pain, and coming for me will do nothing to get vengeance or justice."

He cocked his head to one side and then the other as if trying to decide if I'd made up that story on the spot or if it might be true. "Thank you for letting me know. If I get the chance, I *will* pass it on. It certainly might bring some comfort to the family to know a little more about what happened to Sergey."

"Thank you, Mr. Szarka. That's all I can ask."

His secretary gave me a Zserbó in wax paper to take home. I gave it to a homeless man outside of 555 Montgomery, along with a fifty-dollar bill. It could have been $10,000, and it wouldn't have made a difference to me: not to my finances, nor to my future. I wondered if it would have made any difference to his future.

17

I had the KPMG man book me a different berth, back down in Colma. I loved my campsite, but on the drive back across the Bay Bridge, I had visions of Vernon and Khloe and their little boys being caught in an arson attack on the *Hash*.

Bridge traffic was bad enough that I was able to have a long conversation with the KPMG concierge, who'd been trying to book me in for some "investment strategy discussions" ever since I created my account. I listened patiently as a very smart fellow with an expensive education explained how I could transfer some of my Scottish trusts to the Channel Islands ahead of a new beneficial ownership disclosure rule, and from there, it would be easy to make those firms subsidiary to a new Gibraltar LLC, whose board would be composed of BVI numbered companies.

It only took about ten minutes to realize that this was about five times more complicated than it needed to be and that all that complexity would generate $100,000 in upfront fees to the firm and then an ongoing management fee in the $8,000–$10,000 range that would earn this kid a recurring commission until some other "advisor" charged me a hundred grand more for another restructuring. I told him I'd think about it.

Vernon and Khloe's car was gone when I got to my campsite, so I didn't have to say goodbye. I hitched up the Leaf and hit the road.

I was just getting settled into my Colma campsite when my phone rang. It was Ruth, so I answered.

"Hello, you," she said.

"Hello yourself," I said. I had been about to unhitch the Leaf, but I decided it could wait until morning. Instead, I went into the bus and kicked my shoes off, made myself a drink, and stretched out on my bed.

"It's April 12," she said.

"Uh, happy April 12?" I said.

"Danny Lazer's seventy-fifth birthday," she said. "Facebook reminded me. Don't ask me why I still have a Facebook account."

"Well, happy birthday to poor old Danny," I said. "He was one of the good ones."

"He was," she said. "The assholes I play D&D with won't organize the games over email."

"What?"

"That's why I'm on Facebook. I'm a hostage to Venphira Ghostbane, my level twenty-seven half-elf paladin."

"Sounds like you've got a better reason than ninety-eight percent of the Facebook-using public."

She snorted, then was quiet for a long while. "Where are you, Marty?"

"Colma," I said. "Just relocated my bus."

"Colma's close," she said. "Twenty minutes to San Mateo."

Ah. "Ah."

"Come on, Marty, don't make me beg." She kept it light, but a little bit of intensity slipped in. It made me wary, which made me ashamed.

"I was under the impression that you didn't want a regular thing."

"I don't," she said. "But I'll be seventy-five in ten years," she said. "You know how they say life's too short? When I got that pop-up, I started feeling that way."

"So you made a booty call?"

That made her laugh, a throaty chuckle that was sexy enough to crinkle the skin on the back of my neck. I put down my whiskey, untouched. "I suppose I did."

"What's the drive time, Colma to San Mateo?"

"Twenty-five minutes," she said.

"Text me an address, I'll see you in twenty."

Half her place was in boxes—"I just closed on a place in Half Moon Bay"—and whatever charm she'd managed to infuse it with was long gone. It was a badly proportioned condo that had once been part of a larger unit in a building that was long past its sell-by date. She lived on the third floor, and after waiting forever for the elevator, I took the stairs. I was clearly not the only one, judging by the scuffs and smells. As I reached her landing, I spotted a discarded needle on the floor, and I picked it up with my sleeve over my hand and carefully broke off the tip.

But Ruth herself was resplendent, wearing a pair of blue men's pajamas that made her look especially tiny. She'd left three buttons undone at the top of the shirt, and she smelled of good perfume. She took me in a long hug when I arrived, kissing my neck where my jaw met my ear and then whispering, "I'm glad you came."

"Me, too," I said and squeezed her back, pulling her to me hard enough that her feet left the floor. We threaded the boxes to her bedroom and we had a really nice time.

It was midnight when I roused myself from my dozing and slid my arm out from beneath her. She woke a bit.

"Time for your disappearing act?" she murmured.

"I warned you," I said. "And I was going to leave a note."

"You did. Forget the note; just give me a kiss." I did. She was right, it was nicer than a note.

I turned on the living room light and then opened the bedroom door a crack, giving me enough light to dress by. I stuffed my bare feet into my shoes and balled my socks into my jacket pocket. As I left, I made sure her front door locked behind me.

I took the stairs slowly; the light was poor, and it smelled like I might step in a puddle of something unpleasant. When I got to the ground floor, I started to open the door, and then I spotted a guy in the lobby, leaning against a wall, looking at his phone. I let the door silently swing shut save for a crack and studied him; he was young, maybe even a teenager. Certainly no older than twenty-five. He wore Timberland boots and selvedge jeans, a hot pink Ed Hardy T-shirt with a bedazzled Mexican Day of the Dead skull, a wristwatch the size of a pocket watch, and lots of hair gel. Something was stuck in the waistband of his jeans over his stomach, protruding at an angle: not a gun, wrong shape for a knife, but stuck there in a way that made me think, *Weapon.*

He had one foot on the wall behind him, like he'd been standing around for a long time. As I watched, he sighed and changed feet, looking up from his phone but not seeing me. I got a better look at the weapon. A telescoping baton, I decided. He breathed out another sigh. I let the door close.

The stairwell had a back door as well, signed FIRE EXIT and covered with taped-up notices explaining the rules for disposing of trash and recycling. I softly worked its crash bar and opened it a crack, looked around, and slipped out, crouching behind a dumpster.

The lot was about three-quarters full, the cars dark. The Leaf was under one of the few working lights. That had been both deliberate and a matter of habit. I stared long and hard at the other cars. It seemed there were people in the cars in front of, and behind, the Leaf. I watched until a phone screen lit up one, and then, an instant later, the other. Someone had sent a text message to a pal.

The cars each had a pair of people in them, shadowy, but male. The driver of the car in front of the Leaf was a big guy, head brushing the car's ceiling. Another pair of brief lights as a message ricocheted back from the receiver of the message to the sender.

The big guy opened his car door and unfolded himself, put

his hands on his lumbar and stretched backward, then touched his toes. He walked slowly to the other car, and its driver's-side window rolled down for an inaudible conversation.

The conversation ended with the big guy going back to his car—a sagging Crown Vic—and popping the trunk. He took something out, went back to the rear car, and passed a baseball bat through the window.

As Big Guy got back in the Crown Vic, I thought about the bat, the telescoping baton in the waistband of the kid in the lobby. Five guys, armed. I won't say I never got into a fight. Twenty years before, I might have tried to improvise a weapon from the scrap lumber and other trash out by the dumpster and waded in, got my head cracked, and cracked a few heads myself.

These days, I was smarter. I preferred to have paid professionals apply themselves to that kind of project. The hostiles were a good twenty yards away, and from my vantage point, I could use my phone camera to zoom in on them and get the front car's full plate and the last three on the rear car.

I took a very long look at the rest of the lot. Was there anyone else out there? The shadows were deep. I decided I liked my chances and charted a great circle route around the lot's perimeter, staying out of their sight lines and in the dark, pausing once when I could get a clear look at the rear car's back license plate.

Ruth's building backed onto an alley shared with an office building, four stories and completely dark, even the cleaning crews gone home for the night. I circumnavigated it, sitting on the low half wall at its entrance where the building's address was picked out in big bronze numbers. I noted the address and ordered an Uber.

While I was waiting for it, I dialed in to a call forwarder I used when I wanted to call government sources and then called the San Mateo PD nonemergency number.

"Hi, I don't know if this is the right number for this," I said to the sleepy dispatcher who picked up on the sixth ring, "but I just saw two groups of men doing a drug deal in an apartment building parking lot. They had weapons, too. I saw a couple of baseball bats, and I think one had a gun in his waistband."

That made the dispatcher less sleepy. He asked for the address, descriptions, license plates, vehicle makes and models. I gave it all, working on sounding scared and excited. When he asked for my name, I told him I was Edmund Chowdhury and then said I didn't want to give my number because I didn't want any trouble.

"Sir, can you see these men now?"

"No, I went a ways off before I called. I really don't want any trouble."

"Mr. Chowdhury, you are a witness to a crime. Once officers arrive, they will want to speak with you. Please give me your number and current location, and stay where you are until an officer can come to pick you up."

"No, no!" I said. "The officers don't need to talk to me. Those men have weapons and drugs. That's all they need to know. I was just passing by."

"Sir, they may not be there once our officers arrive. In that case, your ability to identify them might help us—"

"I gave you the license plate numbers for their cars. That should be enough. You don't need me. I'm going now." I hung up. The Uber was just arriving.

I called Ruth the next morning to make sure she was okay. She said she was and asked me if that wasn't my Leaf in the parking lot. I said it was and that I'd be back for it as soon as I could. She told me there'd been a big drama after I left, four cop cars screaming into the building's lot, a lot of shouting, a guy who tried to run, a gun drawn. Arrests. There'd been a cop in the lobby that morning, asking residents if they knew anything about it.

"What a crazy thing. My movers come tomorrow. Not a minute too soon."

"Why don't you get a hotel room tonight?" I asked. "Get away from there."

"I thought about that, but then I realized that means I won't be in if you drop by to pick up your car." She let that hang there for a minute. "Unless you want to come by the hotel room, too. It's my turn to pay, after all."

Be very careful, Marty. Ruth is good people and deserves your honesty. If you say yes to this, she's going to think that you mean it. "Yes," I said.

There was a long pause, then: "Yes, you don't want me here when you get your car? Yes, it's my turn? Yes, you'll see me at the hotel?"

"No. Yes. Yes."

"Oh," she said.

"'Oh, good'? Or 'oh, shit'?"

"Oh, good, certainly, Marty. Very good. I'll do some googling and let you know once I've decided where we're staying tonight. Shall we say six?"

"Sure. City or Valley?"

"I'll let you know."

"I'll be there."

It occurred to me that I could just abandon the Leaf. Literally leave it behind and buy another car. I could buy a car every day.

I wondered how the goon squad had found me at Ruth's. I knew how I would have done it; new vehicle registrations were nominally confidential, but in practice, so many people at so many agencies had access to them that anyone could find out if a given person had registered a new car, and if so, what its license plate was.

From there, it was easy; the private companies that contracted to provide automated license plate recognition to paranoid municipalities and home owners' associations all had side hustles selling location data to marketers and other slime creatures. You could usually run your first five queries at a low teaser rate, less than ten bucks—or free, if they were having a sale—and then an annual subscription cost a couple of hundred bucks a year.

If that was how they'd found me, then they would also find the *Hash* if I moved it again. They might try to get my location data from my cell phone company, but I'd filled in all the opt-out forms after the California Consumer Privacy Act passed, and in theory, that meant they were no longer selling that data to marketing companies, so they'd have to find out what carrier I was with and then bribe someone to get the location fix.

I'd blocked location access on all my apps. That left facial recognition, like maybe from the secondary market Amazon and other smart doorbell companies ran for incidental images captured by their customers' street-facing cameras. I dug out a big pair of sunglasses and a long-billed old air force mechanic's hat that had belonged to my uncle Ed.

What about Uber? They claimed they'd tightened up access to ride histories after a couple of scandals, and the CCPA had made everyone a lot more cautious about who could access that kind of data. But I resolved to do all my ride hailing at least two blocks from my start point and to get my drop-off a couple of blocks away. The walking would do me good.

After all this paranoid noodling, I decided I'd put in a call to Mr. Szarka. His secretary answered.

"Mr. Szarka is with a client, Mr. Hench. Please could I give him a message?"

"Can you just stick your head in and let him know that the San Mateo police arrested five people last night, and I know where the witness who called in the complaint can be found."

The secretary didn't say anything.

"Or slip him a note, if he's with a client. I can wait."

"Please hold," the secretary said. Szarka's hold music was the default Cisco techno track. I nodded along with it while I worked on a crossword out of a fat book of *New York Times* Sunday puzzles I'd thrifted somewhere on the road.

I was chewing on "Settlers of the Yucatan peninsula" (six letters, the fourth was *A*) and was midway in writing MAYANS when Szarka picked up.

"Mr. Hench," he said. He sounded ruffled.

"Mr. Szarka."

"I think you'd better come in," he said. "I have an opening in my schedule at lunchtime. Can you be here at noon?"

"I think I can manage that."

The Uber cost seventy-five dollars, but it gave me an hour for crosswords and a chapter out of a hardcover about the Paradise Papers that I'd bought so long ago that it was now out in paperback. There'd been a time when I'd lived in New York, two years, and I'd gotten so much reading done on the MTA. With the *Hash* beached, I might finally start to catch up again.

I'd booked the car to the middle of SoMa but had it drop me at Civic Center, reasoning that if anyone *was* snooping on my Uber journeys in real time, this would stop them from intercepting me. I handed the driver a twenty-dollar cash tip and wished him luck in his search for an entry-level job at one of the tech companies (we'd chatted while I worked on the crossword).

Traversing the Tenderloin to get to the Financial District was the usual forceful reminder of the city's contradictions, the enormous wealth on display in the line to get into a hot lunch spot, then the pup tents lining a stretch of sidewalk with bottles of piss anchoring their fly sheets.

Smartly turned out young people and weathered homeless people on the nod, or begging, or just staring, miserable and excluded, at the parade. I made a note to myself to find a homeless charity and give them a million dollars.

A block later, it was ten million. A block after that, I was considering one hundred million. What a fucking nightmare. How could a city this rich be this poor? I mean, I knew. I knew: all you needed was financial secrecy so the wealthy could hide their riches from taxation and then loose lobbying rules so they could convert their winnings into wealth-friendly policies.

Szarka's secretary didn't come get me this time. Instead, the security guard sent me straight up. I got out of the elevator a floor early and took the stairs, checking carefully before I emerged into the hallway.

At Szarka's office, I waited until the door was all the way open before stepping in. All of that was prudence, but of course I knew that none of it would stop a half dozen goons from slipping into the outer office while I was meeting with Szarka. But sometimes it's worth looking for your keys under the lamppost at least briefly, just in case you *did* drop them there.

No one offered me cakes or juice. Szarka opened his inner office door and nodded at me. I showed myself in.

"I did some calling," he said. "There are five very unhappy young men who'd like to talk to you now, but three of them will not be able to do so because they violated their parole and are now in custody."

"Maybe I'll visit them in San Quentin," I said. "Assuming they're still inside when this is over."

He pursed his lips. "Mr. Hench, please don't take this the wrong way, but it's probably best if you don't call or visit my office anymore."

"Oh, Sebo, I thought we were friends."

He made a pained expression. "It's not that I don't like you or believe you. Quite the contrary, and that's the crux of the matter. I'm not worried about me. I'm worried about *you*. If you make a habit of dropping by or even contacting me, it will likely fall to me to help other people facilitate an unpleasant interaction with you. I don't want that."

"That's reasonably kind of you, Sebo. Have you ever considered finding a different class of associate, though?"

He looked like a very old man then. "I am near to my retirement, as it happens. And despite what you may think, I am not indiscriminate in who I work with. There are some people whose business I don't need and will not touch."

"But not the Preobrazhenskys?"

"No, not them. Some people I would prefer not to touch, but there is really very little choice in the matter."

I snorted. "What, they came to you and said, 'Help us launder our money or we'll rough you up'?"

"Nothing like that. The Preobrazhenskys have run the Azeri banking system for many years, sometimes overtly through ministerial appointments, and sometimes from behind the scenes. They made things very convenient for people in my line of work, and it came to pass that they held the fortunes of my clients in their hands."

"And your own?" I asked.

He had the good grace to look slightly ashamed. "Naturally. If Azerbaijani finance vehicles are good enough for my clients, why wouldn't they be good enough for me?"

"Fair point. Like they say in the tech world, you've got to eat your own dog food."

He grimaced. "Yes. Well, there came a point when the Preobrazhenskys made it clear that they wanted a more explicit collaboration, and—" He gave me a very old-world shrug.

"I appreciate your honesty. I'll go. But before I do, I just want to point out that the situation you're describing isn't unusual. In my experience, it's absolutely typical. You spent your career as a facilitator of criminals and thought you could define what that relationship looked like, and you were wrong. Moreover, I suspect you knew you were wrong all along, but hand-waved that away because the share of the proceeds that stuck to your fingers was so exciting that you didn't want to dwell on it."

His automatic smile turned sad. "Mr. Hench, I genuinely like you. You and I spent our careers at cross-purposes, but we fundamentally had the same job: without people like me, people like you wouldn't have had a job, and vice versa. Very few people understand what we do, not even our clients. I really am ready to retire, you know. I'm only keeping the office open while I wind down the loose ends of my business. I thought I was going to make it across the line without getting embroiled in something like this, but here we are, thanks to Sethu Lazer, I suppose. But I don't blame her. As you point out, the only person I have to blame is myself.

"Most of my career has been a grand strategy game, pitting my wits against unseen adversaries, thinking up lateral moves to stay one step ahead of them. It's required some very odd hours and even odder predicaments, and as recently as a few weeks ago, I was congratulating myself for having run the whole width of the river on the backs of alligators without losing a leg. Now I have reached the far bank, only to have the ankle of my trailing caught in an old and terrible set of jaws.

"I just want to reach the far bank, Mr. Hench, which is why I don't want to have any further contact with you. I have a wife, a daughter, three grandchildren, and a few decades to enjoy all of them. Please don't take it the wrong way, but I'd like you to leave now, and forever."

I shook his hand as I left. His grip was still strong. "Good luck on your retirement," I said.

"Thank you, Mr. Hench."

I took the stairs two floors up and summoned the elevator, getting out on the second floor and taking the stairs down to the lobby.

Before I entered the lobby, I pulled up a map of the Financial District and picked a corner, then dropped a pin there for an Uber pickup. The arrive time was ten minutes. I confirmed and cautiously eased my way out of the building.

I found my corner and leaned back against the window of a Starbucks, its sill covered in anti-sit spikes to keep homeless people from spoiling the customers' view. A moment later, my Uber pulled up. I double-checked the license plate and the driver's name and got into the back seat, pulling my book out of my backpack and finding my page.

Downtown San Francisco is a mess of one-way streets and no-turn corners, so I didn't think much of the route we were taking at first, but then I realized we were headed up and up the hills, when we needed to be going down, toward the freeway on-ramps in SoMa. I looked at the driver, a Chinese kid whom the app said was called "Clarence," and whose phone screen was all in Chinese.

"Sorry, Clarence, I think you're going to the wrong place."

He gave me a look of incomprehension. I squinted at the phone on his dashboard. He was on the route that the Uber app had specified, but it showed a drop-off time of one minute. As I watched, that turned to zero minutes. I was apparently at my destination. Clarence said, "Goodbye," and when I checked my own phone, I saw that my app was announcing my arrival and asking how much I wanted to tip him and how many stars he rated.

I know about four words of Mandarin, and besides, you can't argue with an app. I gave him five stars and a twenty-dollar tip and got out of the car, my neck prickling.

I was in front of a two-story parking garage advertising $50 ALL-DAY PARKING, NO IN AND OUT and LOT FULL—SORRY. I took stock of my surroundings and spotted dozens of vehicles and people that could be hostiles . . . or could be people going about their normal business on a normal day on a normal street in San Francisco. The precautionary principle dictated that I should treat this as a potential setup, so I resolved to walk quickly and carefully for a couple of blocks and look for a hotel where I might get a yellow cab and pay cash.

I had barely taken a step when an apologetic, middle-aged man stepped in my path. He was dressed like a tourist, an Indiana State sweatshirt and dad jeans. But the sneakers gave it away:

they were the kind of thing you wore if you really wanted to *run*, not just wear something more comfortable than the loafers work made you wear the rest of the year.

He was a white man, brown thinning hair going gray, ruddy complexion with some old acne scars. He had a little silver stud in one ear and a hangdog look. He had a folded piece of paper in one hand. A street map. "Mr. Hench," he said, "could I have a minute of your time?" His tone was light and conversational.

"I'd rather not," I said and started to step around him, looking to see if there was any way I could make a spectacle out of the encounter, something that might make him decide not to take a shot. Maybe if I bolted out in front of that Muni bus laboring up the hill—

He moved to block me. He moved well. "I'd rather not show you my badge here," he said. "But I will if you insist. If, on the other hand, I could ask you to come with me just as far as that doorway, I could be more discreet, and that would be better for both of us."

"What kind of badge is it?"

"I work for the Department of Homeland Security, Mr. Hench."

"That covers a lot of ground. What agency?"

"An unspecified one," he said. He unfolded the map and held it between us, looking down at it. "But I assure you the badge is good. I would be happy to stand by while you looked up the San Francisco field office and spoke to a supervisor about it."

"Goddamn it," I said. "Either you're DHS and able to do things like divert an Uber, or you're a bad guy and able to divert an Uber, or maybe you're DHS and working for the bad guys."

"I'm one of the good guys," he said. "And I want to help you with your problem. I know something about the situation in Jordan's Mill that would be of intense interest to you and several other people." He back-folded the map so the center of town was showing and pointed at a random spot. I nodded and pointed somewhere close by. His fingernails were short and neat. A couple of his knuckles had been broken somewhere along the way.

"And you want to discuss this in a doorway?"

"No," he said, refolding the map. It was a nice piece of business, except that no one used maps anymore. But maybe adding a map to a tourist cover turned it into a clueless, helpless, harmless tourist who was also a potential pain-in-the-ass direction-seeker, and therefore twice as forgettable. "But once you get a look at my badge, I've got a place we can go."

I thought about all the weapons you could hide with a sweatshirt that hung down past your waistband. I thought about whether someone with all those busted knuckles would need a weapon.

Goddamn it.

"Let's go," I said. "Forget the doorway, let's get off the street."

"I thought you'd never ask."

The walk through the parking garage was spooky: enough shadowy nooks to hide a platoon, and far fewer CCTVs than I expected. But the second floor of the garage had a keypad-locked door that opened into the hallway of the expensive residential building next door, and then we took the fire stairs one more floor up, and then into a third-floor apartment that had a much better lock than the other ones on the floor but was otherwise nondescript.

He hit the light switches, revealing a foyer with an exposed metal garment rack bearing a couple of men's suits in dry cleaning bags and a puffy coat. A boot mat had a pair of loafers and a pair of ankle-high brown leather boots.

"Getting out that badge now," he said and slowly dipped his left hand into his front pocket, bringing out a badge case, which he opened and passed to me. It was either a DHS badge or it was a fake DHS badge. It gave his name as Waterman Bates, no rank or title.

"Pleased to meet you, Mr. Bates," I said.

"You want to make that call?"

"If you could gimmick all this, you could also gimmick the call. I'm going to remember your name and do some digging later, though."

He nodded. "Wise. Come in, then."

The living room was mostly unfinished, with bare walls, but there were a couple of good office chairs and a desk, a filing cabinet with a laptop bag on top of it. A bar fridge hummed within arm's reach of the desk, and the blinds were down and cracked just enough to provide dim light. He slapped a switch, and the bare bulb in the ceiling fixture flooded the room with unforgiving white LED light, exposing the smudges and cracks in the white wall paint, the faded spots where paintings had hung and the screw holes for the hooks that had hung them.

"Take a seat," he said, rolling one of the office chairs over to me and then rolling its twin out from behind his desk. He fished in the fridge and brought out a sugar-free Red Bull. "You want?"

"No," I said, thinking, *He's fifty-five if he's a day, but he's living on Red Bulls like a twenty-year-old, and lowering my opinion of him by a couple of notches.*

"The double cross was Maxim Preobrazhensky's idea. He's Sergey's older brother. Half brother, actually. Different mother. He stands to take over the family business when the old man steps down, which is imminent, because the guy's got cancer for the third time and he's down to just one lung. Maxim is a tech visionary, thinks the future of finance is on the blockchain, and he got it in his head that possessing a back door that let him alter an unalterable ledger would make him the Louis Pasteur of crooked banking."

"He's not wrong," I said. It was all sliding into place.

"The job was commissioned by the Zetas' bankers. They had a much more modest idea, wanting to hide their own transactions in the system but otherwise lying low. Maxim wants to offer ledger rewriting as a service, whereas they wanted to use those keys for themselves. Maxim is ambitious, the Zetas are cautious.

"But they are also extremely unforgiving. When they worked

out the cross . . . well, you saw. Frankly, Ales, Jia, and Sergey were lucky they were only dealing with the bankers. The Zetas' enforcers down in Laredo? They'd have been a *lot* messier and more . . . imaginative."

"I'm sure that's a great comfort to their families," I said. I didn't like this guy. He knew a lot but had done very little. If he was who he said he was, he was drawing a public salary and sitting back while some very bad things went down.

"Well, it's all about the families, isn't it? When Sergey got found, Maxim got worried that his old man would find out that Max got him killed. Maxim is a full decade older and is supposed to be a father figure to his little brother. Sergey didn't want to do crime; he wanted to do a start-up, flip it to Facebook, become a VP, maybe end up running the Baku office. Find success without competing with his big brother. Somehow Maxim got wind that Sergey's friends were planning to do the work, and he got Sergey in on it, then talked them all into a little side hustle.

"Maxim was shitting bricks. Then his guys talked to Lazer's widow, got your name, and the plan came together."

"Uh-huh," I said. "So where does that leave me? Should I call the Azeri National Bank and ask to speak to Minister Preobrazhensky?"

He made a sour face. "Don't even joke about it. The reason that Maxim was so scared wasn't just that he got his kid brother torture-murdered—it's that he got Sergey killed by the *Zetas*. The way the Preobrazhenskys operate, they've got to do something about this kind of thing, and anything they do to the Zetas will kick off some *really* bad stuff, stuff that could drag on for years, cost them millions, and end with large swathes of their command structures dead or in prison."

"And yet you sound like you want to prevent this, Mr. Bates. Agent Bates?"

"*Mister* is fine. Yes, Mr. Hench, I want to prevent this, and I think you can guess why."

"That kind of warfare is messy," I said. "With a lot of collateral damage."

"You are every bit as clever as I'd assumed you would be. Right now, we've got informants in both organizations, we've compromised a lot of their comms channels, and we're doing a good job of enumerating their whole distribution networks."

"And you just need some time to wind them all up, huh?"

"Maybe not so clever as all that. No, Mr. Hench, we don't want to roll up these organizations. They have competitors, you understand. If we created a vacuum, these competitors would rush in to fill it, and once again, we'd have a serious mess on our hands, the kind of thing that spills over to the real world. We'd much rather *neutralize* these people: periodically seize their war chests, arrest the odd boss, arrange to have a bunch of uniforms on the street when someone's war party shows up so that they cancel their plans. If we're going to have crime, we want to make sure it's *organized*. When we do the organizing, we can do a lot of harm reduction."

I got out of my chair. "Mr. Bates, it sounds to me like you want me to let myself get killed to protect the reputation of Maxim Preobrazhensky and the fragile peace between a bunch of ex-Soviet oligarchs and the Zetas?"

"Please sit down, Mr. Hench. May I call you Marty?"

"You can call me anything you'd like. It's your secret lair."

"Please, Marty. Sit. Just for a minute. The thing is, this isn't my lair. It's your lair. For now. We can protect you. I understand you came into a lot of money recently. We can help you find a way to enjoy it for a long time to come. Somewhere far from here. A well-earned and safe retirement. Maxim will be in charge of hunting you down, but he'll lose interest eventually and then so will his family, provided you don't resurface. You can live out your days and he can live out his, without ever intersecting with one another. That's a pretty good offer."

It was a disgusting offer. I sat down. "Why are you making it?"

He spread his hands. "I told you, Marty. The status quo is rotten, but it's our kind of rotten. We don't want you to die—our job is to protect you. But we're also protecting all the other people who will be collateral damage if you *don't* die. We have substantial resources—the civil asset forfeiture program means that any time we run short on funds, we just seize one of the many bank accounts we're keeping tabs on. We can afford this, and it solves everyone's problems."

"What about my friends?"

"Which friends? The lady economist? The woman whose ex-husband you ran to ground? We'll keep an eye on them. I don't think Maxim will try to get to you that way. If you had a wife or a kid, sure—but, Marty, you are a sixty-seven-year-old childless bachelor. You don't even have an *ex*-wife. You are the perfect candidate for the kind of disappearing act we specialize in. Give it a few months and you can even start communicating with these old pals of yours, provided you trust their discretion and take care to use self-deleting encrypted messaging tools. Wait long enough and you can meet up for a nice beach vacation somewhere very far from here."

"I don't think I'm interested," I said.

He looked disappointed. "Marty. Be smart. Either you take this offer or you spend the rest of your likely very short life looking over your shoulder. I don't think there's anyone out there who'd have an easier time of it. We'll clear out that bus of yours, ship the stuff along with the contents of your locker to you, and fix things with KPMG so you can keep on spending your money. The alternative is so much less pleasant."

"What if I talk to the Zetas, let them know who was behind the double cross?"

He looked even more disappointed. "While I don't doubt that you have the resourcefulness to reach someone in their organization, it wouldn't help you any. They've moved on. They had a plan, it fell through, they went on to plan B. Unless you wanted to offer to sell them Danny Lazer's secret keys."

"They don't exist anymore," I said. "Danny drilled out the

drive and then dropped the whole machine into an industrial shredder. No one's recovering that data. You'd have to go to his sources in the chip fabs."

"Wouldn't work," Bates said. "We discreetly let them know they'd been compromised, and they cleaned house. So yeah, you're not going to do yourself any favors by going to the Zetas, to say nothing of the danger that once you're on their radar, they'll decide they don't like you, or maybe even worse, that they *do* like you and decide you need to work for them. You have a skill set that they would find useful."

"Mr. Bates, I'm grateful to you for thinking about my welfare, but I'm afraid that this isn't something I'm in the market for. My government's concern for my welfare is very touching, but I'm used to taking care of myself, and as you say, I have a lot of resources at my disposal, just lately."

"Sit *down*, please, Mr. Hench. Marty. You don't have anywhere to go anyway. Your bus has been impounded from the campground in Colma. Happened within minutes of you leaving this morning. Your assets are now frozen. I know you have some pretty good lawyers in your social circle, and, given enough time, they'll probably be able to get the department to give you all your stuff back, but that is a slow-moving process, and it is decidedly unpleasant."

He gestured around at the empty place. "I know this doesn't feel like home. It's not. We don't use this place very often, which is why I was able to offer it to you on short notice. Give me a couple of days, I'll have something better for you, something stateside. It'll be transitional, and a few days after that, we'll find you someplace better, stable, and a long way around."

I opened my mouth to tell him to go to hell, to storm out and find myself a lawyer or a journalist or an ACLU loudmouth who'd blow this whole stupid operation to hell. This guy had made it clear that they'd delved into every part of my life, followed me and spied on me, all because I'd done their job for them—recovered a potentially omnipotent money-laundering tool before not one but *two* international criminal syndicates could weaponize it.

But he beat me to it. "Normally, I'd offer you the chance to think it over. Believe me, I'd love to be able to do that. If I were in your shoes, I'd be beyond furious. I'd be ready to pop off and do something stupid and angry. But I like to think I'd also be smart enough to realize that I wouldn't be doing anyone any favors if I did that, least of all myself. I didn't create this situation, and neither did you. We were cornered into this situation by ruthless predators who are stupidly powerful and over-resourced. Shout at the unfairness of it all later, but in the meantime, Marty, you need to make your peace with things. For starters, you need to call up your lady friend and let her know you won't be meeting her at her hotel tonight." He shrugged. "I'm sorry, Marty, but it is what it is."

It is what it is. An idiot's mantra. The worst part, though, was that he was right.

18

He had business elsewhere. Before he departed, he gave me a long and soulful stare while he impressed on me that this wasn't a game, that I'd best be an obedient fellow and stay where I was put and do what I was told. I swallowed my pride, bit back my scathing retort, and told him I would.

Then I called Ruth.

I'd thought about texting her, but the sad fact was that I cared about her too much to cancel on her by SMS. So I called. She picked up on the first ring with an excited "Hello, *you*," that made me hate myself.

"Ruth," I said.

"Uh-oh." She was always good at reading voices. "Sounds bad."

I laughed despite myself. "From one word?"

"Being married to Lorrie Lin taught me to trust my gut and look for tells, Marty. The way you said my name just now—"

"I'm sorry," I said. "Believe me, I'm sorry. It's not something I can get out of or discuss, but I'm heartily sick about it. I was truly looking forward—"

"Me, too," she said. She was brisk, all business. "Maybe a rain check, then."

"Uh—"

She tsked. "Marty, we're not teenagers. You want just friends, we can do just friends. But come on, be the straight shooter I talked myself into thinking you might be."

"Ruth, something *bad* has come up."

"Something *bad*?" Her tone balanced between concern and scorn. "Something I can help with?"

"I wish," I said. "Sincerely. But I can't even talk about it. Work stuff. I am going to deal with it as quickly as I know how, but until then, I am going to be dropping off the grid altogether. Shit. I'm sorry, Ruth. I don't know how long it'll be, but—"

"But don't get my hopes up. That's fine, Marty."

I could tell it wasn't, and it stung, because Ruth Schwartzburg deserved better. Also, it *hurt,* because as it turned out, some part of me thought *I* deserved better, too. What a fool I could be.

When a sixty-seven-year-old man sulks, it's not a pretty sight. I mean, sure, if I'd been out in the world with my hundreds of millions of dollars, I could have had a whole posse around me to massage my ego and assure me that I cut a tragic figure as I moped around the empty apartment on California Street. But it was just me, and when I had a piss in the empty bathroom—bottle of liquid hand soap and shampoo, Costco pack of six white bath sheets, roll of paper towels—I caught a glimpse of myself in the mirror and I didn't like what I saw. Not at *all.*

The thing is, I'd always been on the red team, the attacker hunting down grifters, fraudsters, and crooks who had to defend themselves from me. When they'd committed their wicked deeds, *they'd* been the attackers, exploiting some weakness in a system of financial controls to exploit it and transfer assets from its side of the ledger to their own.

But that's when the hard part started. These predators now had to think like prey; they had to go from finding a hole in someone else's security to adopting security principles that no one would ever compromise. They couldn't do it. My whole career was a testament to how hard it was to go from attacker to defender.

Once you'd played on the red team, you couldn't go blue team. In theory, playing attack should help you on defense, but in practice . . . it just didn't happen.

What a supreme irony that now, at the end of my own career,

after a payday of absurdly titanic magnitude, I had to make that transition myself. How the fuck was I going to pull that off? I had decades' worth of experience that suggested I was doomed to fail.

God. Fucking. Damn. It.

I took another piss. I looked at myself in the mirror. I saw a sad, tired old man.

Welcome to the blue team.

Some people *love* to play for the blue team. They design careful systems, put in checks and double checks. They run risk-limiting audits. Above all else, they *simplify*.

Complexity is the enemy of security, after all. The more moving parts and seams a system has, the more places there are for an attacker to find purchase and slip inside. Team blue is team minimalism, the Marie Kondo of security. If a procedure does not fill you with joy, remove it and replace it with a simpler one. An ideal security system was a box with only one door with one lock with one key and only one person knows about it.

Come to think of it, the ideal security is a box with *no* doors, *no* lock, *no* key, and *no one* knows about it.

Scratch that. The truly ideal security is *no box at all*.

That was where Danny Lazer had landed, after all. The best way to secure his back door keys was to destroy them so that no one could ever access them—not even him.

I could be very secure from the vengeful friends of the Preobrazhensky family. Just let myself out of the empty apartment, wait for someone inattentive to come careening down the action-movie-steep slope of California Street, texting while driving, and step out in front of his car. Splat. Risk eliminated.

I was in the market for a more intermediate solution.

All right, patience, Marty. All you need to do to defend yourself against this risk is . . . nothing. There's a whole black bag full of G-men out there from undisclosed agencies who conceive of you as a logistical problem, an otherwise inert package that they want to deliver from A to B. Sit back, relax, enjoy the ride. You've got a phone, Wi-Fi, and a fridge full of cold cuts, sliced cheese, and bagged salads. You're a man who thinks nothing of getting behind the wheel of your motor home and driving for sixteen hours. Two or three days in an empty apartment? You can do that standing on your head.

In fact, why don't you try standing on your head? Remember that time your back decided it had had enough and you saw that physio who sent you to yoga classes for a year? That was nice. Relaxing. Getting inside yourself. Granted, it won't be as nice in the absence of lithe young people in stretchy yoga clothes, but that's probably for the best, don't you think?

I spread out a Costco towel like a yoga mat and found a You-Tube video. Then I stopped and made myself a ham and cheese on stale brown bread. Then I went back to the yoga. Then I stopped again.

All things considered, I definitely preferred the red team.

I finally nodded off. The bedroom had an IKEA bedframe and a queen-size mattress I'd heard advertised on a podcast. The box for the frame was in the corner of the room, along with the Allen key that it had shipped with. There was also a Costco pack of white sheets and a fuzzy blanket. Someone had stripped a set of sheets off the bed and thrown them in another corner. I made the bed and put a fresh pillowcase on the pillow and slid under the covers, propping my phone on the mattress next to me, running a playlist of wildlife documentaries, a surefire way to lull me to sleep.

The door chain's rattle woke me. I had a moment's heart-hammering, careering disorientation, and then I came to myself and where I was. The sky was dark outside the blinds in the bedroom window. I climbed out of bed and looked around the room for a weapon. Unless I wanted to put my phone in a pillowcase and try to swing for a lucky head shot, I was shit out of luck.

I moved quickly to the window and lifted the blinds a few inches so I could explore whether it would open, and, if so, whether there was a fire escape or a ledge or—

"Marty? It's Bates. Sorry, you didn't answer your phone."

"No, I suppose I didn't," I said to myself as I let the blinds fall back into place and took a deep breath. "Be right with you," I called.

Bates had brought a midsize backpack of the sort a tourist might carry around with him, and in it was more Costco booty: a handle of bad bourbon, a six-pack of underwear, a six-pack of white tees, a six-pack of socks; more cold cuts, more cheese, an assortment bag of discounted Halloween surplus miniature chocolate bars.

"It's just for a day or two more, tops. We've got an out-of-state place where we're going to stage you, walk you through your overseas postings' options. You'll be near an air force base, and we can get you lifted and dropped direct. Easy."

"An out-of-state place? Which state, precisely?"

He shook his head apologetically. "Need-to-know, I'm afraid. I can tell you that it's mostly rectangular and it begins and ends with a vowel." A weak joke, told with a weak smile. "Sorry for all the secrecy, Marty. It can't be helped, I'm afraid. In the meantime, is there anything I can bring you? Favorite ice cream flavor? Six-pack of something in particular? My PA likes to give his Costco card a workout, but I can send out for something else. Coupla steaks?"

"Some fruit would be nice."

He laughed. "Sorry, right. Gotta get your five a day. Sure. Bag of apples, couple of pints of strawberries. Anything else?"

I suddenly wanted to slug him. It had been many years since I'd been stupid enough to work out my frustrations that way, but I hadn't felt like this since I was a kid—since my old man had picked up my family and moved us from San Diego to Ohio with only a week's notice, my last month of junior high, no chance to say goodbye to my friends or even graduate. That feeling of being a package, a logistics puzzle, shriven of any will or agency.

I made myself take a couple of deep breaths, do a ten count.

He seemed to sense a little of what was going on. "Look, Marty, I know this is a lot to absorb and it's coming at you fast. Believe me, if I could think of another way, I would. But look at it this way, a guy who comes into money the way you just did, you're gonna want to go somewhere for a while and spend it—someplace fancy where that kind of cash gets you the royal treatment. We're just accelerating that process here. You weren't ever going to be able to live a normal life again anyway. Once word got out about your stake, you'd have had to start taking precautions, watching out for crooks and kidnappers. We're accelerating that, too. It's a lot to take in, I know."

"You said that already."

"It's okay that you're pissed at me. All I ask is that you sit tight and let me do my job. I brought you a burner phone; it's got a number in the memory where you can leave me a message. I have a good staff. You need anything, you leave a message and we'll get it to you. Remember, it's just a day more here. Maybe two."

I forced myself to meet his friendly grin with one of my own, forced myself not to ball up my fists. "Thanks, Waterman."

He winced. "No one calls me that. My parents had a thing for fountain pens. Call me Bates. Now, I know you're a grown-ass man with a lot of experience and so am I, and in *my* experience, you're just the sort of person who struggles to do nothing. I can see it on your face now. So I'm begging you, Martin Harold Hench, on behalf of your duly elected government, please just stay put."

"I can do that," I said.

"Can you?"

The rage flash came so hot it startled me. I was standing, suddenly, my fists balled, the rolling office chair I'd been sitting on whizzing away backward, propelled by my sudden rising, then crashing into the wall.

He kept his cool, didn't even startle. If he'd stepped to me, I might have swung on him. I stormed into the bathroom, slammed the door, splashed water on my face, glared at the old, ugly, angry man in the mirror. More water. Pulled a fresh towel out of the Costco package, dried off, went back out to take my lumps.

"I can stay put," I said. "And I'm sorry."

Two short sentences. Two lies.

I assumed there was someone—or several someones—on the main entrance to the building and the parking garage entrance, but there weren't any cameras in the hallway, so I pulled the bill of Uncle Ed's air force cap low and let myself into the stairwell. First, I went up, dead-ending at an alarm-will-sound roof door. Then I went down and had a déjà vu flash: one door led to the lobby, the other to a back alley where they kept the trash, judging from the signs exhorting residents to do a better job sorting their waste. The signs had better grammar and typesetting than the ones at Ruth's old place, but they were definitely part of the same genre. I wondered if there'd be signs like that in whatever building I was destined to spend my years in, in Tangiers or Lima or Stockholm.

I cracked the back door and tripped a motion sensor that turned on flickering fluorescents. The trash room was about the size of a parking space, the two side walls lined with blue and black wheeled garbage bins. The back wall was a loading dock gate, down and locked. Evidently the architect had splashed out and installed a separate fire exit, somewhere else on the ground floor.

Ver-r-r-ry slowly, I cracked the lobby door by a fraction of a fraction and looked around. The first thing I spotted was a camera, squatting on the ceiling like a drop spider. I let the door ease gently shut and padded back to the apartment. At least now I had a sense of the lay of the land. I drank three fingers of bad Costco bourbon and thought hard about how I'd open the roller door in the garbage room in a purely hypothetical exfiltration, a mental red team exercise so soothing it put me to sleep.

The next day was, if anything, even harder. I watched nature documentaries. I searched for exotic Bay Area artisanal ice cream flavors to send Bates's dogsbody out to fetch for me. I read my emails and composed replies, without sending them. I even looked at Facebook, but not for very long, thankfully. I watched the shadows track the rooms.

Raza called, but I didn't answer. Then she sent a text asking if I was still in the Bay Area because her writing project in Santa Cruz was winding up and she was planning to drive up the coast to Oregon and wondered if I wanted to get dinner when she passed through town.

I tried to take a nap. I thought about asking Bates to procure a tin of indica gummies, which put me out like a light. I thought about this until I dozed off. I awoke. It was getting to six o'clock. Bates had said to expect him around dinnertime. Was he a late eater?

I waited. Seven o'clock came and went. Eight. Nine. I sent him a message:

> ETA?

Nine thirty. Ten. No reply.

I repeated my exercise of the night before, verifying that the roller door on the loading dock was still down and that its control box needed a round firefighter's key to open it. I watched some YouTube videos explaining how to pick that kind of lock.

It was surprisingly easy, if you had the right tool. I did not have the right tool.

I put on documentaries and went to sleep.

The next day was a repeat of the previous day. The only difference was that I ran out of cold cuts and that I sent him three more messages without getting a reply. I took another nap and then went back to watching lock-picking videos.

I couldn't fall asleep that night. Maybe it was the napping. More likely it was the frustration. I was way too angry to sleep. Now I was hate-watching lock-picking videos and actively fantasizing about my escape. Red team shit.

I found the answer in 2008. That was the year of the YouTube video I found at 2:00 a.m., in which a lock picker demonstrated a technique for opening a round Kryptonite lock with the barrel of a disposable Bic pen, which, when carefully shaved out with a sharp blade, could be made to fit into the lock's barrel tightly enough to grip and turn the lock mechanism.

The kid in the video was the real deal. I'd started off watching his 2021 videos, in which he was older, heavier, and beardier, and a hell of a lot more polished. The 2008 video was from his prehistory, when he'd been awkward and full of spittle-flecked excitement for his miraculous discovery. I checked out the technique and discovered that it had been a major scandal for Kryptonite and had triggered a ruinously expensive recall.

I also learned that the same technique had been tried successfully on numerous cylindrical security locks in elevators and other industrial control settings.

I was suddenly wide awake and happy as a pig in shit.

The computer desk in the living room yielded an assortment of disposable pens, including a couple with what I judged to be the right-size barrels. The toiletry kit in the bathroom included a Costco pack of disposable razors, and I used a butter knife from the kitchen to pry several of them apart until I had liberated a supply of springy, thin foils. I experimented unsuccessfully with making handles out of my toothbrush, a torn strip of towel, and a splinter of veneer I pried loose from inside one of the empty kitchen cupboards.

Then I hit on the strategy of cutting up an apple and making a handle out of a slice, which worked very well—sinking the blade into a quarter-inch rectangle of apple flesh gave me a sturdy handle that left most of the edge protruding.

Once again, I crept down to the garbage room on cats' paw feet. I had made three pen "keys" in the apartment, and I'd brought down two more pen barrels and two of my MacGyvered razor tools as well. Carefully, drawing on the technique I'd reviewed in the lock-picker videos, I fitted each barrel to the lock. There was a good chance this wouldn't work at all. It had been more than fifteen years since Kryptonite had revised its lock designs to block this attack. But industrial locks had a much longer duty cycle than bike locks, and changing them out was a nightmare, requiring that new keys be made and distributed to the maintenance people, letting agents, owners, et cetera. How much hassle would a building owner go through to make it more difficult to get into the garbage room?

That's what I told myself anyway as I forced myself to work slowly and methodically, using a sour-smelling trash bin as a worktable. One of the pen barrels seemed a perfect fit but splintered when I turned it. I found a blank of the same model and shaved it out and fitted it to the lock and slowly, gently *turned it*. With a clank, the motor controlling the loading dock bay came to life, and the roller door began to lift like a curtain on opening night. It was jarringly loud in the silent fluorescent buzz of the garbage room. I didn't let myself hurry. Slowly, I turned the pen in the other direction, and the roller door reversed its course, gradually lowering until it settled to the poured concrete dock with another *clank*.

After that, I found it very easy to fall asleep.

> Bates, this is getting stupid. Answer me.

I'd risen at ten and done more yoga. I'd eaten the last of the bread and cheese and eaten the last of the junk food. I'd paced. I'd tried to shave, only to realize I'd destroyed all the razors. The stubble made me look different. Rakish? Like a hobo? Maybe both.

It was noon.

> Bates. Now, Bates.

Nothing.

> WATERMAN.

The burner phone rang.

"About fucking time—"

"I'm sorry about this, Mr. Hench." It was a woman's voice, Southwestern. Texan, maybe.

"Sorry about what? And who is it that is sorry?"

"Mr. Hench, I'm Agent Dirks. I am a colleague of Agent Bates. He has been reassigned, and I will be handling your case."

"No offense, but this sounds awfully chaotic."

"My apologies again, Mr. Hench. I can appreciate that this is a difficult circumstance for you, and I assure you that despite the delay, your case is in good hands and being expedited."

"Well, that's reassuring," I said, making it as flat as I could.

"Mr. Hench, Agent Bates's reassignment in no way reflects on the seriousness with which we view your case."

"Yeah, you said."

"However," she pressed on, "the personnel changeover has created an unfortunate delay."

"That's understandable." So flat you could have used it to test a bubble level.

"Not more than a week, I assure you."

"A week." Flat and stony hard.

She pretended she didn't notice. "We'll have someone by tomorrow morning with a resupply. You can text this number if you have any special requests."

"I see."

"Thank you for your understanding, Mr. Hench. I apologize on behalf of the department and the agency for the inconvenience."

"Which agency would that be, again?"

"Goodbye, Mr. Hench."

I went and double-checked my "key" and then made up a go bag and consolidated the remaining food into one shelf on the fridge, ready for a last meal. Then I had my usual afternoon nap.

I woke up at 5:30, ravenous, the nature documentary on autoplay racketing off the bare walls of the empty bedroom. I ate the last of the bread with the last of the cheese and the one apple I hadn't filled with razor blades, had two fingers of appalling bourbon, had a shower, brushed my teeth, looked at my face. I looked old, but better. Red team, baby.

I crept out the door and down the stairs. I hit the ground-floor landing and let myself into the garbage room. That's when my phone buzzed. It was a self-deleting Signal message from an unknown number.

> IT'S BATES. FUCKING TREASURY DICKS DECIDED THIS WAS THEIR TURF AND GOT ME YANKED. ITS SNAFU TIMES A MILLION. MAYBE THEY'LL MAKE YOU WHOLE MAYBE THEY WON'T. THOUGHT YOU SHOULD KNOW. SORRY.

The timer counted down. Signal disabled the screenshot functionality. I could have run up the stairs three at a time and taken a picture with the burner Bates had given me—a phone I had made damned sure to leave behind—but what was the point? Kompromat on Bates in case I ever needed leverage over a black bag/undisclosed agency DHS GS-15?

I didn't wait for the timer. I deleted the message. I fitted my key to the lock. I turned it. The door clanked open. I waited until it was three-quarters up, then reversed it so it started to close, and ducked under it. It juddered to a stop when my body crossed the field of its electronic eye, but once I was clear, it jerked back to life. I heard it clang shut behind me as I reached the end of the alley and turned off onto Montgomery Street.

There were taxis, real ones, the kind you didn't need an app to hail out front of the Japanese consulate a couple of blocks away. I handed the driver a hundred dollars and asked if he was busy for the next hour.

"An hour?" he asked. He was Latinx, middle-aged, and he took the C-note without making it a big deal.

"That's a down payment," I said. "Drop the flag. If the meter goes past a hundred, I'll give you another one of those. If I get out before the meter hits one hundred, you keep that one."

"That's fair," he said. "Any direction?"

"Not yet," I said. "Just not here."

He put it in gear.

I messaged Raza, using Signal. If it was secure enough for Bates to whistleblow on his G-man rivals, it was good enough for me. I set the message to a one-hour destruct, though.

> You in the city yet?

San Francisco traffic crawled by. We hit the Embarcadero and turned toward Fisherman's Wharf, the commuter crowd giving way to tourists.

> Just pulled off the 1 to answer your text. Pacifica. Dinner in an hour?
> Dinner would be great. But things are a little intense at the moment. Related to earlier unpleasantness. What about the W near Moscone? Don't park nearby. Don't use an app to get there, either.
> Roger that. You lead such an interesting life.
> One hour?
> Make it 90 mins. I'll have to figure out BART.
> Pay cash.
> Roger that.

The driver told me to call him Pelon—he was very, very bald—and he was from Michoacán. We talked about Mexican politics for a while. He showed me pictures of his wife and his three grown kids, including a daughter who graduated poli sci at UC Berkeley and now worked for a state senator in Sacramento. She looked formidably intelligent. I congratulated him and told him nothing about my life.

He drove me to SoMa the long way, through Richmond, Golden Gate Park, the Haight, and Castro, then the Mission. I handed him another hundred between the Haight and Castro, and one more when we pulled up to the W, for his daughter's student debt. I handed the doorman who opened the taxi's door a twenty and asked him where the restaurant was.

The restaurant was visible from the street, but he got the message. The twenty dollars got me an escort to the concierge stand, where a fifty got me a table in a back room. I told the nice concierge lady I was expecting a friend who'd ask for the Lerner table, then I sent a quick message to Raza.

Raza arrived looking remarkably relaxed and suave, in a beachy, flowy kaftan sort of thing and strappy sandals. She beamed at me as she slid into her chair.

"The game's afoot, Marty!"

"You are a good friend, Raza, and also very funny. But I'm afraid this isn't a game."

The noise floor in the W restaurant outside the private room was deafening conference-goers from the Moscone Center, well-lubricated with whiskey cocktails, whose brays echoed endlessly off the restaurant's glossy hard surfaces, fore, aft, top, and bottom. I took my phone out and powered it down and Raza did the same, and I put both of them in my backpack and then put the backpack by the door to the main dining room, the noisiest place in our little space.

And then, in hushed tones, I gave Raza the sitrep. I'd had quite a lot of time to think about how I'd do this, and once I got going, it was fast. The server came about halfway through to take our orders and then again, just as I was winding down, with a couple of artichokes and aioli with a habanero-and-vinegar dressing.

We waited until he'd departed, and then Raza had a couple of leaves that she dipped into both sauces, savoring them while she thought it over.

"You lead a very exciting life," she said at last. "It sounds terrible."

That made me snort. It was such a Raza-ish understatement. "Turns out that crime syndicates are dysfunctional organizations that run on bitterness, cowardice, and fraud. I guess I should have cottoned on to that earlier, but I'm a slow learner."

"Better late than never. Also, you must try the hot sauce; it makes for such an odd and lovely contrast with the mayonnaise. I think the fat content blunts the fire and upregulates the other flavors latent in the pepper."

"Raza—"

"I'm not kidding, Marty. First of all, this is delicious, and second of all, you need to take a giant step back from the problem and you'll see the solution. It's not complicated, honestly."

I tried the artichoke. I didn't taste the first one, or the second, but by the time I got to the third, I really did. She was right (as usual).

"Okay, I'm calming down. Thank you, for the perspective, Raza. I'm not sure I agree about the 'not complicated' part, though."

She smiled. Our server came in with mains: saddle of rabbit and sprouts for her, an eggplant parmigiana slice the size of a birthday cake for me. We waited until he left and then—

"Come on, Marty, think. Why are you in danger?"

"Because the Preobrazhenskys are vengeful fucks."

"But why do they want vengeance on *you*? You didn't do anything to them."

"Because Maxim told the family that I—" *Oh.*

"Smart boy." She dug into her rabbit.

For dessert, Raza ordered the cheese board and tiny ramekins of barely sweetened rice pudding that had been finished under the grill, giving it a starchy, crispy cinnamon crust on top.

I was three whiskeys deep and starting to mellow. The W had a much better class of bourbon than Waterman Bates's Costco special. Nothing worth $2,000 per bottle, but absolutely serviceable in every regard and it got the job done. I was feeling a lot more relaxed.

"You think I should call up the Zetas and rat out Maxim, huh?"

Raza nodded and sliced off a generous piece of Point Reyes Toma and spread it on a half oat biscuit and took a cautious nibble, cocked her head while the flavors spread over her tongue, then took a bigger bite. She made a little satisfied moan.

"That is precisely what I think you should do. Finding the Zetas' banker will be a challenge, but it's very firmly in your wheelhouse."

"If I do that, it'll start a war. Bates told me that innocents will die."

She shook her head. "Bates wanted you to help him maintain the status quo, the cozy relationship where they let the crimes go on at a predictable, steady rate. What did you say he called it? 'Harm reduction'?"

"That's what he called it," I said.

"Harm reduction isn't harm elimination. The Zetas are an occupying army, mass murderers. And the money the Preobrazhenskys launder? It's every bit as dirty. The Zetas are retail killers, but the kind of money that passes through the Azeri banks, it comes from people who make their living destroying lakes, poisoning the land, razing forests. Mass murder hidden behind anonymous LLCs."

"*Some will rob you with a six-gun, and some with a fountain pen,*" I quoted.

"Ah, Woody Guthrie. He had such a way with words. You should hear it in French, it's even more evocative. *Plume* has many delicious connotations; you can practically hear the guillotine being sharpened."

"So, what if I get a bunch of people killed—"

"You won't be getting a bunch of people killed. That's what Bates and his archrivals at the Department of the Treasury are doing. Finance crime is a necessary component of violent crime. Even the most devoted sadist needs a business model, or he will have to get a real job. The difference isn't whether there are murders, it's where there are murders: what Bates means by *harm reduction* is 'geographic containment.' The murders take place somewhere else, out of sight, and the dead count less by dint of their brown skin and the fact that they don't speak English."

"I don't know, Raza. I've done my share of things that make it hard to look in the mirror, but I don't know if I could bear it if I knew I'd sentenced strangers to death."

"You haven't passed that sentence, Marty. Bates did. He and his system. They are caught in a contradiction: if they kill offshore finance, they hurt their friends, the 'good guys' whose family offices see to it that they pay zero dollars in federal tax and get to pass on billions to their kids. That's the *real* reason they won't stop the Preobrazhenskys or the Zetas: because doing so would require shutting down the facilitators, and not just people like Sebo Szarka but also your pals at KPMG. Respectable types, the fountain pen set.

"Bates's proposal is a death sentence, only slower. Change your name, abandon your friendships, leave your country, live underground until you die. Not because you committed a crime but because Bates doesn't want to lift his hand to *stop* the crimes that will arise from doing the honorable thing. We have an old Malagasy saying for situations like this: *fuck that guy.*"

"We have a similar saying in America," I said, smiling.

"Truly, our cultures are more similar than we know." She saluted me with a significant slug of bourbon. "So, fuck that guy. Drop a dime on Maxim, find somewhere to lie low, wait for the dust to settle, reclaim your fortune."

I stared off into space for a while, thinking it through. "This is an intriguing possibility."

"It's not a possibility, my friend. It's an inevitability. It's literally your only move."

"You think it'll work, though?"

She shrugged hugely. "Let's see, the feds could try to trump up some pretense to lock you up. The Zetas could just cut your throat for playing an elaborate game of 'let's you and he fight,' or the Preobrazhenskys could torture-murder you."

"Well, since you put it that way—"

She held up her hand. "Let me finish. The feds are in turf war hell, with Treasury and the DHS more interested in their empire-building than fighting crime. The Zetas' psychotic cruelty is a business, not a philosophy, and if they were incapable of making economically rational decisions, they never would have gone global. You know they're partnered with the 'Ndrangheta in Calabria? Someone in that organization has figured out how to get a passport, buy a plane ticket, and cross the globe to do crimes. Find that person, they'll give you a hearing."

"All right," I said. "But what about the Preobrazhenskys?"

She waved her hand. "They already want to kill you and will go on wanting to kill you no matter what you do. They're invariable irrespective of your course of action."

I finished my own bourbon. "Raza, can I be serious for a second?"

All her playfulness vanished. "Of course, Marty. Anytime."

"I'm a little scared here, Raza. These are three very powerful adversaries, and they want to do some very bad things to me. I'm scared for myself, and for you and my other friends. I know Bates said they wouldn't try to get at me through you, but he also thought he could get me overseas and underground without being clobbered by the Treasury Department. I don't want to die, and I *really* don't want to get you killed."

She shook her head. "Marty, I understand. All things considered, I'd rather not die, either. But as you yourself said, you are no good at blue team. The situation is what it is, and you need to deal with the facts as they are, not as you wished they were. This isn't a moment to wallow in feelings of inadequacy over your lack of blue team expertise; it's a moment to lean in to your red team strengths. Go on the attack, Marty. I've watched you run this kind of operation to ground for a quarter of a century, and I've never seen you lose. You are a bloody legend, Martin Hench, and you'd be a fool to forget it."

Raza is five foot two, a heterodox economist reviled by the majority of her profession and beloved by her grad students and the Democratic Socialists of America. She is a war refugee, speaks five languages fluently, and is one of the best cooks I've ever met. She is brilliant, funny, and compassionate. And she gives one *hell* of a pep talk.

"Raza—"

"You know I'm right, Marty, now let me prove it. Let's you and me war-game this little scenario out, map out tactics, and you will see that Martin Hench is more than up to the challenge."

19

It had been decades since I'd camped out. I remembered the experience as a joyous one: sleeping rough, greeting early sunrises, unmoored from the conventions of civilization, a deep nomadic calm settling over me.

Many things separated my last camping trip—in Joshua Tree— from this one, on Golden Gate Avenue, amid a cluster of about fifty tents that had been donated by a homelessness action nonprofit that won a lawsuit with the city over the rights of people without homes to sleep *somewhere*.

Obviously, the night sounds were different. So were the neighbors. And the smells. But the biggest change was my bladder: I suddenly understood all those tents with heavy plastic bottles of urine lined up outside of them. I was up at two, three, and five.

I'd bought the tent and my other equipment for cash at a twenty-four-hour Walmart that I'd gotten to and from in a Yellow Cab I'd picked up out front of the W. Raza booked a room under her name at the W and then left my backpack in the bellman's locker, passing me the claim check.

Once I had my homelessness kit and a bundle buggy to roll it around in, I found a spot a little way off from the main encampment on Golden Gate Avenue, set up the tent, and hit the hay.

Between my bladder and the noises and the smells, what sleep I managed was of very poor quality, and the final straw was the commuter rush, which started before 8:00 a.m.: clacking heels, rolling bags, cell phone conversations. I got up and broke camp, self-consciously pouring my piss bottle into a sewer grate, and then packed everything into my bundle buggy.

Dressed in my night-before clothes, I still looked more like a tourist who'd stayed out all night than a homeless person. I used a tarp to cover my bundle buggy and bike-locked it to a telephone pole around the corner from the W, and then went and claimed my bag with my laptop and phone from the bellman, tipping him twenty dollars. He offered to get me a cab, and I told him I was fine, and hurried back to my cart, which was undisturbed.

I piloted it to the San Francisco Public Library main branch in Civic Center, reveling in my inconspicuousness.

Leaving the country was out of the question: when one of your adversaries is the DHS, border crossings are off the table. That meant I'd have to go underground onshore, preferably close to the action. Homelessness is the American vanishing point, a cloak of invisibility that worked all too well.

Of course, I wasn't actually homeless. I was literally slumming it, a multimillionaire on holiday in a pup tent, pissing in a bottle. Yes, people wanted to murder me, but here in the vast, invisible country of San Francisco's homeless camps, that was hardly a mark of distinction. I wondered if donating $100 million would make a difference. Two hundred million? All of it?

San Francisco Public Library was the first public library branch in the country to hire a full-time social worker. It loaned out suits and ties for job interviews. It had a coat check that would securely store my bundle buggy. And it had privacy-loving librarians who did not allow the city or the feds to monitor connections to its Wi-Fi, a Wi-Fi connection that accepted Tor sessions.

I found a seat near a plug and connected my laptop, manually changed my laptop's MAC address, opened up a Tor session, and started hunting the Zetas' banker.

The key to offshore assets is that they're not really offshore. The money nominally moves from the U.S. to a Luxembourg LLC's account, but that LLC then buys U.S. T-bills or shares in a U.S. real estate investment trust or even a big stake in a private equity fund that gallops through Silicon Valley, scooping up a hundred start-ups to make a giant, unwieldy "roll up" whose primary assets are troll-friendly patents and research tax credits for research that went nowhere.

All that offshore money is all around you, doing socially useless things, making the idle rich even richer. For those whose wealth comes from bone-hard work, like flaying drug snitches alive and dangling their bodies from a bridge in Chiapas, this system is even better, because it didn't just protect the beneficial owners from taxation—it's the only reason they got to keep their money in the first place.

Government agencies like the IRS have subpoena powers, which should put them at a major advantage when it comes to tracking down this money, but they also have a distinct disadvantage: they have to come up with courtroom-ready proof that the assets they've found belong to the person they're accusing of ducking their taxes.

Add to that a sturdy political consensus that tax evasion by the extreme wealthy is (at worst) a slightly sordid sport and (at best) the very purest form of free enterprise, and you can see why they fare so poorly.

I don't have subpoena power, but I also don't have to prove anything beyond a shadow of a doubt. Also, I am a heterodox sort who doesn't accept the consensus vis-à-vis money laundering. Both of these constitute a provable advantage over my opposite numbers in the IRS and DHS.

Also, I know how to search the blockchain. In theory, the transactions there are anonymous. In practice, if you know that the DHS or Mexican Federales shut down a company as a front for a narco gang, you can look at the court proceedings and see the money flows in and out of its accounts.

Those specific amounts are a clue—a key. Find matching transactions in the blockchain—the eternal, unerasable, public ledger of all transactions—and you get a list of suspect cryptocurrency wallets. Look at those wallets' other transactions and see if they have cash flows that line up with other flows in and out of other seized accounts, and you can narrow down the list. Before long, you've got just one account.

Now that you have a positive association between a wallet and a criminal enterprise, fan out: follow *all* of that account's transactions, see where *they* lead. Now, just because a wallet was used in a crime, it doesn't mean that everyone who transacted with that wallet was a criminal. Guilt by association is no crime.

Also, I'm no cop. Some of those wallets will lead to people: people who've posted their identities publicly, seeking donations or offering payments. Those people have social graphs: friends and mutuals on Facebook, Twitter, and especially LinkedIn. LinkedIn has companies. Companies have registration. Registrations lead to registers of beneficial owners. Some names appear in more than one place in this hairball. They are the loose ends that let you untangle the whole gnarly knot.

I left the library for lunch at 1:00 p.m., walking around Civic Center, muttering to myself as I pieced together all the data I'd accumulated in my first four hours' searching. I lined up at a sandwich place and saw that my invisibility shield had added a force field, one that kept everyone at maximum distance from me, the homeless guy. I didn't think I smelled that bad yet: it was just the regular social distancing we give to the very poor, just in case the complete collapse of your life and its chances turns out to be contagious.

The sandwich—tuna salad on a kaiser—was edible, but not much better than that. I ate it on a bench in Civic Center Plaza, wiped my mouth, threw out the wrapper, and headed back to the library. No one was following me. No one cared about me at all, except to the extent that they cared that I stayed far from them.

I'd lost my spot during lunch, and there weren't any more free electrical outlets. I dialed my screen brightness down and lowered my processor speed to conserve battery and started my afternoon's work, looking up from time to time to check for a plug.

None opened. The people who'd acquired those plugs were in a very different sort of trouble than mine, but I won't say they weren't in *worse* trouble. I couldn't begrudge them their jealous camping on the electrical outlets. But it meant that I ran out of juice by 4:00 p.m. and went back out onto the streets.

I pushed my bundle buggy up the hills into the Tenderloin, keeping my eyes peeled for a spot where I might pitch my tent. I'd set up camp the night before after most people were inside their tents, buttoned up and shielded from the world. At dinnertime, though, the tent encampments were lively and social, buzzing with activity. I found a Mexican barbecue place and wheeled my cart in. The cashier told me to take it outside, and I held up my hands placatingly and said I just wanted to buy a whole takeout rotisserie chicken and sides. *Please,* I said and held up two twenties. She frowned at me and told me to wait out front.

A few minutes later, she appeared with my dinner, looking a little apologetic about making me wait outside. "I put in extra beans," she said, taking my cash. "I'll come back with change."

"Keep it," I said. "Thank you."

She looked momentarily surprised, and I could tell she was about to insist, but I waved at her and started pushing my buggy up the hill.

The camp I found was on an empty lot just off Eddy and Van Ness, surrounded by partially collapsed hurricane fencing. I cautiously pushed my buggy in and skirted the main encampment, heading for a rocky corner that no one was using thanks to the piles of broken cinder blocks and garbage. I thought I might move a few aside and create a space where I could set my small tent.

I made my way across the lot, wheels catching in the uneven ground, keeping an eye on the main encampment—five or six tents with tarpaulins serving as sun sails, with a shopping cart parking lot and a living room made from salvaged chairs. A woman emerged from one tent, roused by the clatter of my bundle buggy's wheels. She was Black, old, skinny, hair under a kerchief. She squinted at me with suspicion or maybe fear. I raised my hand and gave the friendliest nod I could muster. She stared a moment later, then went back inside her tent.

A moment later, two men emerged from under one of the tarps. One was shirtless and sleepy, Latinx and middle-aged, paunchy but strong-looking. The other was also Black, quite young, and handsome or even pretty except for the haunted look he gave me.

I repeated my wave and smile. The shirtless man raised his hand in a perfunctory greeting and then started to stroll toward me. I stopped and made myself stay relaxed, though part of me kept thinking of what I might be prepared to do if his life were mine. I thought of myself as a fundamentally decent person, but what if I had to shit in an empty lot and sleep on broken cinder blocks and beg for my dinner? How much of that could I take before I went sour?

He drew up two yards from me, the kid a step behind him, partly in his shadow. "Evening," he said. He had a hoarse voice, barely more than a whisper, an unwell sound.

"Hi," I said. "I'm Milt. I'm sorry if I'm on your spot. I was hoping to pitch my tent over there tonight." I pointed.

"You don't want to do that," he said.

"Oh, all right. Sorry to bother you." I started to turn my bundle buggy around, but he stopped me.

"That's not a nice corner. Lot of piss there. That spot, there, is probably better." He pointed to a better corner, one I'd discounted because it looked like a relatively prime placement.

"Oh. Oh! Thank you. You sure it's okay with you and your friends?"

He shrugged. "Free country."

"Thank you," I said again. "Look, I got a big chicken dinner, and it's more than I can eat. Would you and your friends like to share?" I hefted the greasy paper sack on top of my buggy. He looked at it for a long moment. The kid behind him peeked around and looked, too.

"Yeah, all right," he said.

"Thank you," I said for a third time. "I'll get set up over there and bring it by?"

"Yeah, all right," he said again.

His name was Martín, which took me aback a little, because at first I thought he was using my real name, which I hadn't given to him. I was more on edge than I wanted to admit. The kid was Laquan, and the woman was Tonya. They had another campmate, Tonya's brother Shaq, who had been away for a couple of days, and they were getting worried.

"Maybe he's in jail, maybe a hospital, maybe he OD'd," Tonya said, dry-washing her hands.

"Shaq's been clean for a month or so," Martín rasped. "But he likes Oxys or anything like it. Lot of fentanyl around, kind of thing that you take like Oxy, but never wake up from."

I thought about the vast fortunes that the Sacklers had amassed pushing Oxys, which they claimed was all gone, not available to their victims and their victims' survivors.

I'd spotted some of that money earlier that day, working in the library, tracing a payment from a pill-mill pharmacy that did business with both the Zetas and Purdue Pharma, from there to a Bitcoin wallet, and another, and another, and then it cashed out into the reverse-factoring account of a company that made a payment to an LLC in Kazakhstan that appeared in the New York attorney general's evidence in the Purdue money-laundering indictment. From abstract entries in a digital ledger to the very concrete sight of Tonya's cracked hands, endlessly fretting.

"I hope he's okay," I said. It wasn't much, but at least it was true.

The chicken was very good, and the sides were even better. Martín had beers, cool from the inside of his tent, and he shared them around. The kid barely spoke, but he disappeared into his tent during dinner, made some conspicuous sniffing noises, and emerged a few moments later, with a dreamy, droop-eyed smile. I caught Martín catching me staring at the kid, so I shrugged to make it clear this wasn't any concern of mine, and Martín nodded firmly at me. I wasn't trusted here, and that was as it should be.

"I had to get up really early this morning," I said at last. "So I'm going to go to sleep. It was really nice to meet all of you. Here, give me the garbage and I'll throw it out in the morning." I held the paper sack open and collected the napkins and paper plates and plastic cutlery.

"Thank you for dinner," Martín said.

The kid murmured something, and Tonya put her hands together over her heart and made a little head bow. "Bless you," she said.

It was cold that night, and sleep wouldn't come. I had some gummies, but I didn't want to take them; they made me sleep so heavily that I might not wake if someone tried to enter my tent. I tossed and turned in my mummy bag on my Therm-a-Rest and tried to imagine living this way for the rest of my life. I found it literally unimaginable, despite the fact that I was doing it right then. That was a remarkable realization, the understanding that many, many millions of people, thousands of them all around me at that moment, were living a day-to-day existence that I couldn't imagine, even though it had been my existence for nearly two days.

I wondered how many days it would take for the unimaginable to become the unremarkable.

I nodded off finally and woke a little later than I had the day before, insulated from the *clack-clack* of commuters' shoes and the sound of their phone calls by the lot's setback from the sidewalk. When I did rise, I was sore and gummed-over and desperate for a coffee. I saw Laquan as I packed up, and he gave me a shy smile and wave as I pushed my cart away. I waved back and mouthed, "Thank you," so I wouldn't wake his friends.

As I hit the street, I realized belatedly that I was going to miss out on nabbing a seat with an electrical outlet if I didn't hurry. I hauled my buggy into a convenience store, and before the clerk could object, I grabbed a fistful of jerky from the rack by the register and slapped two more twenties on the counter. He stared me down, and I pushed the money toward him. He rang up my jerky, and I pocketed it and hustled off toward the library, peeling one of the sticks with my teeth and wolfing it as I hustled down Van Ness.

I got one of the last spots with an electrical outlet and realized belatedly that I'd forgotten to grab some caffeine on the way. The realization triggered the psychosomatic ghost of a caffeine withdrawal headache, which would doubtless give way to a real caffeine headache in due course. I made a list on my laptop of necessities to shop for that night: more hard rations—dried fruit, maybe some carrot sticks or other reasonably shelf-stable vegetables; some little energy-shot drinks with caffeine.

Then I closed the document and went back to my hunt for the Zetas' banker, the sprawling spreadsheets where I was crosslinking accounts, amounts, and names.

After a time, I realized that I'd mapped out all the loose ends represented by accounts and flows, and so I turned to my names file. A large number of the people I'd identified were on LinkedIn; from there, I could find their other social media. Looking at their mutual follows turned up their kids and spouses' names and socials.

The kids were the key, as ever. Their fathers and mothers might be hardworking, serious financial criminals, but the kids were reckless, feckless wastrels, the customary—nearly inevitable—consequence of a childhood of fabulous wealth and privilege and isolation.

Their Instagram feeds were treasure troves: not just of their assets and armaments (a surprising number of these little nit-wits liked to pose with serious rifles, expensive handguns, and, in one instance, a surface-to-air missile launcher) but also of their friends, whom they tagged relentlessly.

Working this way, I was able to build a social graph of the crime families I was investigating. Their kids fucked each other, clowned around with each other, beefed with each other, all in plain sight, letting me know who knew whom. If you knew how to interpret it, it was a map of their parents' command structure, and, as I'd hoped, investigating the names told me more about the companies and the cash flows.

I was getting closer.

Whenever my stomach rumbled, I covertly slid a stick of jerky out of my pocket, shoved it up my sleeve so that only a little tip of meat protruded, and nibbled at it. I could tell I was getting dehy-drated, but that also meant that I didn't need to take a toilet break. My plan was to work until I couldn't take it anymore, head to the toilet and give up my electrical outlet, then work off battery for a few hours more before hitting the streets again. Maybe Martín and his friends would let me pitch my tent for another night.

I had an idea of what I was looking for: a banker, someone who looked far too legit to be connected to all these crooks whose lives I was cataloging, but who was nevertheless con-nected to them, densely connected, both through cash flows and social graph. *One of these things is not like the other.*

I kept a file of promising candidates, and as my guts started to twist and demand a toilet break, I gave it a once-over and snapped my laptop lid shut, slid it into my bag, and headed for the men's room. I hadn't gone ten steps before someone else had taken my spot and plugged in their device.

I washed my hands and face in the bathroom sink, then used a wad of paper towels to clean the back of my neck and behind my ears, and to swipe at my armpits. Judging from the mulch of wet towels in the garbage, I wasn't the only one. I dried myself off and then stopped off at the water fountain to drink as much as my stomach would hold before I went off in search of a seat.

They were all taken. I ended up on a bench in front of the library, at the edge of Wi-Fi range, squinting to read my screen in the direct sun. It didn't matter, though: somewhere between the water fountain and the bench, I'd had a hunch.

Theodore Clare wasn't the only Anglo name in the Zetas' inner circles. There were several, as well as Italians and Brazilians and Russians, of course. But something about Clare tickled my intuition. He was a minor cog at a large, white-shoe firm, one with an impeccable client list of Silicon Valley unicorns and the family offices of respected investors and founders. They had more than a hundred associates, of which he was just one, and I could easily see how that position would let him move a lot of money in and out of investments that could paper over otherwise inexplicable fortunes—after all, part of the job of a firm like that was to offer its best clients ultra-low-cost access to other clients' stocks just before they popped, a form of absolutely free money, and an excellent way to hide gains from illegal activities.

Clare kept a very low online profile, but his daughter, Mackenzie, did *not*. Mackenzie Clare was sixteen years old, tall, clever-looking, and popular, with a large circle of friends who were meticulous in tagging each other in their Instagram photos, which also featured location metadata. That was how I learned that the Clare family's favorite vacation spots were primarily in Mexico, and not in Tulum or Cabo but rather in out-of-the-way resorts, "locals" places, which were also frequented by the kids of some of the Zetas' top brass (and, presumably, their more circumspect, social-media-allergic parents).

The more I zeroed in on Clare, the more confident I became. His thin social media profile went beyond the usual boomer reticence and spoke of caution, rather than suspicion or technophobia.

He also had a secret Instagram account.

It was called @PojBu3swof, and it was followed by Theodore Clare and Mackenzie Clare, and a smattering of obvious bots. The only users it followed? Theodore Clare and Mackenzie Clare. Its online activity consisted almost entirely of liking posts about financial engineering strategies at the furthest outer reaches of the legal/respectable landscape. Almost. Only once had it ever replied to a post—one of Mackenzie's: "You're not wearing THAT in public, child." I'd wager $300 million that @PojBu3swof was Theodore Clare. If I was right, then Clare was a lot more interested in money laundering than he had any business being.

Not bad for two days' work: I'd unraveled the internal corporate structure of the Zetas, traced their capital flows, and fingered their banker. Under-resourced the IRS may be, and held to a higher standard of evidence, but sometimes it felt like they weren't even trying.

My battery was dying, and I was hungry. I'd figure out how to call Clare the next day.

The counter-woman at the Mexican barbecue place waved and smiled at me, and when I went to stand in the doorway to call my order, she gestured at me to come in, buggy and all. Other customers stared, but she gave them a fierce stink eye.

"What can I get for you tonight, honey?"

I liked her. She had a wide, open, friendly, lively sort of face, and I could easily believe that she took real pleasure in seeing to it that her customers got fed. I thought she might be the owner or part of the owner's family.

"Same again, please, one whole chicken, one of each sides, paper plates, and cutlery."

"You're having another picnic, huh? I guess you liked the chicken?"

"I liked it, and so did the people I shared it with."

She smiled, then frowned. "You know some hungry people, hey?"

I shrugged. "Lots of hungry people out there."

She turned to the cooler next to her and withdrew a tray of empanadas. "No one's gonna order these after 5:00 p.m. You think you could give them a good home?"

"I'm sure I could. Many thanks, ma'am."

"Thank *you*, sir."

I wheeled my cart up Van Ness and turned onto Eddy, heading for that empty lot, and when I reached its perimeter, I felt a distinct rush of homecoming, like I was opening the door of the *Unsalted Hash*. I hallooed at the lot's edge, and a moment later, Martín emerged from his tent with a face like thunder.

"Milt," he said. "It's not a good time." His voice was somber and even gruffer than usual.

"Oh," I said. "I'm sorry, Martín. I'll go. Uh, I brought some dinner again. Can I leave it here? More than I can eat."

His expression softened a little, and he walked slowly out to meet me. He drew up close and said, "It's Shaq, Tonya's brother. He's not coming back. OD. She's not taking it well."

"Oh, shit," I said. "God, that's terrible. I'm so sorry. Please tell her I'm sincerely very sorry for her loss."

He got a tight little smile that didn't reach his eyes. "I'll tell her."

"I got food," I said again and handed him the foil-wrapped empanada tray from atop my buggy and then the sack with the chicken and sides.

"You're not gonna keep any for you?"

"I can get more," I said.

He shook his head. "Yeah, I expect you can. Tell me, Milt, what's your deal? I can tell you don't belong here, that you don't have to be here. You can afford chicken dinners every night, can't you?"

I thought momentarily about telling him just how many chicken dinners I could afford, but there was no point. "Yeah,

Martín, you're right. I don't have to be here, economically speaking, but for complicated reasons, I still gotta be here. I mean, there's nowhere else I can be. I plan on changing that soon, though."

He set the food down carefully on the ground and stuck out his hand. "Okay, man, I guess I believe you. Thank you for the food and for your nice words. I'll tell Tonya. You stay safe, all right?"

"I'm doing my best," I said. "You got any tips where I could sleep?"

He snorted. "Man, you're nothin' but a baby. Yeah, I got a spot." He gave me cogent, compact directions to his secondary spot, an empty office building whose lobby door was covered in butcher's paper and whose lock could be slipped easily. "Just make sure no one sees you, so I can use it next time I got to."

"Roger that," I said. "Thank you, Martín."

"You take care, Milt."

The deserted office lobby was dry and dusty, but it was warm and quiet. More than anything, it was *private*. Just a few days of being simultaneously invisible and exposed had been a weight on me that I didn't notice until it lifted. I could strip off and give myself a wet-wipe bath, brush my teeth with bottled water, enjoy a dinner of 7-Eleven pizza and a powdered doughnut, both of which sat in my gut like a rock. I did it all in the dark, by the light of my airplane mode phone, whose brightness I turned down to a glowworm glimmer.

The lobby had a working electrical outlet, and I plugged in my laptop to charge.

I inflated my Therm-a-Rest and unrolled my mummy bag, then, on an impulse, I chewed a gummy. Even before I'd swallowed it, I could feel my muscles unwinding in anticipation of the deep, deep sleep I'd just drugged myself into. I slid into the bag, doused my phone, and disappeared into a nameless place where nothing happened and nothing mattered.

20

I woke with the knowledge that my bundle buggy was going to be a liability on the errands I planned to run that day. I thought about ditching it, then taking a cab out to Walmart that night and buying everything again, but my cash was running low: I'd started with five thousand, mostly in hundreds, and had spent that down to less than two thousand, and I didn't know how long I'd have to make it last. I considered trying Martín, seeing if he'd agree to stash it in their camp for the day, but decided it would be an imposition on a grieving household.

So I tucked it into a corner of the lobby and snugly wrapped it in a tarp, making an anonymous rectangle out of it. I exited the lobby door before 7:00 a.m., first checking to ensure the street was empty.

A few minutes later, I was on a Muni bus heading for the Mission. On Sixteenth Street, I paid fifty dollars cash for a room in an SRO and then joined the line for the shared bathroom. Two hours later, I'd showered and shaved and changed into a clean shirt and jeans I'd bought during my Walmart run and carried out in my day bag. I emerged from the flophouse looking like someone who had a home and a bank account, and then I walked up Mission until I found a pawnshop with an old Android phone in the window. I paid fifty in cash for it, and then thirty more at a T-Mobile store for a burner SIM, which they activated on the spot for me.

I hadn't anticipated that all the coffee shops on Valencia would have a no-laptops-before-11:00 a.m. rule. I'd noted a new Starbucks at the other end of the Mission, so I walked fifteen blocks back north and bought a large, unappealing coffee and a couple of pastries, then lucked into a two-top with a working electrical outlet and pounced.

Twenty minutes later, I'd set up @as4obBydrim, a new burner Instagram account. I powered down the phone and ejected the SIM. Five minutes after that, I DM'd @PojBu3swof.

> Theodore, I have something important to tell you about
Jordan's Mill.—A Friend

I suddenly felt very exposed. I snapped my laptop shut and got a bathroom code from the barista and used the facilities. I flushed the SIM down the toilet and left the phone in the paper towel dispenser.

I felt very old. I felt very tired. I wanted to go get my bundle buggy and secure my stuff, but the street would be too crowded to enter the lobby without raising suspicion. I didn't want to cost Martín his spot. I thought through my mental model of San Francisco, a city that once had many public spaces occupied by flower children, bohemians, radical queers. Now the public spaces were like the soccer field over in Dolores Park: places you needed to book in advance with an app, competing with bots created by tech bros who snagged all the best times for their corporate team practices.

I settled my day bag on my shoulders and oriented myself, turned left, and headed for Golden Gate Park.

I found a hipster coffee shop in the Haight that would give me a Wi-Fi password if I bought lunch. I ordered a decent tuna melt and nibbled at it while I logged back in to Instagram. No reply from @PojBu3swof.

I sent another message.

> The cross was by order of the kid's older brother. They're
about to find out who did the retribution. The keys are long gone.

All that's left is settling the score. Just wanted you to know.
Didn't want you to be blindsided.

I went back to the park.

The de Young's Picasso exhibit was packed, but the African wing was criminally empty. I lingered there.

I stopped at a McDonald's in the Western Addition and jumped on their Wi-Fi. The @PojBu3swof account had been deleted. @TheodoreClare was set to private.

I sent Raza an email from a burner account I'd created a decade before and never used, retrieving the login/password from an encrypted file in a plausible deniability partition on my laptop's drive.

> From: Fop7orn@gmail.com
> Subject: Wilma Razafimandimby
> Body: Wilma t.co/lebCon Wilma

Your basic botnet spam. The link didn't work, but "lebCon" was a randomly generated code phrase that triggered Wilma sending an email we'd coauthored to Maxim, assuming she'd managed to find his address while I was probing the Zetas. I had a much easier job than she did, after all: Maxim was a public figure, an executive at an important global financial institution.

Her email was short:

> Zs know about Jordan's Mill. They know about you. You
> don't have much time.

The lobby was securely locked, and a new NO TRESPASSERS sign had been glued to its door. I walked around the back of the building and found my bundle buggy there, bent and wheel-less. A few of my things were there—once-clean underwear and socks, now trampled into the ground. My tent and mattress and mummy bag were gone.

Martín came out a few minutes after I called out his name.

"I'm sorry," I said. "I know it's not a good time, but, uh." His face was closed, stern. "I just—" What did I want from him? "I lost everything," I said. "Tent, sleeping bag, clothes. I left it in the lobby and someone found it. What they didn't steal, they trashed. The lobby's locked up tight, too." I swallowed. "Sorry."

He snorted. "Shit happens," he said. He drew up close. "Look, Milt, you can't do this. This isn't you. You're not suited for it. I get the feeling, you think you're tough, what do they call it? Resilient. Maybe you are. But not here. Not like this. You got a choice not to do this, you should take that choice. You're not gonna last long out here."

I swallowed again. "I'm sure you're right," I said. "And believe me, I'm doing what I need to so that I can stop this, but it's taking some doing."

We just stood there, a few feet from each other. His disapproval was palpable. He wasn't going to offer anything. I was going to have to ask for it.

"I think I can figure something out tomorrow, but I'm kind of at loose ends tonight."

Another long, considering silence.

"One night," he said. "One."

"Thank you," I said. I felt like an idiot.

He bunked in with Tonya. I didn't ask what the arrangements were between them, and it wasn't any of my business. I slept in his tent, on a single mattress that smelled and sagged, under a pile of blankets that had the musky scent of old sweat and hard use, like an animal's den. No one offered me any food, and the third time I got up that night to find a corner of the lot and empty my bladder, Martín rasped, "Fucking shit, will you just *stay in bed*, motherfucker?"

I held it in until 5:00 a.m., and then I packed up the few things I'd taken out of my day pack and slithered out of the tent as quietly as I could. I was about to tiptoe away when Martín stuck his head out of the tent flap and hissed at me.

"Listen," he said in his hoarse whisper. "Milt. It's nothing personal. But you know, if you feed a stray dog, it'll come back for more. We got our hands full, taking care of ourselves. You're a decent guy, I can see that. But we're not your street family, bro. We're not even your friends. You can't come to us for help, because we got no help to give, and if we did, we'd save it for someone who really needs it. I don't know what kind of trouble you're in, but if you think it's better than this, you don't understand what this is."

I paid him the respect of thinking about what he said before I tried a reply. "I completely understand and I don't disagree with a word you just said."

"You're about to say *but*."

I snorted. "Yeah. But. There's some really bad people out there who literally want to kill me, and not even in a fast or easy way. Long and slow. That's what I'm hiding out from."

It was his turn to snort. "You don't think there's people around here, nice people in nice homes, who'd like to kill me nice and slow, too? Just to get me and people living like me out of their nice neighborhoods? Whatever danger you think this is less than, it isn't. Ask yourself, what was Tonya's little brother Shaq shooting up to get away from, and why did he keep shooting up after so many of his people died doing just that?"

Again, I thought about what he said before popping off with a reply. "Okay," I said. "You make a good point. Thank you, Martín. Sincerely."

"Yeah, all right. You stay safe, Milt. Sincerely."

———

One upside of losing everything: no bundle buggy, no bundle buggy logistics. I drank coffee in a shiny twenty-four-hour Mel's Tenderloin booth until 7:00 a.m., taking my bag with me whenever I went into the bathroom to make room for more coffee. The diner clientele was eclectic: a British dad from one of the Union Square hotels, feeding his jet-lagged toddler pancakes; some tired sex workers; a pair of SFPD beat cops who ate corned beef hash and watched the rest of us.

After 7:00 a.m., I switched to a Starbucks on Montgomery, getting there at opening and snagging a window seat with an electrical outlet. I ate muffins and egg-white bites while very, very slowly sipping a venti dark roast that was so bitter it made my sinuses hurt. I watched the 555 Montgomery custodians shine the brass door handles and polish the glass, then power wash the sidewalk out front, sweeping the water into the gutter.

At 8:00 a.m., I packed up my laptop and phone and put one foot on the ground, ready to bolt as soon as—

"Hi, Sebo."

He froze. He'd been lost in thought as he headed for his office, like he was a regular business consultant and not a criminal enabler in the middle of a lethal gang war. That either meant that my and Reza's messages hadn't been taken seriously, or he hadn't heard about it yet.

He did a double take, then a triple take. It was painfully conspicuous, and I had to steel myself to keep from running.

"I won't be long," I said. "Don't worry. Just one minute."

"All right," he said and scanned the crowd. Even more conspicuous. He was a very bad conspirator. Clearly, he did most of his work with a fountain pen, not a six-gun.

"The Zetas know about the Preobrazhenskys. Maxim knows that the Zetas know. It's not going to be pretty. I thought it would be courteous to let you know. I thought you might want to warn some people."

"Jesus fucking Christ," he breathed. His eyes rolled wildly in their sockets, showing white. "That can't—" He mastered himself, heaving a deep breath. "The DHS—"

"Oh, that was you?" I said. "I wondered. They didn't seem competent enough to have gotten all that on their own. Had to be a tip. It wasn't stupid, Sebo. It was even thoughtful, in a way, I suppose. A way to keep everyone who wasn't dead still alive, even me."

"But you fucked it up," he said. Despite his efforts to calm himself, he was panting a little. "Idiot."

"It wasn't me," I said. "DHS dropped the ball. Got into a dick-swinging contest with their archenemies, the Treasury Department, and lost. This is plan B. You warn whoever you think needs to know. Least I could do for you, seeing as how you tried to get me an out."

"You fucker," he said, spittle flying from his lips. "You know that if I warn them, they'll go on the offensive."

"And if you don't, they'll be unawares, and if they survive, and find out you knew and didn't warn them—"

"You *fucker*." More spittle.

"None of this is my fault," I said. "None of it. I didn't talk Sergey into doing a robbery with his rave buddies. I didn't make Maxim design a double cross. I didn't make the Zetas kill those kids. I didn't make Maxim blame it on me. None of this is my doing. I don't owe any of these people anything. Not even you. This friendly warning easily pays you back for the Zserbó, as delicious as it was."

That raised a tiny, sardonic smile from Mr. Szarka. He got a calculating look, and I caught a glimpse of the man who had done so well by himself and his clients. "All right, Mr. Hench. I have some calls to make. You stay safe."

"Everyone's concerned about my safety today," I said.

"Maybe they know something you don't," he said. "Perhaps you should listen to them."

Raza's Muir Beach friend wasn't in when the taxi dropped me off with my bags from Walmart. I set up my new campstool—

catching the plastic wrapping before it could blow away—and got out one of the fat hardcover bestsellers I'd bought off the Walmart remainder shelf. I read it while I waited for him.

He pulled in after 7:00 p.m. and spotted me in his porch light, reading in a cloud of bugs that I'd sprayed myself against several times, with only middling success.

He approached me warily. I didn't blame him. We'd been introduced and I'd lived on his land for a couple of nights, but we were hardly pals. I was just Raza's weird, platonic, middle-aged male friend, and while Raza's vouch counted for a lot with the people who knew her, a stranger on the doorstep went beyond that vouch, though.

"Mr. Flaherty," I said, rising. "I'm sorry to drop by unannounced."

"Uh, that's okay, uh—"

"Martin. Hench. Raza's friend."

"Right, Marty! Sorry, context switch, lost the reference." He was fit but paunchy, tall and ponytailed, with a rumpled navy blazer and an untucked white button-up shirt that he'd spilled something on. "Uh, you surprised me."

"I'm sorry," I said again. "Look, what I'm about to ask you is going to sound weird and very possibly alarming, and you're perfectly within your rights to say no."

"O-kaay." He was doing the math to figure out whether he could beat me to his car. It was stupid to sit between his driveway and his front door, sent a needlessly threatening message, but I'd wanted the porch light to read my terrible book.

"There's something complicated going on right now, involving the work I do, which I believe Raza has discussed with you. That complexity won't last very long, I hope, but I need somewhere I can just . . . hunker down, for a week or two, and I was hoping you might be able to suggest an out-of-the-way campsite near here and that you would be willing to let me drop by every now and again to charge my laptop and use your Wi-Fi."

He gave me a very long, very considering look.

"Mr. Hench—"

"Marty."

"Marty, then. Yes, Raza's told me a little about what you do, and it did sound awfully glamorous, but now I'm starting to see that glamour involves some danger."

"Yes, every now and again. Never like this before, and I can't imagine it will be like this after. It's a kind of end-of-career surge. I'm technically retired, but this is a holdover from my last job."

Another one of those looks. He cultivated the air of an affable doofus, but he'd been a search pioneer, one of the early internet visionaries, and had seen a lot of comings and goings in his days.

"How about if I get us something to drink?" he said. "Scotch?"

"Sure," I said, feeling some relief.

"Wait, you're a bourbon guy, right?"

"Either is good for me."

He brought out two generous pours in lowball glasses with big, clunky whiskey rocks in them and then went back for a kitchen chair, which he set up on the front porch so he could see me and get a look down his long driveway.

"What was this last job, that it's produced this complex and sinister holdover?" he said after we'd clinked glasses and sipped.

"I can't really talk about it," I said.

"I suppose not," he said. "Look, Marty, you know I love Raza, she's one in a million, and any friend of hers is a friend of mine. She's only ever said nice things about you, and I can tell she holds you in high esteem. But this is . . . Well, it's a little much. Not to be blunt, but you're acting like someone wants to arrest you or kill you."

Both. I shrugged.

"Either way, that's not something we know each other well enough for me to get involved with, even in the tangential way I've outlined. I'm not going to tell you you can't go find a campsite, and I can even suggest a few, but as for using this place as a kind of base of operations—"

"Yeah," I said. "Yeah. That's perfectly reasonable, honestly.

I am at a juncture where I've had to improvise, and this was the least improbable gambit out of a dwindling list of even more outlandish possibilities. You're one hundred percent right that this is not anything to do with you and represents a significant overreach in terms of our relationship to one another. No hard feelings at all, and I would be glad to hear any advice you have on local, out-of-the-way campsites where I might pitch a one-man tent." I'd bought some fishing gear and a lot of dehydrated food, and figured I could stretch it all to a couple of weeks if need be.

He grinned. "That's how Raza said you talked. Before you take off, why don't you let me know if there's anything you think you'll need, and I'll see what I can drum up from the fridge and the closet."

"That is a remarkably generous offer, and I'm not going to turn it down," I said, and I toasted him again.

We talked for an hour or more, two more rounds of his excellent bourbon, and told stories about Raza and the prehistory of the dot-com bubble.

Finally, I shook his hand and raided his larder and helped myself to a pair of his high-tech one-piece thermals.

He gave me a long, searching look. "I see why Raza's so fond of you. I have to say, I'm glad to hear this is your last job. You do seem to be one of the good ones, and it would be a shame if you didn't get to stick around for a while."

"I certainly intend to."

"I know you said you couldn't say what the job was, but I'm the kind of hard-boiled mystery reader who can't help but try to figure out whodunit. Can I ask—and you can say no!—can I ask if this is a cryptocurrency thing?"

I snorted. "Easy guess."

"I knew it. Ugh. I *knew* it. Which one?"

I shrugged.

"Oh, *c'mon*. Circumspection is circumspection, but you can't say which cryptocurrency?"

I started to shrug again, then I realized I was just holding back to make myself feel mysterious. "Trustlesscoin," I said.

He punched his open palm with his fist. "No shit! Danny Lazer's thing?"

Before I knew what I was doing, my mouth said, "Yeah, the job that started it all was something for Danny."

"Oh," he said. "*Oh*. Well, that changes things. Danny Lazer was the sweetest, kindest, most *decent* man I ever knew. If it hadn't been for Danny Lazer, I would have quit my job and moved home to Wyoming. Brother, if you're in trouble because you did a solid for Danny Lazer, you just tell me how I can help."

"Seriously?"

"I am as serious as a fucking heart attack." He said it mildly enough, but I didn't doubt him.

"Well, uh, in that case . . ."

My campsite was a quarter mile from Redwood Creek, about an hour's walk from Flaherty's place. He helped me carry out the extra camping supplies he'd rustled up for me, including a cooler of food and a couple of jerricans of potable water, a fold-up solar rig and a storage battery, and a wheelbarrow to move it all with. He showed me how to get to line-of-sight of his place without being seen myself and promised to put an extra Wi-Fi antenna on that corner of his roof in the morning. He asked me which VPN I was using and I told him Tor and he said that would be fine, just fine.

And so it was that my weeks-long stay in the woods turned into a perfectly pleasant camping trip, with resupplies of cookstove fuel and fresh water. It was a chance for me to loll in the tall grass on the riverbank and then go hide in my tent from the odd park ranger or hiker, catching up on my sleep and doing slow stretching to work all the stress and ache out of my old muscles. I swam at the beach a couple of times, fished the river without much success, and then, finally, snuck back to the edge of the wilderness and caught a Wi-Fi signal.

Someone had shot up a house in Bernal Heights. A perfectly nice kind of house, too, not a house that you'd think was associated with any kind of criminal stuff, but in less than five minutes, the people who lived there and the people who'd come to shoot them had discharged hundreds of rounds from some extremely illegal automatic rifles. At least one of the shooters was using high-velocity rounds that penetrated the house next door, which, thankfully, was undergoing renovations and empty.

Eight people died.

The next day, an old man—a beloved local restaurateur—was stabbed to death on his literal doorstep in Little Russia. His family were distraught. Neighbors were terrified. No one saw the killer.

Two days later, an electric vehicle—a Kia—exploded in Sacramento, which would have been noteworthy because that kind of explosion was rare, but even more noteworthy were the criminal records of the two men inside, which were extensive, violent, and international, straddling the U.S.-Mexican border.

I went back to my campsite and didn't leave it for two days. I spent some of that time pondering what kind of digital trail I'd leave if I logged in to my Signal account over Tor from Flaherty's Wi-Fi. I spent even more time working through the big book of *New York Times* crossword puzzles Flaherty had given me. He'd solved the first third or so and had neatly excised the back pages, the answer pages, with some kind of sharp tool and a straightedge. I decided I liked him even more for that.

Bogdan Mikhailovich Maslennikov was a careful man. He'd come to the U.S. as a political refugee in 1986, having escaped a gulag and crossed over the Finnish frontier, living off the land, hunting animals with an improvised spear and snare. He was a legend, the subject of a well-received documentary film by some surprisingly talented USC film students who'd gone on to good things after their Maslennikov picture tore up the festival circuit. He'd also given an oral history of life in the gulag and of his escape.

When SFPD got a report of an active shooter in Maslennikov's surprisingly large Twin Peaks home, they'd responded in force, nearly killing Maslennikov and his "secretary" before learning it had been a false alarm. When they got another alert the *next* night, they came in a lot cooler and managed to verify that it was a false alarm without nearly killing anyone. The *next* night, they sent out a patrol car, letting the Delta Force types go about their usual business.

The night after that, someone came into the Maslennikov household and butchered Maslennikov, his secretary, and four very large young men who were known to law enforcement.

> This is going to get worse before it gets better.

The Signal message was unsigned and from an unfamiliar number.

> Keep your head down. People are plenty pissed, but as far as
I'm concerned, there's nothing else you could have done.
> Turf wars are bullshit.

I used another of my dwindling supply of burner email addresses to send Raza another "spam," this one a prearranged code that meant, "I'm safe." She had sent another of my accounts a "spam" with a code that meant, "I checked on Ruth, and she's fine, as am I."

I went back to the woods.

One week later, I used Flaherty's bicycle to ride up the coast to a beach parking lot with a pay phone and fed it quarters and then called Szarka's office. His front-office man answered. "Is Sebo in? It's an old friend calling about Max P."

I heard the intake of breath as the secretary recognized my voice. "One moment."

I stared at the seconds counter on the two-dollar digital alarm clock I'd bought at Walmart, the second time I'd stocked for camping. I'd mentally decided to give him ninety seconds. At the ninety-second mark, I decided to give him thirty more. The pay phone had a view of the waves, and the surf was pretty. I could watch it for another thirty seconds.

"What can I help you with." No question mark, no old-world charm. He sounded beaten.

"Just wanted to get a situational update."

He grunted. "The situation . . . is bad."

"The situation's always bad for someone."

"The older brother is dead."

"That is a shame," I said. "Please give my condolences, should you speak to the family."

"I will," he said. "Look, I must go—"

"I know the brother had something he was hoping to say to me," I said, interrupting him smoothly. "Do you know if any of the other family members have a message for me?"

"No, Mr. Hench, no one else in the family has any interest in speaking to you about anything. Ever, I should think."

I wonder if I should believe you. "I wonder if I should believe you."

He sighed. "I don't really care if you believe me, to be perfectly honest. You were never anything but an innocent bystander in this. I know that. Everyone knows it now. But there are many innocent bystanders out there, and today, they face an appreciable risk, even as your own risk has fallen away."

"I'm sure you're right," I said. "Still, if you do speak to the family—"

"I'll give them your condolences."

"Yes. Thank you."

21

I pumped up the tires on Flaherty's bike and oiled its chain, then put it away in his garage/shop. I used the wheelbarrow to cart all the camping gear back and cleaned and laid it out on and around the workbench next to the bike.

Flaherty was out, so I locked up and put his spare keys in the hidden lockbox around the back, then I took out my phone and powered it up for the first time in what felt like a lifetime. I watched it go through its boot cycle, then unlocked it and watched the icons in the notification bar flicker as it found a signal and connected to it. I thought about all the people who would know that this phone was on and where it was right then.

I realized I was holding my breath. I made myself breathe deeply. I tapped the Uber icon. The nearest car was twenty-two minutes away. During my campout, I had lost track of time for hours at a stretch. Right then, twenty-two minutes seemed like forever. I ordered the car. I got out the spare key again and retrieved the book of crosswords, now three-quarters finished. I borrowed a pencil from a cup on the workbench and went and sat on my campstool on the front porch, my day pack between my knees, and forced myself to concentrate on the clues.

Nineteen minutes later, I put the book and the pencil back, locked up again, restowed the key, folded the stool, and walked the quarter mile to the top of Flaherty's driveway, just as the little gray Prius pulled up.

The driver was an older woman, Black, with a hair kerchief that reminded me of the one Sethu Balakrishnan Lazer had worn when she'd come out of her bedroom, and also the kerchief that

Tonya had worn when I'd first met her. The app said the driver's name was Jasmine.

"Hello, Jasmine," I said.

"Hello, Marty," she said, looking at her screen.

"I hope you don't mind a long drive. I'm headed all the way into the city."

She shook her head. "I don't mind at all. I'm retired, and the drive is pretty, and sometimes the passengers make pretty good conversation."

"That sounds like a hint, or maybe a request?"

"Something like that. Get in. We got a long way to go."

At first, I was worried, and I kept sneaking looks at her phone screen to see if the destination had changed. But she was funny and had led a fascinating life as a Linotype operator on a Pittsburgh Black daily newspaper, and her stories were both interesting and well told. I mostly forgot my anxiety, except that a few times it rushed back, sudden as a seizure, bringing with it the conviction that I was about to die and take this lovely, funny woman with me.

An hour later, we were pulling up to the Fairmont. I found the reservation number my guy at KPMG had texted me, but I didn't need to. The doorman greeted me by name as soon as I stepped out of Jasmine's car. I gave him my backpack and day pack to hold and then bent down to Jasmine's open window.

"Thank you, Jasmine. It was really a pleasure to ride with you."

"Thank *you*, Marty. The pleasure was mutual. You look like you're about to have quite a nice time."

"I hope so," I said. "Drive safe now."

I didn't want a bath. I didn't want room service. KPMG and the concierge had magicked up a decent suit, a pair of jeans, a pack of underwear, a T-shirt, and some sweatpants and gray tees for pajamas. I didn't want to wear them.

It was a clear night. On one side of the suite, the balcony presented a view all the way to Treasure Island. Follow the balcony around the corner and there was Alcatraz's lighthouse light and the Golden Gate Bridge. At the far end of that leg, Golden Gate Park and the improbable inverted pyramid of the de Young. All of it in distant miniature, far away and irrelevant from that great, great height.

I wondered if anyone had ever jumped off one of the Fairmont's balconies.

My cell phone rang. I felt a feeling of dread so intense it bordered on nausea. I went inside, took the phone off the desk where I'd plugged it in, and looked at the screen. Breath whooshed out of me. I sat down in the cushy office chair.

"Hello, Raza," I said.

"Flaherty said you'd left."

I winced. "He wasn't supposed to be talking to you about my presence," I said. "For his benefit."

"I think he assumed that if you'd left, it no longer mattered one way or another."

"That's a fair assumption."

A silence yawned between us down the line.

"It's over, Raza," I whispered. "All done. At least, my part. I have a feeling the other part—the part I got caught in the middle of—will go on for quite some time yet."

"How are you feeling, my friend?"

"Good," I said. "Or at least, not bad. Numb. Maybe guilty. Overwhelmed, I suppose."

"Well," she said, "you've always been pretty good at observing your own internal weather. A lot of people can't."

"Yeah," I said. "Yeah."

"Look, Marty, you have just managed something quite impressive and are about to enter a new phase in your life. Retirement, the chance to do something new, and the resources to do it with. You are completely within your rights to feel overwhelmed. It would be very odd if you *weren't* overwhelmed. I'm back in Missouri now, got some grad students who needed hand-holding, and they've talked me into teaching an Econ 101 course next semester."

That actually got a laugh out of me. "How on earth did they convince Wilma Razafimandimby to get back in the mud with *undergrads*?"

She sighed. "They compared it to the Feynman Lectures, told me that they'd record the series and make it open-access."

"Well, I can see that, actually. Leaving a legacy sounds pretty good to me right about now."

"I can imagine. Marty, you know how you've been saying for years you wanted to get some theory, some econ, into your data banks?"

"Raza, you want me to drive to *Missouri* to audit your *undergrad econ course*?"

"Of course not. You can fly. Mothball the *Unsalted Hash*, and I'll help you find a short-term rental here. You can afford it."

"I have just lived the weirdest month of my life, and even by that standard, this is a genuinely weird suggestion."

"Is weird the same as bad?"

"No, Raza, weird is not the same as bad."

"Marty, you are the best forensic accountant I've ever met. You understand the nuts and bolts of money in ways that none of my academic colleagues can touch. I've learned a lot from you myself. But—and I'm going to be honest in a way that befits our long and significant friendship here—I've also been repeatedly shocked by just how little you understand about economics. You're like a virtuoso savant mechanic who knows everything about internal combustion engines but hasn't the slightest idea about the physics of it and just acts as though his pistons are full of fire demons who make it all work with phlogiston. No offense, Marty, but you're an economic ignoramus."

"No offense taken, Raza, but as you've just pointed out yourself, I'm retiring. None of that matters anymore. Why bother to learn it *now*?"

"Really? Just a minute ago, you were talking about legacies. You are sixty-seven years old and have had a professional career that lasted four decades. Your work affected hundreds of millions—maybe billions—of dollars' worth of cash flows. That *is* a legacy. Don't you want to know what it means?"

"When you put it that way—"

"I *do* put it that way. Plus, Marty, you are very, very bad at switching off. That's an asset when you're a driven professional, but it's a huge deficit when you're retired. I shudder to think of what you'll do if you're left to your own devices."

"You want me where you can keep an eye on me."

"Sure. And if this *is* my Feynman Lectures moment of glory, then I want one of my oldest and dearest friends in the world on-site to witness it. It would be a favor to me."

"You make a compelling case, Raza. I have some loose ends here, but I'm going to seriously consider it."

"You do that, Marty. And while you tie up those loose ends, go slow and pay attention to that internal weather of yours."

My KPMG guy found my Leaf in an impound lot and arranged to have it bailed out of car jail, detailed, charged, and delivered to the Fairmont's valet. The claim check for it was centered on the desk blotter when I got back from my morning swim and breakfast.

He also found me a lawyer who filed a motion that got my assets unfrozen.

I left messages for some of the best phys-sec and electronic countermeasures people I knew, and then when they returned my calls, I asked them obliquely about who they'd hire to sanitize the *Unsalted Hash* and confirm that it was free of cameras, implants, mics, malware, and other nasty surprises, including the kind of stuff that unspecified DHS agencies had access to.

The consensus was not to even bother trying. Sell it or scrap it, but don't trust it. At a minimum, take it to a trustworthy security mechanic to have the firmware on every assembly and sub-assembly re-flashed, right down to the tire-pressure sensors and their integrated wireless interfaces. Even then . . .

I walked down to the DHS lot on Golden Gate Avenue. My lawyer had negotiated intensely for the *Hash*'s return, and the DHS lady who signed it out to me was impressed with what a cool piece of rolling stock it was.

The *Hash*'s exterior, mirrors, and windshield had accumulated a convincing coat of grime, and the air inside was compellingly stale, but still, driving it back was a spooky, jumpy experience, and there was a moment at a red light where the crashing sound from some nearby construction site convinced me that a bomb had just gone off in the bus and I was about to die. By the time I realized I was still alive, the light was green, and six drivers behind me were leaning on their horns. I pulled over.

When my hands stopped shaking, I got it the rest of the way to the Fairmont. The valet took the keys, and the concierge invited me into his office to discuss my needs. He assured me that it would be no problem to contract with some bonded packer-movers to attend the *Hash* at the Fairmont's loading dock (it was too tall for the underground garage) and get everything aboard transferred to a nearby storage locker. He offered to get three competitive quotes. I passed him a $1,000 tip and said I'd trust his judgment, but I wanted it done fast. He pocketed the money with a straight face and calmly thanked me. I thanked him right back.

22

It took me three more days to work up the nerve to call Ruth. That said something about my internal weather. I tried to decide what, but I couldn't.

"Hello, you," she said. It came out cold.

I was suddenly very self-conscious, and not just about what I might say to her—I was convinced that Waterman Bates and maybe his Treasury rivals were listening in, recording, analyzing. As paranoid fantasies go, it was more plausible than most.

"My thing, the thing I couldn't talk about? It's over."

"I see," she said. "Well, I'm sure that's a big load off your shoulders."

"As a matter of fact, it is. It wasn't pleasant, and the fact that I couldn't see you or call you made it even more unpleasant."

"You say the nicest things." She didn't sound like she meant it.

"You've got every right to be pissed."

"Yes, I do."

"Yes, you do."

"Marty, I was just in the middle of something. Is there anything else?"

"No. Yes. Just . . . I'm going away for a while, but no mystery this time. I'm, uh, I'm going to go audit a freshman economics class at UMKC."

She laughed. It was a merry sound, and hearing it was a balm. "That is either the weirdest lie you've ever told, or the weirdest truth."

"The latter. I'm flying to Kansas City the day after tomorrow, through O'Hare."

"Marty, *why*?"

"Ruth, I can't say I can explain it. It's a dear old friend's last year teaching, and she's giving it a lot of effort. But that's not the whole story. I feel like I spent forty years cultivating a hell of a worm's-eye view, and now that it's over, I want to go and get the bird's-eye view. Like finishing up a long hike by pulling up a map and seeing all that terrain you just covered."

"When you put it that way, it almost makes sense."

"Yeah," I said. "On a good day, it makes sense to me, too." I drew a breath, then let it out. "Like I said, my last job, the one for Danny Lazer, it set me up pretty well. I'm about to start a new phase of my life, and after the stuff that I just went through, I need some kind of formal terminus."

"You make it sound like you're in mourning. Marty, you're rich, retired, good-looking, and you've got all your teeth and all your joints. There's damned few people who can say the same."

"That's a good way to put it, Ruth. To be honest, that's kind of what I was hoping for. I knew you'd be the friend who could tell it to me straight."

She sighed. "My dear old friend Martin Hench, I will always tell it to you straight. Text me your address in Missouri and I'll send you a postcard and maybe you can send me one back, and maybe when you've finished your postgraduate economic studies in the frozen Midwest, you and I can get together and celebrate your liberation from toil."

I felt a pang so sharp I couldn't talk for a moment. I was entirely certain that by the time I got back from UMKC, Ruth Schwartzburg would be romantically spoken for. How could she not? I almost canceled the trip right then. But I didn't. Instead, I told her how much I was looking forward to our correspondence, and after I hung up the phone, I texted her the address of the house that Raza had found for me and that the KPMG kid had rented for me.

The guy who worked on the *Hash* was an ex–Cult of the Dead Cow hacker who'd done a turn in the NSA before starting his own consultancy, recruiting about twenty of the brightest kids he could find at DEF CON and HOPE. His name was Hamish, but he insisted on calling himself Baron Von Rijsttafel and painstakingly correcting people's pronunciation so they'd be sure to get the pun. You'd think a fifty-year-old man would have gotten tired of that joke, but you'd be wrong.

The Baron's kids had worked on the *Hash* at NIMBY, an East Bay hackerspace that was the winter home to a couple of dozen large Burning Man mutant vehicles and art cars. They were still swarming it when I pulled up in the Leaf. They reluctantly dismounted her, slid their mechanics' crawlers out from beneath her, and used cordless power drivers to rivet the access hatches back into place, disconnecting funny-looking cables from networking and diagnostic ports whose existence I'd only dimly suspected.

The Baron himself came out to give me a tour, detailing all the different subsystems they'd triple-checked and restored to factory defaults. They'd added up the power consumption of every component and then painstakingly checked to make sure that every microwatt was accounted for, and they'd done a close EMF and physical sweep.

"If there's anything bad in there, it's small, independently powered, and intermittent," he said.

One of his kids, a Black girl with Afro-puffs and a ripped Palantir T-shirt, added, "Course, there's plenty of bad stuff that fits that description." I assumed the T-shirt was ironic.

The Baron nodded solemnly. "There are," he said. "There certainly are. That's the problem with blue teaming it—you need to be perfect, while—"

"The red team only has to find a single error," I finished. "Yeah. Send me an invoice?"

"Course," he said. "Net sixty, but I'll knock two percent off if you pay in fourteen."

"I'll pay you today, you send me the invoice now."

"Sold," he said. I shook hands with each of the kids who'd worked on the *Hash*, and then aimed it across the Bay Bridge.

I unhitched the Leaf back at the Fairmont and handed the keys to the valet and then drove the *Hash* into the Tenderloin. Parking it was hard, but after a half hour's circling, I found a spot only a couple of blocks away from the empty lot on Eddy. Before I debarked, I walked its length. Empty and freshly stripped and reassembled, it was revealed as the ridiculous rock star's confection it had always been—an overpriced toy, finished in marble, mirrors, and tropical hardwood. I should have called it the *White Elephant*. It was still worth mid–six figures, on paper, but what kind of idiot would pay that?

I stood at the edge of the empty lot for a moment. I'd been half convinced that the tents would be gone, had wondered whether a private eye could find three homeless people on the streets of San Francisco with nothing more to go on than their first names.

But the tents were there, the carts, too. I drew up on the tents and called out: "Martín? Tonya? Laquan?"

"Gimme a minute," came Martín's rasp from deep inside the tent.

He got out and stretched painfully, then limped over to me. He saw me watching him limp and grimaced. "Fucked my leg up," he said. He looked me over. "You look like your troubles are over."

I started to say, *Well, I wouldn't put it that way,* and then I stopped myself and said, "Yeah, I guess they are."

"Congratulations."

Tonya emerged from the tents then, followed by Laquan. She looked like she'd aged a decade since I'd last seen her, grief still etched into her features. Laquan didn't look more haunted than he had before, but he'd been plenty haunted then.

"Hi, folks," I said.

"Hello, Milt," Tonya said.

Laquan managed a shy nod.

"Look," I said, "it's like this. I'm leaving town, and one of the things I need to deal with before I go is this mobile home I'd been living in, a bus. And, well . . . I thought you folks could help with that, if I was to turn it over to you."

"You want to sell us your bus?" Martín said.

"No," I said. "I just want to sign it over to you."

"Why do you want to give us a bus, Milt?" Martín's suspicion was palpable. I hadn't really considered the possibility that this would come up.

"I guess it's because you did me a kindness, and you have things pretty rough, and I don't need the bus anymore."

"Don't be rude, Martín," Tonya said. "That's very nice of you, Milt."

"It's all right," I said. "The bus is a couple of blocks away."

"Let's go see it," Tonya said. She was pretty when she smiled. It took ten years off her.

They toured the *Hash* in solemn silence, and I encouraged them to open the cupboards and fold out the beds. "It's supposed to sleep eight," I said. "Three should be fine. You can divide it up with these—"

Martín waved me silent and stared at me. "Milt, what the fuck are you doing?"

"I told you," I said. "I'm leaving town and parting ways with this monstrosity. I tried to figure out what I could do with it, and I decided I wanted you three to have it. If you want it, that is. I, uh, well, this is a prepaid gas card that should keep it on the road for a year, depending on how many miles you put on it."

I held it out to him, but he didn't take it, so I put it on my—

his—kitchenette table, next to the title slip that I'd laid out before I'd gone to find him.

The three of them were staring at me now.

"You a rich guy, Milt?" Martín asked.

"Yeah, Martín. I guess I am, now. There was some bad stuff that I had to get past, but now that that's done, I'm a rich guy."

"Congratulations," Tonya said. She said it quietly, like someone talking to herself.

"Anyway, I'm a rich guy who doesn't need this bus. I don't care what you do with it. Live in it, sell it, abandon it. And if you don't want it—"

"We want it," Tonya said. "Don't we, Martín?"

He was quiet for a long time.

"We take this bus, anyone going to show up looking for it?"

"No, nothing like that. Here's the papers, and here's my ID." I dug out my driver's license.

"Martin Hench?" Martín said.

I hadn't thought about this part, either. "Yeah," I said. "Milt was a name I used so that the trouble I had wouldn't come for you. But now I'm Martin again."

That made him laugh. "Pleased to meet you, Martin," he said and held out his hand. We shook. His grip was strong, his hand callused.

"Pleased to meet *you*, Martín."

"One problem," Martín said. "I don't have a driver's license."

"I do," Tonya said.

"And then there's insurance—"

"Paid two years in advance. After that—" I shrugged.

Laquan spoke up, startling all of us. "Come on. Sign the paper. I *like* this bus."

We did it.

As I turned to walk away from the bus, Martín leaned out. "Hey, Martin!"

"Yeah?"

"What the fuck's an *Unsalted Hash*? That some kind of drug thing?"

"No," I said. "A math thing. You can change it, if you want."

"Naw," he said. "I like it. Sounds like one of those fucking yuppie ice cream flavors."

23

The taxi from the Kansas City airport dropped me off at my rental house. Raza had wanted to meet me at the airport, but I told her not to be silly, I'd see her for breakfast.

I slept between a stranger's sheets that night without bothering to unpack my toothbrush. The next morning, as I was digging through my suitcase for it, my doorbell rang. I pulled on last night's pants and tee and descended the unfamiliar stairs.

I pulled back the curtain on the living room door to see who it was, but the house had a mudroom vestibule and the front door was a couple of feet away and its windows were fogged over, so I braved the ice-cold tiles in my bare feet and opened the door.

It was a delivery kid, wearing a big down parka, heavy boots, a woolen hat. One of his gloves was tucked under an armpit, and his blue, bare hand was holding a pen. "Morning," he said and passed me a clipboard and the pen.

"What am I signing for?" I asked.

"These," he said, pointing to an odd-shaped paper-wrapped parcel at his feet. I gave him the clipboard back, and he carefully picked up the parcel and handed it to me. It sloshed. It was a vase of flowers, carefully wrapped against the cold.

I thanked him and brought it inside and cleared the binder full of household instructions, rules, and tips off the scuffed coffee table and set down the parcel and unwrapped it. Two dozen very large, very red roses, with a card:

> Now you've got something to write about in
> your first postcard.
> —Ruth

And an address in Half Moon Bay.

Raza asked me about the flowers halfway through breakfast. I played it coy at first, but then spilled, and for the whole semester, she took every private opportunity to grill me on the process of my postcard-based romance. I got up to six postcards per week, at the end.

Raza was brilliant, by the way. I knew she would be. How many times had she explained something to me that I'd never understood, in a way that was so clear that I understood it forever, so clear that it seemed *obvious* in retrospect.

But these *were* her Feynman Lectures, the last big job she'd spent her whole life preparing for. She started with the origin of money, Roman emperors, and their conquering armies, and worked her way forward.

At first, the kids in that class were the ones who had to be there. Econ 101 was a prerequisite for several UMKC majors. But word got around, and by midsemester, I was getting filthy looks from undergrads who tramped into the hall in their snow boots and parkas and saw some weird old dude taking up a seat in the front row. They moved Raza to a bigger hall. Then they set up an overflow room. As victory laps went, it was a hell of a success, and her YouTube numbers started in the hundreds of thousands and quickly went to the millions.

Her last lecture was more triumphant party than seminar, with cake and tears and a song from her TAs. She kept a straight face through most of it, but by the end, she was beaming, just the biggest and most radiant smile I'd ever seen on her.

And with all that, and the karaoke they took her to, and the late night, she still drove me to the airport the next morning, with a stack of postcards in Ruth's handwriting in my carry-on. I wanted to reread them on the flight, and more importantly, I didn't trust the airline not to lose them if I checked them.

I was antsy after the long flight, but the hour-long cab ride down the peninsula to Menlo Park was a kind of meditation. The cab driver was an older Black man, and he'd actually grown up in the area, in Oakland, and with a little prodding, I was able to get him to point out the ghosts of landmarks long torn down to make way for the new, the newer than new, and the newer still.

Raymond recited the names of the departed places, and it gave me comfort, because if all those places could vanish into the murky depths of history, then all the places I was seeing now might likewise slip beneath the wash and sink out of all human recollection.

The KPMG guy booked me a room in a boutique hotel near Stanford. It was a cross between a B and B and staying with a gracious old friend, and the landlady made me feel very welcome, brought me a little plate of local cheeses and rustic crackers and port, and wished me a good night.

I rang the buzzer on Ira Hermann's storefront office at ten o'clock the next morning, full of the delicious breakfast of berries and yogurt and a very flaky croissant and drinking a six-dollar coffee from a place two doors over where they prepared it in a fancy, showy siphon.

Zoe answered, and I could tell it took her a moment to recognize me, then she did, then she did some kind of mnemonic trick that let her fish my name out of the recesses of her memory. "Mr. Hench! Marty. What a lovely surprise. Come in, come in."

The office was different, somehow, the furniture rearranged, different prints on the walls, a striking abstract bronze on a plinth in the corner. I didn't think it was Ira Hermann's style.

"I'm sorry I didn't call, Zoe, but I just got back into town, and there was something I wanted to discuss with Ira in person."

She got a serious look and clasped her hands in front of her. "Ira retired a few months ago," she said, "and I'm sorry to say that his health has been poorly since, and has just taken a bad turn for the worse."

"I'm so sorry," I said. I was. I liked Ira Hermann. I could see that Zoe felt bad about it, too—it wasn't just a show of professional gravitas.

"I was always going to take on Ira's clients, and this has accelerated things. If there's anything I can help you with—"

"As a matter of fact, there is."

She got me settled on the sofa in the internal office, Ira's old office, which she had redecorated, including another bronze that had to be from the same artist as the piece in the lobby.

"My husband," she said, catching me admiring it.

"No!" I said. "Really? It's fantastic work."

"Really," she said and got a hugely proud look. "He's very good. He's got a studio in Woodside. Does his own casting."

"It's really wonderful stuff."

"He's got a show coming up. He teaches part-time at Stanford, and he and some of his students are taking over a gallery in Palo Alto. I have a flyer for it, here." She handed me a quarter-cut sheet of photocopied office paper with a spare, nicely laid-out invitation. I carefully pocketed it. "What can I help you with, Marty?"

"Do you remember when Ira asked if I'd be paying tax on my windfall from Danny Lazer?"

"I do," she said and got a smile when she saw where this was going.

"I want to."

"All right," she said. "That's a very admirable choice. I can work with your financial planner to facilitate the transfer of the assets into onshore vehicles for assessment and—"

"No," I said. "That's the thing. I want to pay tax on them

offshore. I want to give the IRS all the accounts, all the structures, all the plans. All of it."

She looked puzzled, then alarmed, then curious. "I see," she said. "And when you do that, you will be implicating many other people besides yourself—people who avail themselves of the same structures and systems."

"Yes," I said. "I will."

"In that case," she said, "you won't need my help."

"No," I said, "I won't."

She studied me for a long time. "You never struck me as a gloater," she said.

"I'm not," I said. "I like to think I'm an honorable person. I knew that Ira's clients—your clients, now—would be exposed if I did this, since he set up the vehicles. I wanted to give you warning. I'm going to the IRS in a month. That should be plenty of time to figure out exciting new ways to hide all of that money from Uncle Sam and any other governments that might take an interest in it."

She cocked her head. "It certainly is." She looked at the bronze. So did I. It seemed almost molten, full of pent-up energy.

"Why, Marty?"

"I guess it's an object lesson—for the IRS, not you. You once asked me if I thought I could untangle your knots, and I told you I could but the IRS couldn't. The fact of the matter is, they *should* be able to. You're good at your job, but you're on the blue team. They have red team advantage and they're squandering it. I want to rub those Treasury G-men's noses in their own lack of imagination and maybe inspire them to do better. Your job really ought to be a *lot* harder."

She thought about that for a while. "I'd be up to it, and it would clear the deadwood out of the competition. Sound. All right, Marty, the warning is appreciated."

"If you speak to Ira—"

"I'll give him your best. You take care, Marty. Enjoy your retirement."

The front desk security at the Camino Real braced me and made me wait outside the lobby until they got Sethu on the phone. New security protocol, after someone came in pretending to be a courier and tried to bum-rush the elevators.

Once Sethu cleared me, though, they were absolute gents . . . and they still accompanied me in the elevator to make sure I rode it all the way to the top. On Sethu's behalf, I was both glad that they were so diligent and sad that they had to be.

She answered the door in the same wide slacks I'd last seen her in, with a long linen shirt overtop, a pair of businesslike reading glasses in her hair, which was cut short with interesting texture at the tips.

"Marty!" Her smile was warm and went right to her eyes. She gathered me in a delicious-smelling hug that went on and on.

"Sethu," I said once I'd disentangled myself. "You are looking fabulous."

"Oh, bullshit," she said, leading me into the living room. It wasn't magazine-photo ready anymore: covered in files, with a big printer in one corner and a whiteboard in the other, it was the secondary command center of a busy CEO. "I'm a wreck. I used to get on Danny's case about the hours he pulled. Now I wonder how he ever managed to take time off."

Her PA—a young woman fresh out of Stanford with a tight ponytail and a toasting of freckles over her forehead and nose— took my coffee order and brought it, along with Sethu's tea, out to the roof garden and then retreated.

"So?" she said, looking at the empty streets of Palo Alto.

"So," I said. "So, the business in Jordan's Mill is over, for me and you. It might not be over for some other people, but I don't expect your path will ever cross theirs." I thought for a moment. "Actually, some of them might be Trustless customers, come to think of it."

She shook her head ruefully. "It's possible. I've fired three compliance heads, but I think I've finally found someone who understands that my goal is to *be* clean, not *plausibly deniable*." There was a new canvas on her easel, but it was blank. She saw me look at it and shook her head again. "Too busy for that sort of thing now. How about you, Marty? Are you too busy for the good things, or are you truly retired now?"

"I guess I'm about to find out. I took a little trip and only just came back to town. I've got an idea that might keep me busy for the years to come."

"Would that have something to do with Ruth Schwartz-burg?"

I guess I'm losing my poker face, because whatever happened to my expression made her burst out in giggles that were so much younger than her outfit and haircut.

"I approve, Marty," she said. "She was my first boss at Key-pairs, and I got to know her pretty well. We still stay in touch, and the subject came up. You're a lucky man."

"I am," I said. The awkward supposition that they might have compared notes about me and my performance arose in me, and I forced myself to disregard it because a nearly sixty-eight-year-old man shouldn't indulge that kind of foolishness. However, my poker face failed me again.

"I didn't think it was necessary to talk about the favor you did for me the last time I saw you. It was a kindness, and I appreciate it."

"I will always think of it fondly."

She lightly slapped my wrist. "Fondly, but sparingly, sir. Ruth deserves your undivided attention."

"She does," I said. I looked at the blank canvas, the empty city streets, the beautiful and mature woman that Sethuramani Lazer Balakrishnan had become. "Thank you, Sethu."

"Thank you, Marty."

Ruth had bought a beautifully restored craftsman on a big lot. I parked the Leaf in the driveway and sat in it for a moment, looking at the stained glass set into the front door, the neat herb lawn, the crossed battle-axes where a door knocker might go.

I picked up the gift box from the passenger seat and opened the driver's-side door and let my feet bring me to her front door. I hesitated again before knocking, and she opened it, wearing a blue silk blouse with the top two buttons undone, a pair of loose harem trousers, and a jeweled scarab clasp that kept her long, gray hair off her shoulders.

"Hello, you," she said. Tears stood out in her eyes. She squeezed me so hard my rib cried out. She smelled *wonderful*. I buried my face in her hair and squeezed back.

I got a jumbled impression of her house, the bookshelves and the fantasy art and a fat gray cat, but before I knew it, I was in the bedroom, and then my conscious mind stopped registering anything except pure sensation and warm affection.

"You seem to have brought me a gift," she said, tracing a hand lazily down my chest in a way that made me shiver.

I looked at the bedside table where the small box sat. "I did," I said.

She picked up the box, contemplated its size and weight. "Not jewelry, I hope. Jewelry would be decidedly premature."

"Not jewelry."

She undid the ribbon, carefully removed the loose tissue packing, then lifted out the small, tissue-wrapped item and unwound it delicately.

She looked at it for a long moment. "It's, uh—"

"I'm reliably informed that this is what a level twenty-seven half-elf paladin should look like. The sculptor I commissioned it from is very highly rated in these things. And the painter—"

"It's Venphira Ghostbane?"

"It's Venphira Ghostbane."

"Martin Harold Hench, you are something fucking else."

"It's very mutual."

Finally, after the last of the movers had gone home, toting the last of the broken-down boxes and packing material, I considered the small pile of things from the storage locker near the Fairmont, the items that had been on the *Hash* at the end, there.

I'd gone through it as the guys had unpacked, setting stuff aside that I no longer needed for them to take to the thrift shop. So much of the stuff I'd stored in all my storage lockers had turned out to be things I didn't need, things I'd entombed for years in windowless, anonymous spaces around the country. Consolidating it all together had been a kind of Buddhist revelation about how little the material world mattered.

But it wasn't all meaningless. The self-portrait Sethu had given me stared at me, stern and fierce and brutally self-critical. I'd forgotten all about it, and then I'd thought about hanging it in the living room, but I couldn't imagine unwinding with a crossword while she glared at me.

It couldn't go in the bedroom. Not the bathroom or the kitchen. The little guest room I'd mentally dubbed "the office"? Perhaps in there. I picked it up and started up the stairs to see how it looked when the doorbell rang.

"Agent Bates," I said, standing aside so he could come in. He was back in his lost-tourist dad-jeans costume, but his eyes were hard behind his bifocals.

"Mr. Hench," he said.

"Drink?"

"No, thank you," he said. He considered the painting. "Beautiful woman," he said. "Wouldn't want to get on her bad side, though."

"No, you really wouldn't."

"Sebo Szarka died yesterday. Flipped on the San Mateo Bridge, went over the guardrail."

"Ah," I said. "That sounds familiar."

"It does, doesn't it. In case there was any doubt, the spot was within a couple of yards of the spot where Jim Hannah's Bugatti went over." He looked deep into my eyes. "We think that might be the end of it. We think that might be the last loose end snipped away. There's been a lot of death, and we're thinking they're finally losing their appetite for it."

"Well, that's something."

"Marty, what you did was reckless, and it got a lot of people hurt."

"Yeah," I said. "I know that."

"But I understand why you did it." He swallowed. "I just wanted you to know that." He swallowed again. "And my Treasury colleagues got something out of it, thanks to your extremely comprehensive tax return."

"It was the least I could do, given how easy it turned out to be to unfreeze all those assets and spring my bus out of the impound."

"I may have helped with that a little," he said.

"I figured as much. Thank you, Waterman."

He smiled. "You're welcome."

The meeting with the homeless charities went late, and I didn't have the heart to rush them. They were spending a *lot* of my money, and they wanted to show me just how far it was going. But it meant I got to Ruth's craftsman late.

"Happy anniversary," I said, handing her a bouquet. Two dozen fat red roses, as had become customary with us.

She took them from me, put them in water, gave me a long kiss and an even longer hug while Sméagol, her fat gray cat, twirled around our ankles.

She brought me a bourbon in a lowball glass and a little wrapped present.

"I thought we said no gifts," I said.

"It's not from me. It's from Sethu."

"Sethu?"

"She sent it over today."

I opened it up: a flat box whose lid lifted to reveal a layer of tissue paper. I moved it out of the way and found a pair of beautiful, thick regimental-stripe pajamas in a dense-woven cotton. They had a monogram over the pocket: *DML*.

"Dead man's pajamas?" Ruth wrinkled her nose.

"He wore them with a lot of style," I said. "And he didn't get to enjoy them as long as he deserved to."

"He certainly didn't," she said.

"But I plan to," I said.

"You'd better."

acknowledgments

Thank you—as ever!—to my incredibly patient wife, Alice, who put up with me spending lockdown in a hammock, furiously distracting myself from the end of the world by writing books and listening to obscure Talking Heads remasters over and over. And over.

Also and forever, of course, thanks to my agent, Russell Galen, and my editor, Patrick Nielsen Hayden.

Thank you to Steve Brust and Bruce Schneier for your early encouragement on this one.

Finally, thanks to every crypto grifter for giving me such fertile soil to plow.

**Turn the page for a sneak peek at
Cory Doctorow's next novel**

Available Winter 2024 from Tor Books

1

Avalon is a chocolate-box town on an enchanted island, twenty-two miles from the Port of Los Angeles. Catalina Island: the redoubt of the Wrigley chewing-gum fortune, acquired by William Wrigley Jr. in 1919, and developed as *the* chic spot for Hollywood's smart set.

For years, starlets, leading men, producers, and directors plied the channel on wooden ships out of Long Beach, drinking cocktails on the three-hour crossing, vomiting discreetly over the railings.

They caroused at Old Man Wrigley's "Casino": the largest building on the island, a twelve-story art deco roundhouse with a ground-floor cinema with its own pipe organ, and, above it, the largest ballroom in the USA, known to a glamour-hungry nation as the source of a weekly broadcast live from "high atop the Casino on beautiful Catalina Island."

The one thing the Casino didn't have? Gambling. Wrigley fancied himself a sophisticate, and his casino took its name from the Italian word for "gathering place." The fact that this confused everyone who visited the place, for the rest of time, only reinforced Wrigley's superiority.

There was no gambling at the Catalina Casino, because gambling leads to crime, and there's no crime in Avalon. That's what the tourist brochures tell you. It's what the four thousand year-round locals tell you. It's what the two-thousand-odd beautiful people who own summer homes on the island tell you. If you're one of the members of the thirty-five-thousand-strong

July Fourth weekend crowd, you'll come home and tell it to your friends.

There's no crime in Avalon.

Scott Warms brought me to Avalon in 2006, one year after he sold InterPoly to Yahoo! and became a millionaire at twenty-three. Scott had been forced into the sale by his investors, and I'd helped him, a little, untangling their creative accounting so he didn't get crammed at the sale time and lose the equity he'd bargained hard for at twenty-one, when he founded the company.

Scott didn't want to work at Yahoo!, and truth be told, Yahoo! didn't want Scott working there. But Scott's Yahoo! shares wouldn't fully vest for three more years. He was already a millionaire, but if he hung in—or got fired—he'd be a decamillionaire. Corollary: if he quit, he'd *lose* tens of millions of dollars. At twenty-three years of age, three years felt like an eternity to Scott, but he had plans for those remaining millions—$20 mil if Yahoo!'s share price held, maybe more if it went up.

So Scott and Yahoo! were playing chicken. He wanted them to fire him, but not for cause, and so he became an expert on California employment law—Scott could become an expert on any subject in six months. California employment law only took him two. He made sure that he engaged in precisely as much fuckery as the law allowed and not one nanogram more.

Which is how he ended up on Avalon. Scott was formally a vice-president, as was typical for the CEOs of the dozens of companies Yahoo! bought with billions pumped into it by Soft-Bank's Masayoshi Son. That meant that he was entitled to five weeks of paid vacation every year, which no Yahoo! exec came close to taking. Not even the French ones.

Scott took every single day he was entitled to. Twenty-five days of paid leave translated into 12.5 four-day weekends per year. Add in federal and state holidays and sick days, and that number went up to twenty-four four-day weekends per year. Then there were the conferences, off-sites, and team-building retreats, at least one of those every month, and then the time off in lieu of the travel days and overnights, and Scott was taking thirty-two short weeks per year, plus two weeks at Christmas.

He was entitled to a plush office, which he generously allowed other teams to book as a meeting room or getaway space, because it was so often empty. Scott liked microbrewed beer, and his grateful coworkers often brought by a bottle of something they'd taken home from a brewpub or made in their garage, and they'd put it in his grocery-store-style glass-door refrigerator with a post-it of thanks and tasting notes.

Scott was part of an executive committee that was supposed to evaluate possible acquisition targets, companies like Inter-Poly. The only times Scott came close to quitting Yahoo! and forfeiting his $20 mil were when a really promising start-up came through the door. The combination of a smart founder and a great product made Scott pine for all the time he was wasting. Even worse was his dreadful knowledge that if he gave an honest assessment of the start-up he'd just heard pitched, he'd trap some other naïf like him in the Yahoo! quicksand.

He had a good nose for this stuff, and he'd use the preliminary documents to schedule his long weekends, making sure he was in town and present only for meetings where they were hearing from stupid companies making stupid products. He found it physically painful to sit through their pitches without tongue-flaying their founders. But at least he could honestly sit down with the rest of the committee afterward and recommend that the company stay the hell away from the wretched start-ups they'd heard from that day. Generally, the committee would all agree with him.

The sole exception was CabCandi, a start-up that wanted to fill taxi drivers' trunks with candy and use a web-based dispatch to turn major metros' cabdrivers into a circulating snack-delivery service for hungry stoners. Scott correctly pointed out that this was a profoundly stupid idea. The other committee members pointed out that CabCandi had much better fundamentals than its rivals, the successors to Kozmo.com. Scott replied that Kozmo had collapsed and the post-Kozmo stoner-snack dot-coms would do no better. The committee overrode his objections and offered a term sheet to CabCandi, $7 million on $12 million, pre-money. But they were outbid by Battery Ventures, who offered $9 on $14.

After CabCandi, Scott decided to use one of his sick days and go to Avalon, and he invited me down for the long weekend.

"Fly into Long Beach, Marty, and we'll chopper over." He was deliberately breezy, clearly wanting to impress me. I'd been in helicopters. They're noisy. But Scott was as eager as a puppy and he just wanted me to have a good time.

"It's a date," I said. "Let me check Expedia for flights from Oakland."

"Southwest is your best bet. They're not on Expedia, and they've got a website that doesn't suck."

It didn't suck, which was quite an accomplishment for an airline, to be frank. I caught the 5:15 and we touched down in Long Beach at 6:07, four minutes ahead of schedule. Scott met me at the baggage carousel, bouncing on his toes with excitement.

"Marty Fuckin' Hench!" He grabbed me in a big hug. He was still ninety-eight pounds soaking wet, tall and bony. He'd gotten rid of his ponytail and gotten a millionaire's haircut, something that transformed his cheekbones and prominent teeth from skull-like to aquiline, and he'd replaced his crooked wire-rim glasses with a pair of aviators with clear lenses, which was a statement, though I couldn't tell you what it was trying to say.

He released me from the hug. "Scott Fucking Warms," I replied. "You're looking good." Sky-blue Hugo Boss blazer with turned-up cuffs, striped shiny lining, and orange satin accents at the slash pockets; obligatory Japanese denim as stiff as cardboard; some kind of designer sandals that looked like something Salvador Dalí would put on Jesus' feet.

"I'm so, so, *so* glad you came, buddy. Catalina is crazy, like nowhere I've been before. They've got *bison*. Oh, here are the bags!" There'd only been eight people on my flight, and only four bags spilled onto the belt. I grabbed for mine, but Scott got it before me and shot the handle. "Come on!" He took off for the private airfield.

I followed him out the door and into the cool, sea-scented Long Beach night, across a couple of crosswalks and then up to a gate where a private security guard checked his ID and mine against a list on his screen.

I was just a forty-something forensic accountant back then, with a good line in unwinding high-tech scams, and I was far from a rich man, but I'd flown private a few times—sometimes clients claim they can only fit in a meeting on their bizjet—but I didn't see the attraction, not then, when it just convinced me that I was working for someone with more dollars than sense, and not much later in life, when a big score set me up with enough money to fly private any time I want.

I keep waiting for the day when private fliers are subject to even one percent of the indignities of a TSA checkpoint, but every time I fly, it's the same. I could have brought a wheelie-bag full of C-4 and packing nails through that checkpoint and they wouldn't have known about it.

I sure hoped no one mentioned this to Osama bin Laden.

The helicopter was waiting for us, Scott's bag already aboard. We climbed in using the little running-board, and the pilot—a grey-hair with the bearing of an ex-military pilot gone to fat—welcomed us aboard and showed us to our headphones, giant earmuffs with curly-cable umbilici that plugged into armrest one-eighth-inch jacks, reminding me of my old high-school hi-fi set. Once we snapped into our five-point harnesses and opened our complimentary mineral waters, Scott toggled some switches on an overhead panel and we were on a channel with the pilot.

"We're all ready, Captain," he said.

"Roger that," the pilot said in perfect air force monotone.

"Going private now, Captain," Scott said.

The pilot gave us a thumbs-up and kicked in the engines and my whole skeleton began to buzz with the chopper's roar. We lifted off and Scott let out a *whoop!* and drummed his thighs.

"Oh, buddy, I can't *tell* you how bad I needed this," he said. "And it's *so* good to see you."

"It's good to see you too, Scott. How's life in the punctuation factory?" That's what we called Yahoo!, in tribute to that asinine exclamation point.

"Don't ask. Let's talk about this weekend instead. Normally I stay at a friend's place; there's about a half dozen people I know with summer places there and they've all got guest rooms, but I thought it might be awkward for you to crash with a stranger, so I booked us rooms at the Zane Grey Hotel."

"As in the author?" Zane Grey pretty much invented the cowboy novel. My old man had dozens of his books and would always circle the *TV Guide* listings for the movie adaptations—there were more than a hundred of them, and he loved every one, but insisted that none of them came close to the books.

"Yeah! It's his old house! He built a summer place there, old Pueblo style, and just kept adding onto it every time he got a fat check. It's a hotel now. Gorgeous. I got us the penthouse. Four balconies, a patio, harbor views."

Maybe I made a face. My business did just fine. The dot-com bubble had sucked in billions for every harebrained scheme you could imagine, and some of that money disappeared into creative spreadsheets. Hardly a month went by without my being called upon to find a couple of million that had been made to disappear through a black hole in one of those spreadsheet cells. My take was 25 percent of whatever I recovered, and I recovered a *lot*. But even so, I didn't have punctuation factory money. This Zane Grey place sounded pricey.

"It's on me," he said. "My invitation, my tab. I insist. I've wanted to stay at this place since I first laid eyes on it. Man, I can't wait."

We were high over the channel now. The deepest channel off any coast, anywhere. It's a crime scene. There's no crime in Avalon, but just offshore?

That channel is the final resting place of tens of thousands of barrels of DDT, dumped there by Montrose Chemical in barrels that were thoroughly, utterly incapable of maintaining their integrity at the bottom of a three-thousand-foot saltwater channel.

Down in those depths, there's crimes whose perps belong in front of the International Court of Justice for crimes against humanity.

The sun was just setting, right in our eyes, the Pacific-blue sky turning the color of fresh blood, then dried blood, and then— that flash of green, just as the sun dipped over the horizon.

"There it is!" Scott pointed and bounced a little in his seat. From the air, Catalina Island was a rugged Mediterranean hillscape with a picture-postcard seaside village nestled in its little harbor, where ranked yachts bobbed and a ferry backed and filled to turn around. The towering Casino anchored the town to the right: a cream-colored squat cylinder topped with a dark rice-paddy hat of a roof whose red-brick color flared in the last rays of the sun. To the left, the harbor turned into a beach road that girded a cliff. We banked that way and there was the helipad, lit up with spotlights.

The pilot angled us in, leveled off, and sank down, both skids kissing the ground at the same moment. A couple of ground

crew in hi-viz ran out to tie us down, and then the pilot un-
buckled, stepped into the passenger area, and opened the door,
stretching out his arm in an "after you" gesture. We stepped out
into the Catalina night.

2

Old Man Wrigley launched his chewing-gum fortune in 1891. Company lore says he was a door-to-door soap salesman who had the bright idea of putting a free piece of gum in with his soap and the gum was so popular he got out of the soap biz and jumped into gum.

Wrigley might have been good at gum, but he was better at business. Specifically, he was extremely good at convincing investors to back him as he acquired 95 percent of the world's chicle-tree forests. All the gum in the world was Wrigley gum: either Wrigley made it, or someone else made it and paid Wrigley for the privilege.

In 1890, a year before the Wrigley Company was founded, Congress passed the Sherman Antitrust Bill, named after its primary author, Senator John Sherman, William Tecumseh's baby brother and a man almost as grimly determined once he set his mind to something. In his impassioned speech to the Senate, Sherman said, "If we will not endure a King as a political power we should not endure a King over the production, transportation, and sale of the necessaries of life. If we would not submit to an emperor we should not submit to an autocrat of trade with power to prevent competition and to fix the price of any commodity."

The Sherman Act was law when Wrigley set out to corner the market on chicle, but it was a weak and struggling thing. Sherman's main target was a robber baron who cornered the market on something far more precious than chicle: John D.

Rockefeller, who owned the oil, the railroads, the banks, and the state lawmakers who oversaw them. Rockefeller's Standard Oil company fell to antitrust law in 1911—twenty-one years after the Sherman Act's passage, and eleven years after they put Sherman himself into the ground.

That buying 95 percent of the world's chicle violated the Sherman Act is beyond doubt, but is it truly a crime if no one prosecutes you? What if you spend your fortune in harmless and charming ways, say, by buying the Chicago Cubs (they call it Wrigley Field for a reason) and then bringing them to your celebrity weekender island for spring training every year?

Clearly this is not a crime, because there is no crime on Catalina Island.

The Zane Grey sent out a driver in a liveried golf cart to take us in. The island had strict limits on cars and the waiting list was more than a decade long, but the golf-cart policy was more generous. The driver was a kid named Antonio who told us he was a local, whose great-grandpa moved there before Wrigley bought the island. Graduated Avalon High, the local K–12, and married his high-school sweetheart. Antonio told us all this as he drove us away from the rotor wash that blew our hair and found its way up the cuffs of our pants.

Once we were on the long, quiet curve of the sea road, Scott leaned forward. "You an In-N-Out fan, Antonio?"

Antonio looked around at us so quickly that the golf cart actually swerved a little and he had to look forward again to get it back in the middle of the lane. "Sorry, sorry!" he called. "In-N-Out?"

Scott said, "I bought a sack of burgers in Long Beach before we took off. They might even still be warm. Fries, too."

"Really?" Antonio said. "Damn. I mean—Sorry, I mean—Sir, could I possibly buy one of those from you?"

Scott smiled and clapped him on the shoulder. "They're for you, Antonio. Six double-doubles, six orders of fries. No milkshakes, I'm afraid. I couldn't figure out how to pack them so they'd keep cold."

Antonio slowed the golf cart, pulled onto the shoulder by a chest-high railing. "Seriously, sir? I mean, that's very generous of you."

"It's not my first time on the island. I usually stay with friends out in Hamilton Cove. I know enough locals that I know what to bring."

Antonio's smile was wide enough to lift his scalp and send his chauffeur's hat askew. "Thank you, sir! Thanks very much!"

He got the golf cart back in gear and we sped down the road, past the ferry docks, through a tiny roundabout and onto a beachside tourist strip of souvenir shops and breakfast places and busy bars open to the night, then swung onto the town streets, lined with pretty little vacation homes and locals places. At a Ralph's Grocery, we turned left to parallel the beach road for a few blocks, then descended to the beach again, fronted now by a seawall. Another cute roundabout got us onto a steeply pitched driveway walled in with whitewashed rustic plaster.

The golf cart struggled up the hill and creaked into the hotel's entrance court, where another employee in matching livery hopped to and helped us out of the cart and unloaded our bags. Scott interrupted him, got his bag back, and unzipped it, producing a grease-spotted In-N-Out sack, which he solemnly presented to Antonio, wide-eyed and grinning. Antonio took the sack and pumped Scott's arm in energetic thanks, while the bellman took custody of Scott's bag again, looking jealously at the sack.

No need to stop at the check-in desk; we were expected. The bellman and one of his colleagues humped our bags up the stairs to the penthouse while we followed. They showed us around the three bedrooms, the four patios, the kitchen, the dining/living room, switched on lights, and accepted a twenty each from Scott. I got the distinct impression that either of them would have preferred a burger.

Once we were seated on the patio with beers from the ice bucket that had been waiting for us on the kitchen counter, Scott clinked with me and we both drank and watched the little shore boats run people around the moored yachts in the twinkling harbor below us.

"About those burgers," I said.

He laughed quietly. "No fast-food chains on the island. Local council's orders. Preserves the character of the place. I happen to think they're right, but a weird side effect is that the locals fetishize In-N-Out and McDonald's. Forbidden fruit. Did you see how that guy's face lit up? Absolutely worth having everything in my suitcase stink of hamburger for the weekend."

There's no In-N-Out in Avalon.

We stayed up late chatting and watching the moon paint a milky river on the ocean, and slept in the next morning. Scott woke me to let me know that room service had just arrived with breakfast, and I joined him on the patio for muesli, sourdough toast, unpasteurized honey, cold German breakfast sausage, and fresh-squeezed orange juice and a press-pot of Kona coffee. We ate it while the high sun baked the patio tiles and made our flesh sting, and then we put up the big shade umbrella.

"You brought a sun hat, right?"

I had, my uncle Ed's old air force mechanic's hat.

"You'll need it," he said. "Lots of open space on the bison tour."

Antonio was our tour guide. He had a permit from the island trust, which the Wrigley family had created and then donated 98 percent of Catalina Island to. That let him drive us—this time in a four-wheel-drive jeep, not a golf cart—up to high ground, past the country club and the zip lines, and through the gates into the wildlife reserve.

"The bison were brought over in the twenties, for a Zane Grey movie shoot," he said, as we climbed a winding country road. "The director wanted big suckers, so he brought males. Now, your male bison doesn't much like other males, won't stay in their company for long, so they busted out and took off.

"Old Man Wrigley liked how they looked, so he brought over thirteen females, so they could have Christian relations." He smiled to let us know he also thought this was foolishness. "But bisons are more pagan than Christian, they get together in harems, a bunch of lady bison and just one big old bull."

He downshifted the jeep as the road got steeper. "Now, this was once the stagecoach road," he said. "Visitors headed for Two Harbors would take a horse-drawn coach across the island, about a day's journey. Can you imagine how those horses had to work on this hill? You see those trees there?" He gestured at the evenly spaced, mature, straight trees running along the outside edge of the road. "Either of you gentlemen recognize them?"

Scott smiled. "I've had this tour, so I'm not going to answer. What about you, Marty?"

I've been a Californian ever since I dropped out of MIT, got my accounting certificate, and lit out for the West Coast, where all the computer companies were. I have a pretty good grasp of California plant life, though mostly focused on the Northern California varieties. These ones had strange, streaky bark, like they'd been partially peeled.

Unmistakable. Still, I could tell Antonio was busting to show off, so I said, "Sorry, I can't place them."

"That's because they're Australian," he said, looking over his shoulder to grin at me, then looking back in time to keep the car from crashing into one of those trees. "Eucalyptuses. They were Ada Wrigley's idea. We call 'em the guardrail trees. See, they're spaced close enough that a car can't squeeze between them. A few cars have crashed into them, but they never went over the edge." He downshifted and cranked the wheel around a hairpin, then put his foot down again. The engine revved. "Ada liked them because they're also called 'gum trees,' and she was a Wrigley. Beautiful, aren't they?"

They were. Australia has a lot of beautiful plants and animals and most of them are, frankly, monsters. The eucalypt is no exception. Its reproductive strategy is to drop those heavy, oily leaves around its base until the trapped heat and the highly flammable oil consummate their tragic love affair and burst into flame. The ensuing forest fires reduce the eucalypts to ashes, but the same goes for all the plants that might compete with them. The difference is that eucalypt seedpods *need* fire to open up and release their seeds, and the fires that coax them open also eliminate all the canopy cover that might compete with them for sunlight, while the ashes of the fallen competing trees enrich the soil with nutrients.

That life cycle played out in Australia for millennia, but it's been playing out in Southern California since the 1850s, when nitwit settlers imported them and planted them in an act of slow-motion arson that gives PG&E a run for its money in the competition to see who can burn down the state first.

We saw our first bison half an hour later, after driving past a few hikers with tents on their backs, heading to an inland campsite. It was a cow, a big one. She was standing on a distant hill, placidly contemplating the dry gulch that separated her from the dusty road Antonio had been traversing.

We came to a stop and watched her. Scott rolled down his window and got out his SLR and a long lens and snapped some pictures.

"The Tongva people lived here for eight thousand years," Antonio said, in his tour-guide voice. "They called the island

Pimu. They traded with people from all over the Americas, and anthropologists have found artifacts made with materials from thousands of miles away."

In 1924, the "amateur archaeologist" (that is, grave robber) Ralph Glidden opened his "Indian museum" in Avalon Harbor. It was a "museum built of bones," filled with the desecrated remains of Tongva people and their grave goods. It remained in operation until 1950. The looted remains—including thirty thousand teeth—sat in storage until they were given a Tongva burial in 2017.

The conquistadores enslaved the Tongva, used them to build the missions that every California schoolkid studies in the fourth grade. Their children were kidnapped to those missions and forcibly stripped of their language, culture, and faith. Later, the Americans enslaved them again—this time through indenture, after the act of being an "Indian" in California became a crime in a dozen petty ways. Tongva convicted of crimes were sold to white settlers under the 1850 "Act for the Government and Protection of Indians."

The Tongva were never put on a reservation. They learned Spanish and styled themselves as Mexicans, and in 1921, the *Los Angeles Times* declared they were extinct. Meanwhile, their children were still kidnapped by federal agents and sent to the Sherman Indian High School in Riverside, where they were tormented beyond all reason.

The Tongva of Pimu had a front-row seat for all of that. They were forced off the island in 1930 by the Spaniards, who renamed the island after Saint Catherine of Alexandria, whose fourth-century martyrdom took place sixteen hundred years *after* the Tongva settled Pimu.

There are fewer than four thousand Tongva left on this Earth today. None of them live on Catalina Island.

There is no crime on Catalina Island.

about the author

CORY DOCTOROW is a regular contributor to *The Guardian*, *Locus*, and many other publications. He is a special consultant to the Electronic Frontier Foundation, an MIT Media Lab research associate, and a visiting professor of computer science at The Open University. His award-winning novel *Little Brother* and its sequel, *Homeland*, were *New York Times* bestsellers. His novella collection, *Radicalized*, was a CBC Best Fiction of 2019 selection. Born and raised in Canada, he lives in Los Angeles.

craphound.com
pluralistic.net
Twitter: @doctorow
Mastodon: @pluralistic@mamot.fr